~ Liv Unravelled ~

A Novel

by

Donna M. Bishop

~ *Acknowledgements* ~

Firstly, from the bottom of my heart, I would like to acknowledge the immeasurable support and hard work of my editor Lissa Millar, who helped me edit and transform a jumbled mess of a manuscript into what I hope is a unique, insightful, enjoyable novel.

Undying gratitude and love to my wonderful husband Paul, whose unwavering support and encouragement enabled me to retire from my job, giving me the gift of time to pursue my dream of writing this story.

Kudos, love and belief in my children, Jasmine, Heather, Nick, Mitch and Barb, for growing into fantastic adults in spite of the sometimes tumultuous family life I lead them into. I like to think children choose their parents, so thank you for choosing me.

Heart-melting thanks to my beloved grandchildren, Andie, Bowin, Tess, Joe, Dylan and Cohen for being the perfect, joyful little distractions I needed to lift my spirits through some tough writing moments. I love each of you with my whole heart — and no, you are not allowed to read this story until you're grown up!

To my women friends, my lifeline in times of trouble and my source of laughter and lightness always, my gratitude to you for being my early readers and offering so much encouragement and inspiration to write, re-write, revise and send this story off into the world. It belongs to all of us: Deborah Mabee, Cheryl Hurley, Katrine Winter,

Lorraine Winter, Lissa Millar, Valerie Owen, Maureen Brown, Lisa Puharich, Wendy Nordick, Anita Swing, Darlene Jennings, Sally Haywood-Farmer, and so many more whom I have been honoured to be in friendship with throughout my life, especially Nancy Bingham, who tragically passed away in 1998.

Thank you to friends and fellow humans from the Himalayan hills in India, Ireland, Scotland, Norway, Thailand, Australia and beyond, who have inspired and shown me that we are all connected.

Deep gratitude to my counselling clients, who trusted me with their stories and showed me that telling your truth and reinventing yourself on your own terms is essential to healing.

Many thanks to Karen Hofmann, published author and English professor at Thompson Rivers University for sharing her writing prowess and to Maxine Blennerhassett for helping with line editing.

Last but not least, thanks to my eclectic and multi-talented writing group, The Cauldron, without whom I would not have come to identify myself as a writer and learn the discipline of sitting in the chair and doing it!

I acknowledge the land on which this story was written, and upon which I am honored to live, is the unceded territory of the Tk'emlups te Secwepemc nation.

This story has been fictionalized — while it is based on true events, characters, names, places and some circumstances have been altered to fit the story's time line and to protect individuals. The stories of past lives through hypnosis sessions are for the most part imagined.

Cover photos by Luizclas, Pexels

Authors quoted in this novel: Winken, Blinken and Nod, by Eugene Field; God is our refuge and our strength, Psalm 46, Verse 1 in the Holy Bible; On Joy and Sorrow by Kahlil Gibran; Cauldron of Change and Back to the River, ancient pagan chants; Satyagraha by Mahatma Gandhi; and Do Not Be Dismayed, by L.R. Knost.

~ Dedication ~

This story is dedicated to all the brave people who have come forward with their own stories of sexual assault and abuse, and to those who are willing to hear, believe and support them.

I must say this story had been burning inside me for many years but without the kindling — the courage of people like yourselves — it would have remained untold.

Let's all join the movement to change the world and weave it well, one story at a time.

Table of Contents

~ *Prologue: Weaving The Wyrd* ~

In ancient Norse mythology there are three sisters, the Norns, who live beneath the Yggdrasil tree, or the Tree of Life, keeping it alive with magical mud whilst weaving the fates of humankind. The first sister, Urd (past) arrives at the birth of a child, and weaves the new life from threads of the past. The second sister, Verdani (present) steps in at midlife, ensuring that the path is true. And finally, Skuld (future) appears near the end of life to tie the loose threads and weave the story of that person's life in such a way as to ensure it carries through to the future. The Norns twist the threads into horizontal strands and these cannot be altered. They are fate. It is the vertical threads, those which represent each short lifetime, that can be altered through choice, belief and circumstance. The colourful result of all this weaving becomes the fabric of existence they call the Wyrd.

These beliefs are represented in many other cultures as well. The Persians, Romans and Mayans, to name a few, have crafted their stories into tapestries for centuries. In ancient China, it was common belief that an invisible thread connects those who are destined to meet, regardless of time, place or circumstance. They believed the thread might stretch or tangle, but could never break.

I have come to believe these representations are truths about life and love, war and loss, death and redemption. I have come to see that if we pay close attention, we can follow lines of consciousness from our past into our present and forward into our future.

This story is a work of fiction, loosely based on events in my own life, unravelled, fictionalized and tied back together with my own blue threads, imaginings and dreams of possible past lives.

May we all be open to each thread that comes into our lives — the smooth ones, the tangled ones, the "weird" ones — and with love and support, may we weave them all into brilliant and beautiful lives.

~ *The Way It Is* ~

There's a thread you follow
It goes among things that change. But it doesn't
change.
People wonder about what you are pursuing.
You have to explain about the thread.
But it is hard for others to see.
While you hold it, you can't get lost.
Tragedies happen: People get hurt or die: and
you suffer and get old.
Nothing you can do stops time's unfolding.
You don't ever let go of the thread.

— William Stafford

1

~ *Fury* ~

Fallen twigs snapping beneath her feet, Liv rushes along the tree-lined trail at the river's edge. One might be inclined to look behind to see who is chasing her, but she's alone. It isn't fear that drives her, but fury. The crisis has been building for a long while — her suspicion that Ross has been having an affair has been hanging between them like a dead cat for months. Last night he confirmed it. She's still reeling from all of this, and the incident with the bicycle this morning has toppled her over the edge.

Her arms fling wide in a clumsy attempt to balance as she manoeuvres a twist in the trail, which wends around great grey trunks of the towering cottonwoods that stand in formation like the legs of sleeping elephants. Their sprawling roots threaten to trip her. She clutches a sapling as she rounds a corner on the path — it bends crazily, and she staggers off course into the prickly underbrush.

Goddammit.

Her face grim, her faint blonde brows drawn with concentration, she carries on.

What the hell, you bastard — the kids are out of control? You're out of control! You almost run over our daughter and then you yell at her! I hate you so much right now! Were you in that much of a hurry to meet your girlfriend? You are the most narcissistic, selfish, cold-hearted asshole I have ever known!

Her left sandal slips on a soggy root, turning her ankle painfully. The thrust of the pain evokes a loud sound from deep in her chest — a prolonged, wounded moan. She drops to the ground and rubs her ankle, then pulls herself into a tuck and hugs her legs, rocking gently.

His cruel words from this morning reverberate in her mind, forcing her to relive that moment again.

She is washing dishes at the sink when suddenly he's close behind her, his breath moist and sour with the smell of coffee.

"I told you not to ask if you didn't want to hear the answer." He hisses the words in her ear, so the children, playing nearby, cannot hear. She instinctively flinches away but he holds her arm and she can only press her body against the counter.

Bile rises in her throat. She numbly continues scrubbing the plate in her hand, searching her mind for a response. But then he releases her and he's gone.

She registers the sounds: the door slamming as he leaves; his footsteps on the porch; the car roaring to life; the Volvo spitting gravel as it accelerates in reverse; a metallic crash; her daughter Molly screaming — she launches herself toward the door, mentally accounting for two of her children on the way. In her peripheral vision she can see Micah has dropped his toy bulldozer and is running to the window with his sister Leah, who has abandoned her finches mid-feeding, leaving the cage door open. "Mommy!" they both call, but are transfixed, looking in horror out the living room window. Liv can't stop to look. She knows something horrible has happened and she just has to get there.

"Molly!" She screams as she flies out the front door. Molly had asked to go outside after breakfast to have a quick ride on her bicycle. "Molly!" she screams again.

Tearing down the steps, Liv looks further up the long gravel driveway and sees the twisted, pink metal of Molly's bike beside the car. Folded in on itself, wheels side by side, it looks more like a wheelchair — the rainbow handlebar streamers flap pointlessly in the warm summer morning breeze. Liv's heart is a thumping cold stone, her legs are wobbly, and her brain is in some kind of reptilian mode — she screams "Ross!" and his head turns towards her and then away. She's still too far away to read his expression. Her vision is blocked by the car, so all she can see is the top half of him. It looks like he's bent over Molly, maybe shaking her or holding her. Doing CPR? Liv moves in what feels like slow motion down what seems like a never-ending driveway toward what she's certain is her dying daughter. *Get there, get there.*

Now Liv's hearing kicks back in and she hears Ross shouting, berating Molly. She sees his large hands on her small shoulders, forcing her to look at his steel grey squinting eyes.

"This is your own fault. I've told you kids a hundred times not to leave your toys and shit on the driveway."

Molly sobs, "Sorry Daddy, it was only a minute, I had to go pee. 'Member, you passed me on the steps and didn't say bye. Then you drove backwards and you…wrecked it."

Liv can finally breathe. *She wasn't hit.* Her voice is choked as she pushes past Ross to embrace Molly, kissing the top of her tangled copper hair, "Oh my god, are you okay, sweetheart?"

Molly is fine physically. The look she gives her Dad as she turns to Liv for comfort is haunting… her bright blue eyes flash both anger and sadness.

"Look at my birthday bike, Mommy, it's ruined!" she wails. Liv wipes away her daughter's tears with her sweater sleeve and tries to comfort her, "It'll be okay Molly, this isn't your fault."

"You need to discipline these kids, Liv. They're out of control." Ross glares at her.

"She could have been on this bike — you just weren't paying attention. You could have run over our Molly," she retorts furiously. She wants to scream at Ross or hit him — this man she doesn't even recognize as the man she married — but she can't, not in front of the kids, who are surrounding Molly and the broken bike now.

"I think I can fix it, Molly," Micah offers, his voice soft with empathy.

"They don't deserve new things," Ross says. And with that, he kicks the bike out of the way, pulls a cigarette out of his shirt pocket, sticks it in his mouth unlit and gets back in the driver's seat. He tears up the driveway past the barn, sending Rhode Island red chickens squawking, feathers and dust flying as they scramble out of his way. He's onto the highway and gone without a goodbye, sorry or see you later.

Revisiting this memory fuels a surge of angry energy. Liv gets to her feet and raises her face to the late-summer, leaf-mottled sky. She speaks aloud to the unhearing forest, her voice thick and hoarse with exertion: "I've spent my whole life immobilized by other people's anger. I've swallowed up betrayal after betrayal since I was a small girl. I will not live like this any longer."

She stands still for a moment in the dappled light, feels a slight release from her outburst — instead of being crazed, she has the conviction that she is going to change things.

She straightens her twisted flowery skirt, takes a deep breath and resumes her journey at a slower pace.

My rage has forged something in me that I didn't know existed. If this is the thing that will push me into action, then thank you, Molly, my love, for sacrificing your bike and your trust in your father.

She ducks through the barbed wire fence that runs perpendicular to the river, separating her property from Celeste's. She's done so a hundred times before, but today she's careless and a barb catches her favourite sweater — the sky blue one her grandmother knitted for her when she was sixteen. She feels the tug as the wool begins to unravel.

"Fucking hell!" This is the last straw. It makes her cry. Through all of this, she hasn't cried. She stops and bends, places her hands on her knees and gives in to the sobbing. Her curly, flax-blonde hair clings to her overheated, freckled face.

Throat raw and emotion spent, she reaches up to pull her hair back off her face and neck — the light breeze cools her slightly. She flashes into a strong memory: her grandmother, her namesake, Olive, smiling fondly and softy rasping, *"Sometimes you've got to let yourself come undone a bit Liv."* Then, *"You can do this, sweetheart."* Remembering that dear woman's gentle love and wisdom, Liv composes herself.

She bunches up her cotton skirt and uses it to mop the tears and sweat from her face. Straightening up, she follows the strand of yarn back to the fence, rolling it into a plum-sized messy ball, which she tucks into her skirt pocket. *Later*, she thinks, *much later, I will mend it.*

She carries on. Where the path rises from the river into the meadow, she begins to run again, anxious to see her friend. Jumping over a tree root, her right foot lands full force on a snail's shell, making an awful crunching sound. She cringes and calls an apology to the snail she's certainly killed. Her long limbs and rapid heartbeats slow as she passes through Celeste's garden and approaches her bright green door.

Celeste has been watching for her. The door opens as she mounts the step.

"Oh god, Liv, I could barely make out what you were saying on the phone! Give me a hug."

She steps into Celeste's arms gratefully for a strong, enduring hug that makes Liv want to cry again. She draws her hand down her friend's strong, broad back and encounters the single braid of her dark hair. She grasps it briefly, appreciating the woven strength of the soft twists of hair.

"What the hell happened?" Celeste pulls back and looks into Liv's eyes. "Is it the affair? Did you finally confront him? Did he admit it?"

"It doesn't really matter, he can screw his damned student all he wants for all I care." Anger brings the words tumbling from her. "But now he's hurting the kids too and that's where I draw the line!"

"Ah, Liv. Yes, you do care. You care about all of it. I'm so sorry. Come on inside. I'm making us some tea."

Liv kicks her sandals off onto the porch and enters. As her friend readies the tea, she lowers herself into a chair at the table, handmade out of glowing yellow cedar by Celeste's husband, Jacques. The dining area is set in a nook surrounded by leaded glass windows and affords a serene view of the of Celeste's vibrant garden. This place calms her.

"Will Jacques get any days off this fall?" she enquires. It's always been ironic to Liv that her earthy friend would find happiness with a logger, but she likes Jacques — for all his rough edges, his devotion to Celeste is unquestionable. While she gently restores her clients' hearts and minds as a hypnotherapist in their country home, he's out there pillaging the forest. And yet it works.

"Yes, he'll probably get home for Thanksgiving — and you know you're changing the subject. You're here to talk about you."

"Okay, I know I tend to do that, Celeste. It's because I am literally unravelling! Look at my sweater!" They laugh easily, like they always do, but for Liv, the laughter borders on hysteria. The emotional release threatens the equilibrium she's trying to maintain and tears well up again. Her fair skin is blotchy from crying and her eyes are all the more brilliant blue in contrast with her flushed complexion.

Joining Liv at the kitchen table, Celeste places a box of tissues beside the tea pot and meets her friend's gaze with affection and frank concern.

"Now tell me exactly what happened."

"Last night I avoided looking at him or talking to him until the kids went to bed. Then I got up my courage and finally did what you've been advising me to do for months. I sat him down on the porch and asked him flat out whether he's having an affair with Anya."

"And…?" Celeste's amber eyes are wide.

"He said 'Do you really want to know? There's no going back.' I said yes. I figured if I could get him to admit it or deny it I could at least know where I stand. Then in this cold voice he said 'Yes.' That was it — then he left and didn't come back for hours. He probably went to Rob's to drink. I heard him return and creak around the house. He slept on the couch and I lay awake all night, agonizing.

"This morning he threw it all in my face as if he'd done nothing wrong and slammed out the door, where he proceeded to back his car over Molly's beautiful new bike. For a few heart-stopping moments I thought he'd run over Molly! Then he tore into her, telling her she was a spoiled brat for not putting her bike away. He was merciless."

"Oh, my god." Celeste's expression is shocked.

"Molly was absolutely traumatized — she actually wet her pants, which she hasn't done in years. I managed to calm her down and give her a bath by the time Kat came to pick the kids up for summer camp. I was surprised she still wanted to go. I promised her I'd be there to get them this afternoon and we'd go directly to Cutter's Gorge and get her a new bike."

"Poor little Moll. That must have been terrible for her. And you."

"Yes, sadly, the bike can be replaced, but I think her tears were more about the way her dad treated her. I will never be able to repair that and I'm afraid he won't either. He used to be such a positive, energetic dad and husband — there have been times he's been strict, but he's never been cruel, not like this. Over the last few months he's been making excuses to stay in town — now I know it was because of the affair — but he's also been drinking way more and suffering from terrible migraines. I've been trying so hard to shield the kids from all of it, but now he's broken trust with them too. I can't live like this anymore."

"Of course you can't, Liv. I can see how devastating this is for you. Look at your puffy eyes, and when we hugged I could feel every rib on you."

"Ha, yes, *now* I get skinny! After all the cabbage soup, grapefruit and Jane Fonda aerobics classes we've endured to lose weight, turns out all I needed was a nervous breakdown."

The aroma of freshly picked mint wafts from the steam as Celeste pours the hot tea. She places the honey pot and a plate laden with fruit, crackers and cheese prominently in front of her friend. Liv's stomach clenches in anticipation and she realizes this will be her first nourishment of the day. She'd had no appetite this morning.

"I am so damned angry with that husband of yours after all the crap he's pulled." The soft features of Celeste's tawny brown face, are drawn briefly into an exaggerated scowl.

"When you first moved here I admired what you two had — you were so in love and both absolutely committed to the rural lifestyle, raising organic veggies and free-range kids. And Ross was such a brilliant, charismatic guy. Remember the parties you had? He was so much fun."

"It's all fallen apart, Celeste. He's not the same person anymore. You know, when I was lying awake last night it came to me that everything started to change when he ran for the nomination. It was like he was swept up by the political possibilities — sometimes he seemed too exuberant, too fired up about it — and then he was shocked and devastated when he lost. It's like it took away his sense of himself somehow — his commitment to us, his family, has been eroded."

"I think you're right. He's lost it, and I wonder if he realizes he could very well lose you. Sometimes I think the most helpful thing your women friends could do would be to posse up and run him out of town."

Liv smiles as she visualizes this scenario.

"You know that whether you decide to work things out in your marriage or leave him, you have my full support."

"I'm such a mess, Celeste. I feel so beaten down and weak. I've always been able to feel happiness and joy in my life and now, it's as if the plug has been pulled and it's all draining out of me. I think I really need you, not just as a friend, but as a therapist. I don't think I can make it through this without some help."

"I'm always here for you. You know that. I'd be honoured to be your therapist, but do you realize what that means? You've always been a bit quiet when I've talked about the techniques I use in my work."

"I admit I've been a bit skeptical. But if we were to do it, what would you suggest?"

"We could do some sessions talking about what's happened lately, and in your past."

"You think I need to work on some things from my childhood? My problems are now, Celeste. Do you really think I should be looking at the past?"

"I do, Liv. In my work, I often see that looking at the past, even going back to past lives, can give a person insight into their strengths and find the courage to move forward. You've never really told me much about your life before you came here to Little Mountain. You've alluded to traumatic incidents, but you've never elaborated.

"Your past is who you are — it shapes your personality, your decisions and how you respond to everything. I believe our past lives also have relevance. Somehow you became this amazing person, and I would love to explore that with you using hypno-regression. Do you think you'd be up for that?"

"Childhood and past lives? Really? I'm afraid I'm a bit dubious about that, but maybe it's fear as much as anything." *As if I don't have enough to worry about without adding past incarnations to the mix.*

Liv suddenly realizes this wise woman is the only person she's willing to trust at this moment. She's not some New Age snake oil salesperson, she's her closest friend and a respected therapist who has helped many people through far worse situations. She thinks of her dear friend Thomas, who sought help from Celeste to cope with his fear of death when he was diagnosed with AIDS. *If Celeste could help him, certainly she can help me.*

"I guess we could give it a try."

"Your hesitation is natural," Celeste says with a smile. "We've all been trained to think of hypnosis, reincarnation and past lives as kooky. But I think you'll find it helpful. It will always be your choice what we talk about or where we go in our sessions. It's also absolutely fine if you decide it's not for you."

Liv has another flutter of interior panic. *What am I getting into?* She pushes it aside, choosing to have faith in her friend.

"Okay. Yes, for sure, I do want to try this and I will keep my mind open." Having spoken the words, she feels lighter.

"You're the most wonderful friend, and you've been here for me since the first day we met. I don't know how I would have survived this far if I hadn't had you to talk to and help me figure things out — not just with Ross, you've taught me so much about gardening, parenting, even canning and rural living. I trust you, and I really do feel this is the right time for me to do this. I'm ready."

Celeste beams — the confidence she exudes and the crinkles around her eyes are all that belie her age as a decade ahead of Liv.

"When can we start?" Liv asks, keen to begin now that she's finished wavering.

"I have two hours free tomorrow morning, starting at ten."

2

~ Blue ~

As she retraces her steps through Celeste's vegetable garden on her way home, Liv absently snaps a sprig of rosemary from one of the bright yellow herb pots and inhales its scent. She tilts her face to feel the warmth of the afternoon sun. Through the trees, she can see the glint of sunlight on the river.

She notices with surprise that she feels almost at peace. The anger that drove her to Celeste's has been assuaged. In its place is a strange feeling of purpose. She has a plan to make a plan. Celeste, who has always been her ally, will now bring out her superpower to help her deal with this — and at last she is dealing with it. As she carries on along the trail, thoughts of Ross invade her mind. She always thought if a man ever cheated on her she would kick him out. But it's not that simple.

We've been together nearly ten years, mostly happy. I still love him, I think. But I hate him right now. We've worked so hard to make this farm perfect for us. He's wrecking all that. It doesn't seem like he's even sorry, for the affair or for any of it.

Given Ross' behaviour, anyone else would probably have intuited that he was having an affair long ago, but she didn't — she had felt secure in their love. Their relationship had never been wildly sexual, so a lessening in that department hadn't concerned her. It wasn't until she'd seen Ross and his student at a faculty party last spring that she had the uneasy feeling there was something going on. There was a kinetic energy between he and Anya — he looked entranced with her. There was joy in his eyes.

Maybe the kids and me and the farm have never been enough to keep Ross happy. Maybe he's always been seeking more, one way or another. This may not even be his first affair.

The thought makes her blush with humiliation and bile rises from her stomach into her throat. She swallows hard.

Her pace quickens as she approaches the meadow at the edge of their property. She begins to wonder how the kids are doing at the camp. Molly tends to find a spot and fall asleep if she's emotionally distraught. Once she even crawled under the table at her own birthday party. On the rare occasions when Ross is minding the kids lately, Molly can be found asleep upon Liv's return, no matter the time of day. Molly lost her trust in him long before he ran over her bike, Liv realizes sadly.

Liv doesn't worry about Leah, she'll be looking after other kids, reading or tidying the art supplies. Five-year-old Micah is a different story — whenever she leaves him with anyone, there is an element of stress. When left unsupervised for a moment, he's been known to wander up to the highway or down to the river. Once he got himself into the back of a truck being loaded with bulls and nearly got stomped. Another time, she ran across the kitchen just in time to prevent him from sticking a fork into a light socket.

She realizes with a deep regret that she has never really trusted Ross to keep any of the three kids safe. Her thoughts bounce back and forth. *Is this because he's always been untrustworthy or do I just have a problem with trust? Did he actually change or get worse, or did I just stop being able to make excuses for him?*

Ducking under the fence, she recalls snagging her sweater earlier that morning. She imagines the whole garment unravelling until it becomes nothing but a messy pile of blue threads. *Is my marriage unwinding the same way? Is my whole life coming undone? Losing trust, losing hope, losing the whole ball of yarn. I feel like I'm emptying out. The energy I had for propping myself and this marriage up is dissolving. My heart has cracked open and it hurts like hell, but maybe it had to happen.*

As she passes the asparagus patch, she casts a deep sigh. Another of Ross' big ideas, it looks ragged and weedy. He wasn't happy to just plant a few asparagus plants for the family. No, he had to plant a full acre and dream up a scheme to supply French restaurants in the city — which never happened.

Approaching the house, Liv's apprehension grows. She hopes Ross won't be there — she doesn't want to have to deal with him without the buffer of the kids between them. She should have picked them up by now and if he's home, he could delay her. The children are already off kilter from the scene this morning, they don't need the added insecurity of wondering if their mother will ever come back for them.

She dodges through the rose garden like a spy, trying to see if Ross' car is in the yard. She just wants to duck into the house and grab the car keys. She makes a mental note to remember to water the roses — they're limp with drought but amazingly still willing to share their wonderful scent. Liv has a flash of guilt. This garden was her romantic vision — fragrant roses planted with clumps of lavender and hollyhock. Ross thinks it's a waste of time growing temperamental roses and he hates lavender — he says it's a repellent used by women to remind men of the scent of the sachets in their grandmothers' underwear drawers. A sure-fire turn-off, in his opinion.

Painfully aware of how cowardly she's being, sneaking around the corner of the house, Liv musters up some maturity, if not courage. *If he's here I'll deal with him*, she thinks, but all the same, she sighs with relief when she sees his car is not there.

Her children are not sleeping or huddling in the corner pining for her when she arrives to pick them up, demonstrating that her worst fears are realized only very occasionally. When Micah and Molly spot her they launch themselves into her arms for hugs. From eight-year-old Leah she gets a big smile and a tug on her sleeve. They show Liv some cool dough art they've made. Leah's looks like a map of Canada, Molly's looks like a baby doll in a cradle, and Micah's looks like a dinosaur — possibly. Not wanting to hurt their feelings by hazarding a wrong guess, Liv says, "My artistic kids, I love your creations! Now we're off to the hardware store, as promised."

Molly chooses a two-wheeler bike identical to the one Liv bought the month before, except it's blue. There wasn't another pink one. Micah talks her into buying Skittles candy too. Molly skips around joyfully, the painful incident that morning seemingly forgotten.

At home, she makes her nearly famous grilled cheese taco pizzas and serves them with wedges of Russet apples straight off their tree. After dinner, the kids seem tired and irritable. Molly shoves Micah out of the way when he drives his grader right through the area she has set up for her doll to sunbathe. Leah rolls her eyes when Liv asks for help with the dishes. "What, are you a teenager already?" Liv teases Leah into submission.

They all seem edgy — they know there's a storm brewing, threatening to shake their world, and they need some kind of assurance that everything will be okay, but Liv can't find the words.

Throughout the evening, the kids don't ask where their dad is. They've grown used to him being away all day, or in bed with a migraine. It's such a change from their normal routine. In April through August, when Ross has no classes to teach, he's usually a fount of fun, creating projects and adventures for all of them. Even Liv hasn't given him much thought — she's been focusing on the kids.

Leah seems more subdued than usual and she says she doesn't want a bedtime story — she wants to read her own book, *James and the Giant Peach.* She's more than halfway through and she wants to try to finish it tonight. Liv's heart beats with both pain and pride as she reflects on how grown up her oldest daughter has become, and then as Leah climbs into Liv's arms for a hug, Liv breathes out those thoughts.

"Mommy, what does it mean if somebody is 'on something'?" she asks softly.

"What do you mean, Sweetie?"

"Well, the art camp teacher, the tall one, was talking on the phone, and I could tell she was talking about you and Daddy, and she said, "What a shame about Ross, I swear he is on something.""

Oh man, Liv thinks, *she's too young to know about this kind of stuff.*

She distracts Leah by brightly saying: "I don't know what she meant, Hon, but I know we better get on some jammies and some tooth-brushing, because it has been a super long day!"

Instead, Leah tightens her hug and holds it a little longer. It's so like her eldest child to intuit that her mother needs a little extra love today. She's a caregiver — an eight-year-old with the sensibilities of someone much older. There are times that Liv worries that she's marred Leah's childhood by counting on her way too much to look out for the younger two. *And now she's looking after me*, she muses.

As she's getting ready for bed, Molly asks, "Does Daddy know I got a new bike? He didn't think I 'zerved one."

Liv can't bear to tell her that Daddy probably hasn't given her broken bike, or any of them, another thought since this morning, so she just says, "I don't know, Sweetie, but I can hardly wait to see you ride it tomorrow! We'll take the rainbow streamers off the broken one, they'll look pretty on it."

"Is blue a boy colour, Mommy?"

"No way, Molly," Liv replies, "Boys can't have blue all to themselves — it's one of the best colours and it's for everyone."

Molly smiles a little as she dresses her favourite baby doll in blue sleepers and wraps it up tight in a soft pastel pink baby blanket. "I love *you* to the moon and back," Molly says to her baby doll. Liv smiles, "Well, by golly Miss Molly, I love *you* to Mars and back," she says, lightly tickling Molly's ribs and eliciting her purely joyful laugh.

There's an odd sound coming from the kitchen — Liv rushes upstairs in time to find Micah in his froggy pajamas, diligently sawing at the leg of the oak dining table with a pruning saw. She thought he was asleep!

"No, no, no…" she cries, running to intervene. "No tools inside!"

She coaxes the saw from his tight little grip, scoops him up in her arms, and carries him downstairs to his bed, kissing the angry tears from his cheeks. He's not upset about what he's done, he's upset that

Mommy's taken the saw away. As she re-tucks Micah into his bed, Liv has a flash of irony — that beautiful wooden table should be marked by the children. It was too perfect anyway.

Stories told, monsters banished, kisses delivered, Liv closes their bedroom door and returns upstairs to throw on a load of laundry in the utility room off the kitchen. This is the first time in her life she's had her own washer and dryer. Prior to her marriage, it was laundromats all the way. She tidies the kitchen, even wiping down the wood cook-stove — she calls it Elmira — buffing the nickel trim until it gleams. She loves this room with its rich oak cupboards and the deep indigo countertops set off by splashes of rust, yellow and blue in the inlaid Mexican tile floor.

Ross won't be coming home tonight — it's 8:30 and there's no way he'll be sober enough to drive the hour and a half home. *I've always thought Ross had a problem with alcohol, and I know he takes a lot of pretty strong medication for his migraines, but what if he's 'on something' else?*

Which is worse? The idea that her husband has a drug problem and she doesn't even know it? Or the fact that people — the woman at the day camp and how many others — have observed his behaviour, are talking about it, feeling sorry for her? Do they know he's been cheating on her too? It makes her feel cut off and alone. And beyond exhausted.

3

~ *Into the Deep* ~

Celeste draws Liv into the living room and ushers her to the overstuffed, burgundy velvet couch. Liv has spent many a happy time in this room, but today she feels awkward and nervous. Celeste is different in her role as therapist, a bit more business-like. They hugged as usual when Liv arrived, but Celeste moved directly to the purpose of their meeting. Liv had hoped to chat until she felt more comfortable. She feels rattled as she takes her seat on the couch. Celeste pulls an oriental brocade stool into position in front of Liv and sits.

"I know — it feels weird, doesn't it? Don't worry, Liv. All hypnosis is self-hypnosis — I'm only teaching you how to access your unconscious mind. I promise I'm not going to make you bark like a dog or anything." Their laughter washes away most of Liv's apprehension.

"Okay, Liv, remember that you can stop me at any time. You'll still be right here with me — just your consciousness will be doing a bit of travelling and you're in charge of the journey. It may not always be easy — there needs to be some dying in order to get some rebirthing."

Celeste reaches for Liv's right hand.

"Please take this soapstone pebble and hold it in your hands. It was passed down to me from my Métis birth mother. See the thick white band that goes completely around it? To me, it's a symbol of all things being one. The stone will help you to stay grounded and free at the same time. Are you ready to do this?"

"Yes," she murmurs, flashing a quick smile at her friend. *Not so sure, but at the same time willing.*

"Past, present or future? What do you think?"

"Let's give the past life thing a try," Liv replies, trying to sound brave.

"Okay. Speak out loud to me and I'll record it, so you can revisit it later." She presses the button on the recorder and Liv's heart contracts. *We're doing this thing now.*

"Take a deep breath and relax into the softness of the couch. Look around at your surroundings. Notice the Buddha stained glass in the window on the left — yes, the one you're always begging me to make for you — and the red begonia hanging in the window on the right. Notice how its lush green leaves are reaching for the light. Feel how the roots are stretching down for the nourishment from the earth. Every living thing is the same in this way, reaching for the light above and growing from our roots beneath."

Celeste adjusts the position of the stool, places her strong hands on Liv's knees and continues.

"Plant your feet firmly on the floor. Imagine them heavy on the worn old carpet, strong and sure like the feet of an elephant — grounded and remembering all. Focus for a few moments on the intricate warp and weft of the rug. Imagine your past like a beautiful woven carpet, filled with the stories and adventures of the people who wove it and those who walked upon it.

"Breathing easily, you are moving deeper into relaxation. Your conscious mind is gently falling to sleep, making room for your sleeping mind to slowly wake up."

Liv feels her body relax as if collapsing, while simultaneously her mind opens and focuses solely on her friend's calm, level voice.

"Walking down, down, down a narrow forest trail, green cedar branches swaying lightly in the breeze. Smell the cedar and feel the soft mulch under your feet as you go further down, toward the sea. You arrive at a set of wooden stairs and you can see the shoreline and the distant ocean. Count your steps down, starting at twenty…nineteen, eighteen, seventeen, sixteen…. There you are…fifteen, fourteen, thirteen…through the light mist…twelve, eleven, ten…feeling the rhythm of the ocean…nine, eight, seven, six, five…moving gently across the sands of time… breathing out…four, three, two, one…here you are. Breathe it in….

"Take a few moments to become grounded, Liv. Notice your body, breathe evenly and connect with who and where you are, knowing that you are safe. Let yourself be open to meeting a past version of yourself. Can you see yourself in this place? Where are your feet? Ground them. Where are your hands? Watch them move in this place. Look for the luminous spirit line that is your connection to another from your past. Follow it and you will find someone who is connected to you.

"You are facing several paths to different horizons, with the ones on the left being the far distant past, moving towards the present as you look to the right. Your strong intuition will help you to choose. What is your soul seeking? To heal or to shed light within itself? What are you curious about?"

Indeed, Liv sees the paths. Before her are sandy trails through waving grasses, swimming in blue light. She is drawn to one trail on the left that curves over a rise, out of sight. Under her gaze, the light converges, illuminating this route more intensely than the others. She steps toward it with her mind and her consciousness follows suit. Her body floats.

"Now that you have chosen, you become acutely aware of your senses. When you feel like speaking, Liv, tell me what you see and feel and hear."

Session No. 1 transcript, Aug. 30, 1987
Hannah, 1855

I hear the sounds of birds overhead — sea gulls, I think. When I talk, my voice sounds distant in my head.

I smell and taste the salty air. I feel a gentle wind on my face and it's blowing my hair. I feel like I'm in between one place and another, and also like it's all only in my imagination.

"Heart to heart, mind to mind, body to body, soul to soul," Celeste says gently. "Let yourself be in this time and within this being that you have chosen to explore."

My feet are in sand right now. I'm being drawn toward the sea. The mist parts and shows me the watery route I will travel.

I'm not afraid at all as I step onto the path and move through the tunnel of swirling blue light across, across and across an enormous body of water...like I'm crossing a huge, long bridge.

Now I'm slowing down. I have arrived at my destination in the middle of a dark, cold, stormy sea. Far below me, a wooden barrel floats slightly off kilter, bobbing in rough waves.

I feel like I've been turned into fluid and I'm being poured into a vessel from a great height. Everything is black — no, my eyes adjust and I see a child. I join this child — in a barrel in the ocean. I suddenly share her senses, I actually feel her body, feel her emotions, think her thoughts. She seems vaguely familiar.

The sky that is visible through the top of the barrel is bluish black. The only part of her body that is feeling warm are her wet, leather-clad feet. She's sitting in a few inches of whiskey, from the smell of it.

Her hands are small and blotchy and icy cold, clinging like lobster claws to the sides of the cask as it's tossed around in the angry sea. It's dark and loud with the thumping of waves. She's terrified. Her name is Hannah and she's lost. The language she's thinking in is Dutch, but somehow I'm able to understand.

Celeste, I'm panicking. I have to say your name so I know you're still there. How did this little girl get here?

"Breathe Liv, remember to breathe and remember everything is as it should be. Let her tell you her story. You are only there to see and feel, not to change anything."

Okay. It's as if I see with my eyes and think with my mind but her fear and despair overwhelm me.

Hannah begins to sing. Her voice is heartbreakingly sweet, surprisingly full for a child so young, although the flow of the song is broken by her shivering. It's a children's poem — a lullaby.

Winken, Blynken and Nod, one night, sailed off in a wooden shoe;
Sailed off on a river of crystal light into a sea of dew.
"Where are you going and what do you wish?" the old moon asked the three.
We've come to fish, for the herring fish, that live in that beautiful sea.
"Nets of silver and gold have we," said Winken, Blynken and Nod.

She thinks if she sings loud enough she'll be heard and someone will rescue her. She's singing for her family, whom she fears are lost under the cold, dark sea.

The old moon laughed and sang a song as they rocked in the wooden shoe.

And the wind that sped them all night long ruffled the waves of dew.

Her throat is a mass of raw nerves from trying not to cry. She can no longer contain her fear and pain — her small chest is heaving, tears are running down her face. She is struggling, forcing herself to sing, trying desperately to project her voice out of the barrel.

Now the little stars are the herring fish that live in the beautiful sea:

"Cast your nets wherever you wish never afraid are we!"

Some folks say 'twas a dream they dreamed of sailing that misty sea.

Now she's remembering the last time she heard this song. Her mother was tucking her and her little brother into their yellow-painted trundle beds in the bedroom they shared. She's envisioning it, and I can see, I can feel her memory — how lucky she felt to have the best Mama and Papa and brother and home in all of Amsterdam. Soft blue curtains frame the windows of the two-gabled room. Down in the cobblestoned street, the clip, clop of wooden shoes and horse's hooves. The wonderful aroma of apple cinnamon streusel wafts through the window, which is open just a crack, causing the curtains to billow inward. Her memory is so detailed....

Now she hears her mother humming downstairs as she prepares supper for Papa, the murmur of them sharing a joke she cannot hear and their light, warm laughter. Hannah longs to linger in this lovely memory forever, but this thought brings the present crashing back. She takes a fortifying breath, deep into her diaphragm, and resumes singing.

Now Winkin and Blynken are two little eyes and Nod is a little head.

And the wooden shoe that sailed the skies is a wee one's trundle bed.

So close your eyes while mother sings of the wonderful sights that be.

And you shall see those beautiful things as you sail on the misty sea,

Where the old shoe rocked the fishermen three – Winkin, Blynken and Nod.

As she sings the last verse, there's a fullness, a harmony — there's the sense that her mother's voice is accompanying her, completing the sound, and their journey together. Suddenly, and with terrifying clarity, Hannah knows that her mother has drowned. Her spirit has come to say goodbye. She feels the loss like a stabbing pain in her heart and she slumps into the depths of the barrel.

I can't let her give up. I have to try to encourage her to survive. I reach into her mind with mine, trying to emanate hope and positive energy. She rouses slightly. I urge her to sit upright, further out of the whiskey that sloshes in the barrel.

She begins to rub her freezing hands together to warm them, but it hurts terribly. With difficulty, she unbuttons her fine woolen coat and tucks her icy hands under her armpits. They begin to feel a tiny bit warmer. Her mind returns to the near certainty that her Mama and Papa and little Finn are dead. In her heart, she feels that this is so.

She's getting too weak to balance against the rocking barrel, which lurches and reels in the waves. I want to help her, but a particularly large wave slams the vessel to one side, knocking her sideways. Her head cracks heavily against the hardwood cask. Hot pain in her skull, then sickening dizziness.

The sky — at least the small part of it she can see — turns purply black, then a blacker black. She's passing out.

4

~ *Swallowed* ~

Session No. 1 transcript continued, Aug. 30, 1987
Hannah, 1855

Celeste's soft voice echoes distantly in her consciousness.

"Breathe, Liv, breathe. You're in a safe place. Feel the cool smoothness of the soapstone in your palm. Have you had enough?"

No, I want to stay. It's so good to hear your voice, though.

"I'm right here. We'll stay with Hannah. You're doing well at telling me what you see and feel."

The sun is coming up — I can make out the edge of the barrel. Hannah is awake again. She stands and tries to climb up to the rim. Every movement threatens to tip it. Finally, she manages to peek out. She gasps the fresh, salty air — such a relief. The surrounding ocean has calmed.

Now that it's brighter I can see what she looks like. She's pale, and her chestnut-coloured braids hang limply.

Overhead there are hundreds of birds — all sorts of birds that I don't recognize. Some look a bit like the seabirds I've seen in Europe and others look strange and cartoonish, purplish grey with long red beaks and pink eyes. They're swooping and whooping and screeching.

Hannah calls out to them in a sing-songy voice, "Help me, help me, birds." It's like she's trying not to scare them — she wants to befriend them so they'll help her. "Pretty birds, fly me out of here. Our ship has sunk, my parents are drowned and my brother is lost like me."

She's just making up the mournful words as they come to her.

"Can you see Finn? Fly to him!"

She's going through all the possible scenarios in her mind — maybe the ship didn't sink after all, or her parents were able to survive and are floating nearby. Surely the lifeboats are drifting close to her and will spot her and reunite her with Finn. She starts to sing again — Finn's favourite lullaby, just in case he can hear her.

Slaap Kindje Slaap
Sleep, baby sleep,
Outside there walks a sheep,
A sheep with white feet,
Who drinks his milk so sweet,
Sleep, baby sleep.

The song complete, she succumbs to despair. She conjures an image of a ship sinking below violent waves, voices screaming in the dark, splashing sounds and then nothing. Nothing but the incessant thunking of waves drumming against the barrel.

"Swoop down, bright birds! Lift me up, magical wooden shoe! Lift me and my family out of this cruel sea! Take us home, take us home!" She's singing even louder, her voice now raspy. I'm amazed by this little girl's fighting spirit.

A sudden wave makes the barrel sway dangerously and Hannah is jolted sideways, losing her footing. Afraid that the unsteady barrel will topple and fill with water, she slumps back onto the floor. At first, I think she's losing consciousness, but her mind is still working away. She escapes into memories again — no, more like a dream world that I seem to be privy to.

I see her mother's face, then her father's, then Finn's. Fleeting images, sort of scrambled. A beautiful old wooden steamer ship. There's some kind of lounge, with plush seats and polished wood. I can smell the polish, it's like the stuff in the tins we used when I was a kid.

Hannah sits with her father. He's a dignified looking man, well-dressed, with dark hair and a trimmed beard.

"Papa, how much longer will we be on this ship?"

"We will arrive in Edinburgh tomorrow morning. Your Aunt Rachel will be at the dock. She can't wait to finally meet you and Finn." His voice is rich and deep, his dark brown eyes are serious, yet kind.

"It seems like we've been moving forever and we're still in the middle of nowhere," she says.

He laughs fondly.

"It may seem so, my little one, but we're really in the middle of everything. If you go that way, you would find France, and over there is Norway."

"I know about France because it's next door to Holland. I've never heard of Norway."

"It's a vast, wild country. Its coastline has many fjords — long, winding ocean bays surrounded by steep mountains. Many years ago, it was the home of the Vikings."

He has piqued her curiosity.

"What's a Viking, Papa?"

"They were a warlike people who were farmers, but also accomplished sea travelers. They built long wooden boats with great tall dragon heads carved on the front. They navigated by the stars and traversed the world by sea."

"Like pirates?"

"Yes, very much like pirates. Only they had metal hats with big horns on them."

"I wish I was a Viking so I could explore the world — but I don't want to wear horns on my head."

Papa laughs and reaches to lift her into his lap, where he hugs her close.

"You are such a delight, my dear child. Please don't ever change." Oh, the feeling Hannah has when he holds her — protected, adored.

Beside them, Mama is reading a story to Finn, who sits enrapt, clutching a small wooden flute. Hannah gave him that flute. She flashes onto a memory of the two of them at home, her coaching, him doing his best to keep up. She has a grand dream of being a brother/sister musical duo — she envisions Finn becoming a virtuoso flautist, and pictures herself seated at the piano, mesmerizing audiences with her fluid fingers and her voice.

What was that? Strange noises. A loud cracking sound and then a thump that vibrates throughout the entire ship. It tilts abruptly, causing a few people to lose their balance. Papa holds Hannah more tightly. Mama flings her arm and pins Finn protectively in his chair. Her eyes are wide with alarm.

The crew is running in all directions, struggling to stay upright against the increasing angle of the ship and barking orders at each other.

"I am sure it is nothing serious, darlings," Mama says, her voice wavering. "The captain is probably having some trouble cutting through this icy water."

Distressing shouts and creaking noises. It's serious — the crew are in a panic, and the passengers, in response, begin to push out onto the deck. Everyone is talking at once — in the jumble of words, the rumour spreads that the ship has run aground on submerged rocks and the hull has been damaged severely.

Everything is chaotic — all I can see is a crush of people. Mama and Papa are trying to protect Hannah and Finn, but it's terrifying.

Papa finds a small alcove out on the deck in the shelter of a stairway. He corrals Mama and the children into the area and clutches the stair railing and a pipe, encircling them with his arms.

A sailor comes by and shouts at her father to keep his family together, stay put and not go below deck to their stateroom.

I get an image of Hannah's mother in her long black coat, its soft grey fur collar buttoned up tight. Her dignified, upswept hairstyle is being ravaged by the wind and wisps fly across her face. She is trying to smile for the children's benefit, but she's pale and her lips are trembling.

Finn begins to whimper with fear. Despite being very scared herself, Hannah tries to distract him with a clapping game.

"Peas porridge hot, peas porridge cold, peas porridge in the pot nine days old." Finn smiles tentatively as he tries to keep the rhythm, clapping his hands against hers.

She tickles him under his chin, making him smile, but fear is still evident in his wide eyes. His dark brown curls are damp from the sea spray, his chubby cheeks are rosy. He squirms and buries his face in Mama's coat.

All is noise and turmoil — the other passengers are screaming, crying, or huddled together in frozen silence. Hannah is watching a woman and a young girl nearby. She recognizes the girl from the dining room the day before. They were seated at the same table and Hannah was entranced by the girl's honey coloured ringlets and ivory skin. They were English, so Hannah couldn't communicate much with the little girl, whose name was Winnie — but she hoped they could become friends during the voyage.

Winnie's mother is clutching a rope that dangles from the deck above and her daughter is desperately clinging to her legs.

Then the worst happens. The ship shudders and drops suddenly, jarring everyone. Winnie loses her footing and her grip on her mother and falls onto the tilting deck of the ship. The sound of creaking, breaking timbers, high pitched squealing of steam and howling wind makes it hard to hear anything else but Hannah can hear Winnie's pleading voice. Hannah watches her slide as the ship creaks and tilts further — Winnie is flailing to stop herself, but there's nothing to stop her — and she rolls under the ship's railing and disappears.

It happens in slow motion — yet it happens so quickly that no one can stop it. All the way down the deck and falling through the air, she cries, "Mummy, Mummy, Mummy!" Her mother is screaming and lurching after her. She's grasping the railing, looking down in horror and then her knees buckle underneath her.

No one can move to save Winnie or help her mother or do anything. Other people have fallen and are screaming for help — people cling to the railings, metal and rope cables or iron rings. Hannah's family is clustered in their corner, anchored by Papa's strong arms.

Winnie's mother is pleading to God now. She's on her knees, shaking her fists at the sky — her frazzled red hair has come unpinned and she looks like a wild woman. She tears off her wool coat and throws it over the railing and shouts "Winnie, take my coat to keep you warm," which makes little sense, but only Hannah seems to be listening.

Mama and Papa are trying to shield their children's eyes from witnessing all of this, but it's too late, they have already seen. Hannah's eyes are locked on the woman, who is frantically scanning the water for a glimpse of her daughter. I feel a flash of outrage, and in the same instant, angry tears blur Hannah's vision.

"We have to help her, Papa!"

His eyes transmit his mortification. "There's nothing we can do, my love. If I were to go out there I would have to leave you."

Papa catches the arm of one of the ship's crew, a tall man with a scruffy moustache and a deep voice, who breathlessly tells him to remain here with his family and that a lifeboat will soon be ready for them. Winnie's mother now cries out angrily to all those around her.

"Why did you not help my daughter?"

Hannah ducks under her father's arm, scrambles over to the woman and takes hold of her skirt.

"I am so sorry." She says it in Dutch, crying. "Winnie was so nice and so pretty, I wanted to be her friend." Of course the woman doesn't understand the words but she pulls Hannah to her body and holds her tightly.

Hannah's parents rush over, with Finn between them. They grip the railing and each other, enclosing the distraught woman along with their family. Bowing their heads, they recite a prayer aloud. Winnie's mother joins in and they speak together to the same God, in their different languages.

The pitching of the sea threatens to topple them off their feet, so they return to their alcove, drawing Winnie's mother with them. She crumples into the corner. The family is observing the mayhem around them. It is as if they hope that by standing quietly together amidst the wrecking ship and raging water, they will be safe from harm.

There are multiple cries from further back on the ship: "There are not enough lifeboats for everyone! Stand aside! Let me through! My children!"

Papa turns ashen. His strong, square jaw is set in a grimace and his eyes are misty and dark. He pulls his yarmulke out of his inner coat pocket and puts it on his head, but the wind immediately catches it and dashes it to the deck at his feet. He picks it up and holds it against his face, shielding his family from his fear. Then he gathers them in his arms and they sink to their knees, bracing against the movement of the lurching ship, and pray through their tears.

"Women and children first!" a crewman calls, and all is pandemonium as people clamber along the deck, dragging their loved ones along and jostling others out of the way. Great waves crash against the ship and run down the deck in cascades that wash people into the sea. A huge pile of heavy chain slides thunderously past, unwinding like a snake, knocking people down as it slithers violently across the steep slant of the ship's deck. It goes the way of Winnie, under the railing and into the sea, without the anchor that was meant to hold it fast.

A sailor strides over and scoops up Finn and sets off into the throng of people surging toward the lifeboats. Papa grasps Hannah and Mama and they burst after him. The sailor passes the squirming, wailing Finn to an old woman at the front of a lifeboat. Papa has pressed forward into the crowd and manages to catch a fleeting glimpse of his son's contorted face before the woman passes him back, out of sight, into the crush of women and children huddling within. Papa is pushed back by the mob and clambers across the deck to rejoin his wife and daughter.

"My Finn!" Mama calls.

"At least he will be safe," Papa says. He picks up Hannah and looks into her eyes. "I need you to be brave, my love, and look after your brother."

He begins to move once more toward the lifeboat, hoping to get her on also — but the crew has swung the boat out over the edge of the rail and are lowering it into the sea. The three watch in shock and horror.

"Sir! Come this way." Another sailor is gesturing for them to follow. He leads them toward the rear of the ship, where there are fewer people. Father makes sure Hannah and her mother have a safe place to wait and goes over to the crew, who are rigging a barrel to ropes and a pulley. They talk agitatedly for a few moments.

When he returns, he whispers briefly in his wife's ear, then bends to talk to Hannah.

"Hannah, we love you so much. These men have a plan to save you, but you must be strong. The lifeboats are all gone, but they'll put you in a barrel to escape the ship. Find Finn and look after him for us. When we are rescued, God willing, we will soon be united again."

Hannah's mother joins them and she takes her daughter in her arms. Her face is drawn with sorrow and panic. Hannah tries to focus on her words.

"God has blessed you, Hannah. Remember always who you are and what gifts you bring to the world. God is our refuge, our strength and our path."

Watching this breaks my heart — these are the last words she spoke to her daughter. And now Hannah is meticulously remembering the whole horrendous event, looking for meaning in every word, every action.

The three of them are on their knees, entwined, on the deck. Their faces pressed together, her parents kiss her on the cheeks simultaneously. Mother buttons up her daughter's wool coat just before Hannah is scooped up by one of the crewmen. He tells her not to be afraid, and then he lowers her into the barrel, which still contains several inches of whiskey.

As she is being lowered in, she can see her parents holding each other — bracing themselves to lose everything and everyone they have ever loved. From the darkness of the barrel, she thinks she hears their voices joined in prayer. Shivering uncontrollably, she recites it in her head.

God is our refuge and Strength
Therefore we will not fear,
though the earth does change and
though the mountains be
moved into the heart of the seas.
Though the waters thereof roar and foam,
though the mountains shake at the swelling
Thereof... Shela.
There is a river, the streams thereof make glad the city of God
The holiest dwelling place of the Most high.
God is in the midst of her, she shall not be moved:
God shall help she, at the approach
of morning... Shela.

Hannah is jostled as the barrel is hoisted aloft and lowered into the sea. Her heart pounds and her stomach wobbles with nausea. She scrambles up and grips the rim of the barrel, hoping to see her parents one last time — but the ship shifts again, rises ponderously, and with an ominous groan, capsizes fully onto its side. The resulting turmoil of the water causes her vessel to lunge and change direction and she's thrown to its bottom, so she doesn't see what must certainly be the death of her parents.

"Liv, I'm going to bring you back. One, two, three, four...pull yourself away...five, six, seven... coming back to the present...eight, nine, ten. You are alert and feeling refreshed, calm and safe. Wow, Liv, what a journey that was for you. Me too, actually. Let's take a few minutes to get grounded here again."

Celeste is there, right in front of her, leaning forward and looking at her attentively.

"Just take a few big breaths. Plant your feet firmly on the floor and look at my eyes. Recognize our connection and the work we are doing together. Do you feel okay, Liv? Do you feel safe now?"

"I just need a few moments to gather my thoughts and feelings. That was so intense. I feel extremely cold, like my spirit has been drowned in icy water."

Celeste reaches for the well-worn Navaho blanket beside her on the couch and wraps it around Liv's shoulders.

"There's so much to take in. It feels like this little girl has so much to tell me — things I already knew at some level, but have forgotten."

Liv begins to relax back into her present surroundings — the artful clutter of Celeste's home, the chatter of birdsong through the open window. No angry sea, no danger, no death.

"I'm not surprised, Liv," Celeste responds, "Our subconscious minds are chock full of memories, images and symbols relating to our struggles in this and past lives. Dreaming and hypnosis both bring them to the surface."

"I need to go back to see Hannah again. I have the strong sense that she survived. And she seems so familiar to me, like I really did live as her."

"Your connection to her was so vivid and full of emotion," says Celeste, "It's so amazing that Hannah took your visiting spirit back to the ship to share those last moments with her family. I've never seen anything like that before."

"I don't get it. How could I have been a little Jewish girl in a past life? I don't think my family has any Jewish connections."

"Nobody really knows how it works, Liv. There are lots of theories. The prevailing belief is that souls are reborn into situations that will teach them the lessons they need to become a more enlightened spirit. Souls are reborn again and again, inhabiting any number of bodies.... It would be rare, I would think, for one to be reborn into the same family."

"Okay, I sort of understand."

"There are enough books written on this to keep you busy for the next thirty years. I kind of like the idea that when we die, our spirits go to a place that some people might call heaven. I see it as a vast, magnificent library in the sky."

"That's a cool image."

"I have a picture of it in my imagination: there's no ceiling, and the walls are lined with books and intricate tapestries and paintings depicting the lives of all souls. This is the place where spirits from the past, present and future gather. It's here that we determine which body we'll be born into, which life lesson each person will learn this time around. It takes centuries. Sometimes a lucky soul gets to stay in the library and venture back to a suffering existence only when it needs a break from the pure bliss of being there. Sorry for the long explanation, but you asked...."

"So, who decides where a soul goes?"

"The soul chooses where it will be born next."

"So, I chose my parents?" The idea makes her laugh and wrinkle her nose.

"Yeah, if this concept of reincarnation is true."

"I guess I like that better than if it were just random — like a giant assembly line of souls needing bodies on one side, and bodies needing souls on the other. I can't believe I'm talking like this! A few hours ago, I didn't believe in any of this past-life stuff. But now I can see how this experience might help me tie some loose ends together."

Liv thinks for a moment, and then leans toward Celeste.

"There's one thing that makes me question all this. Starting when I was young, maybe four or five, I had a recurring dream, until I was a teen, that my bedroom was engulfed in a ferocious storm and I was riding my bed like a life raft, adrift in the waves, far out to sea. Out of the mist and the wind, a girl would appear, clinging to a piece of wreckage from a ship — holding on for dear life, strong, brave and singing. I would pull the little girl onto my bed and together we would weather the storm."

"Hannah." Celeste's eyes are wide.

"Yes. I wonder whether, when you hypnotized me, maybe I just called up that old dream and made it into a story."

"It's possible, Liv. In my experience, it would be unlikely under hypnosis, but you certainly tapped into something from your past, if not a past life." Now she sits forward, looking into her friend's eyes.

"What most concerns me is your dream. For a child to have a recurring dream like that implies you were in danger — it sounds to me like you were a little girl with something terrible to deal with. Can you tell me what it was?"

Liv pauses, then speaks tentatively. "You know, I don't really want to go there right now. I always figured I must have created that little girl to be my imaginary friend."

"It's possible," Celeste says thoughtfully. "Or maybe she created you."

The two of them digest this statement silently, and then Liv gives a little shiver. She rises, laughing nervously.

"At any rate, Hannah's story is incredibly compelling," she says brightly. "I really do need to find out what happens. Is it possible to pick up this same life, later on in another session?"

"Normally I wouldn't be sure about that, Liv. But you have remarkable abilities under hypnosis — you're able to convey Hannah's story as you observe it and spin it out in such colourful detail. I suspect you'll be able to steer yourself wherever you want or need to go."

5

~ Lost and Found ~

"Hey Liv! You're looking fresh today. Did you actually get some sleep?" Celeste greets her on the porch. Her gaze is concerned as she assesses her friend.

"A little bit — I managed to take the time to have a bath this morning, and I'm less tense because Ross hasn't been home for the last two days," Liv says with note of irony.

"I know he's okay because I called the university and talked with his great, gossipy secretary. Sometimes I think she revels in spreading rumours, although they do seem to be true. She said he was there yesterday, prepping for classes and raising a ruckus with the union. One of the other profs has been charged with sexual misconduct and Ross is defending him to the hilt, even planning a protest, she thinks. Christ, these guys are having affairs with students, screwing other people's husbands and wives. It's a hotbed of scandal — and Ross and I are centre stage at the moment, I suppose."

"Man! Life here in Little Mountain is pretty tame in comparison."

The two women enter the house. Celeste turns to go into the living room, but Liv holds back.

"Would it be okay if we just had a little visit before we get into the session? I'm feeling so overwhelmed with my own life, I think I need to talk for a while before I'll be ready to face Hannah's life too."

"No wonder you're feeling overloaded. Tell me about it," Celeste says as she heads for the kitchen.

"When Ross is away like this, I can't stop torturing myself, imagining all these sordid scenarios between him and Anya. She's so cool compared to me. She's like a cross between Annie Lennox and Sinead O'Conner — her head is shaved, but it's perfectly shaped. She's skinny and she wears impossibly tight black jeans and a leather jacket. Both of her arms are covered in tattoo sleeves with gorgeous Celtic designs. Of course, she has everything pierced — her ears, her nose, her tongue and probably her clit too," Liv says mournfully, hoping for a laugh.

She cringes as she thinks about her own lack of "coolness." She's always felt somewhat confident in her physical appearance and in her ability to carry on witty, intelligent conversations. But put her in a room with a bunch of artsy extroverts and she's sure to feel frumpy and shy with nothing to say.

Celeste grabs Liv's hand and says, "It's time for you to get it out of your system — it's not even about you, what happened. You need to let go of that insecurity."

"I imagine the two of them locked in passion on his desk with students lined up outside the door. Him performing fellatio on her in the back of our car, doing things he'd never want to do to me — or I'd never let him. I imagine how it would feel if we broke up and she became my kids' step-mom. What if they just love her?"

"Liv?" Celeste asks, "It might help to do a little exercise to help you let go of those thoughts. It's just not helpful for you to torture yourself! Here's a pen and paper, I want you to write down the worst of the worst images, right down to clit rings and whose parts went where and how."

Bent over the page, Liv's face becomes red and rashy and she has tears in her eyes as she writes down the scenarios that have been playing in her head. She reads them aloud to Celeste and somehow the daggers are taken out of them, and they sound more silly than painful.

"I'm pretty sure you can't even put that there unless you're a contortionist," Celeste snorts, trying to suppress her laughter, and both women laugh until they're holding their sides.

"Now carry that paper to the fireplace, rip it up into pieces, strike a match and light it on fire and say 'I release these images'."

She feels a bit silly doing this, but as she sets it alight the paper evaporates quickly into flame and a black tongue of smoke slips up the chimney, taking with it some of Liv's angst and anger. She sits back on her heels and breathes out a sigh.

"I've been thinking so much about Hannah – did I truly visit my past soul or did I just dredge up a childhood nightmare and cook up a story in my imagination?"

Celeste smiles, "Does it matter?"

"No, like I said, it's weird, but I think it's helping me find some kind of inner courage and let go of some of the things that are not in my control. I really want to find out if Hannah gets though this."

"Okay Liv, we won't need to do the full prologue to the hypno-session today, as your mind will remember how to be hypnotized and you'll know where you're going — that part is scientific, by the way. I could show you my brain diagrams if you like.

"Direct your mind back to where we left off…"

Liv imagines she's walking on a path through a magnificent forest. Her mind is clear and observant as she follows Celeste's voice and her heart quickens with excitement rather than fear this time as she arrives at a series of stairs leading down to a white, sandy beach. With each step she goes deeper, deeper into relaxation. Her heartbeat slows now and her mind's eye becomes focused and clear. She feels the wind as it gently rustles the leaves of a stately arbutus at the foot of the trail… seven, six, five, four… she's breathing comfortably… three, two… down, down…finally at the last step… she can smell the sea and feel it lapping at her toes.

A cool mist surrounds her as she stands grounded on the sands of time. The mist parts to the left, and again she's with her spirit sister, Hannah.

Session No. 2 transcript, Sept. 12, 1987
Hannah, 1855

Hannah is still in the barrel. She's awake, trembling violently from the cold. It's just past dawn and the sky is pinkish grey and cloudy with just a tiny patch of blue directly overhead. The barrel is rocking more gently now — there are fewer waves. I hear seabirds calling very close — they pass through the view above, wheeling around. Perhaps their squawking is what roused her.

She's so weak, but she's pulling herself up, trying to peek out of the barrel. It tips dangerously with her movements.

She glimpses the dark silhouette of land on the distant horizon, then drops down into the icy liquor again. She spreads herself wide to try to steady the barrel. I can feel her giving up hope — the land is too far away, there is no one to save her. She's crying now. Images — flashes of her parents, of Finn — haunt her mind, driving her tears.

She's all crumpled up and sitting in six inches of whiskey, now fouled with her own urine.

I feel her giving up, slipping away. The chill in her limbs is creeping into her core. There is an ominous quiet. She's fading away.

It's so awful, but I feel like I have to let her go. Things have to happen as they're meant to....

Delirious and as if in a dream, from below the surface of the water, I hear a squeaking sound, or more like a tiny horn blowing. Swimming in the bluish haze in Hannah's mind, I see two shining white sea creatures emerge from the darkness. Their bulbous heads glow — one comes in close, then turns and I look into an intelligent black eye. They are beluga whales — beautiful white belugas — and they swirl around the barrel, bumping it playfully. I can't tell if they're real or in Hannah's imagination. There's an actual sensation of movement — the barrel is travelling as opposed to just bobbing suspended in the water.

The movement makes her empty belly whirl — these strong, magnificent creatures are transporting the barrel toward what looks like a giant green rock in the sea. Hannah's body is numb, her mind is barely conscious. But somehow I'm still here with her, bound by the luminous thread joining our souls.

There is a jarring crunch — the barrel connecting with the sea bottom. Hannah stirs. Miraculously, I think I hear people talking and the sounds of splashing.

The voices grow louder, the barrel suddenly tips on its side and a small round face surrounded by a halo of blonde curls peers in.

For an instant Hannah thinks this is the girl from the boat — Winnie, the one who fell overboard. She's so excited — her mind screams, "She is alive!" But I can see it's not Winnie — this girl is much paler, a little older, skinnier, and taller than Winnie. Her heavy wet clothes make her look comical. She reaches into the barrel, trying to pull Hannah out and she's smiling and sputtering. She turns and shouts to someone behind her.

Two older girls come and help her drag Hannah's limp body out of the barrel. Wading through the surf, they carry her to shore and set her on the beach. The taller one strips off her cloak and wraps it tightly around Hannah. The little one is quaking with cold, but talking excitedly, non-stop, in Norwegian.

The two older girls carry Hannah between them up a steep path that winds up the craggy hillside, followed by their shivering, wet little sister. At the top they travel along a forest path to a clearing with an old ramshackle farmhouse, its whitewash peeling with age. It sits too tall, leaning slightly to the right — perhaps this is the pervasive direction of the wind and over many years the house has shifted. It looks as though it just may fall down with one strong huff or puff. I see smoke coming from the chimney — they'll be able to warm Hannah and hopefully nurse her back to health. The little girl — the others call her Ingaborg — is chattering away to Hannah. She doesn't yet realize that Hannah is barely conscious and can't understand her language anyway.

The door opens, and there stands a stern looking woman with her hair pulled tightly into a bun. She's dressed in a dull grey cotton dress, a fishy smelling, bloody apron tied around her waist. The three sisters all begin talking at once. When the mother has deciphered their story, she scoots them inside. Hannah is deposited on the wooden floor in front of a large stone fireplace. The woman begins to undress both Ingaborg and Hannah and then wraps them up, skin to skin, in scratchy wool blankets. She sends one of the older girls outside to fetch more wood to make the fire hotter.

She's a dour figure — all of this she has performed without a smile, but there is kindness in her actions. Now satisfied that the girls are warming, she begins preparing food, all the while issuing orders to her two eldest daughters, Oline and Alexandria. Ingaborg, meanwhile, is still talking to Hannah, but now she's whispering into her sodden, smelly hair. Hannah is drowsy and only vaguely aware of where she is, but I feel a tremendous sense of comfort in her as the warmth slowly ekes into her core and Ingaborg's animated voice reminds her what it is to be alive.

It is a cold, bare room, with little furniture other than a table with benches where the woman and her daughters are working. From time to time, one of them stirs a kettle suspended over the fire.

Hannah has fallen asleep. She's safe and I think she's going to be okay.

From far away, Celeste says, "Yes, Liv. She's a tenacious little spirit. Do you want to see how her life plays out? Try to cast your spirit line forward — you can touch down in different places, like a stone being skipped over the surface of a pool."

Alright.

Whoa! You're right. It's like time slipped ahead, just a little bit. So strange! Hilde — that's the mother's name — is bending over, feeding Hannah tiny spoonfuls of broth. Ingaborg is no longer tucked in — she's at the table, where she and her sisters are devouring freshly baked biscuits and milk.

Hannah can't swallow the broth — she's sputtering, it's dripping down her chin. But with each spoonful, a little makes its way down her parched throat.

Nothing in her life has ever tasted so good. Her hands are throbbing as they begin to thaw — her belly contracts and groans as the food arrives. Now the tears come.

Hilde doesn't acknowledge her crying or try to comfort her, but Ingaborg comes back and curls in beside her, murmuring in her language that everything will be all right. Tears of sympathy trickle down her round cheeks.

Suddenly it's as if I'm watching a movie playing at fast speed — I'm hearing and seeing so many things at once it's overwhelming. I don't know if I can describe it, but I'll try.

"Liv, turn the stone to help you manage the speed. Your breath is your view into the soul, so breathe evenly. Take it in…. Focus on that thread of light that binds you to Hannah. Carry on. Cast forward — I have the recorder running."

~ ~ ~

Hannah and Ingaborg are walking hand-in-hand along a trail on a ridge high above a stunning fjord. It's warm and sunny and they're dressed for summer in plain cotton shifts. I can see houses here and there through the trees, as well as goats and sheep grazing on green grass. The girls are talking and giggling. They're speaking Norwegian. Hannah speaks slowly, but they understand each other fairly well, so I must have jumped forward in time several months.

They're excited because they've finished their chores and Ingaborg's mother Hilde has given them a basket of food to take to Great Uncle Olav, Hilde's mother's eldest brother. He's just returned from a long fishing voyage — even though he is very old, Ingaborg explains, the fishermen welcome him along because of his almost magical ability to find the best fishing grounds.

He's a very lonely man, she says. His beloved wife and daughter died from influenza many years ago. Since then he's lived in semi-isolation in a stone house he built under a massive granite ledge on the edge of the Lutheran settlement. He's a storyteller, and he loves to share tales about his family to keep them alive in his mind.

When they arrive at Uncle Olav's curious house, Hannah is shy with the old man — she's never seen so many wrinkles, and he's thin and bent. His faded blue eyes shine in the dim light of his grim, cramped home.

Uncle Olaf settles in to entertain his guests — but Ingaborg eagerly asks him if she can first share a story of her own. She describes the day she found Hannah — how she spotted the barrel bobbing off shore and how she knew right away there was treasure inside. Her sisters forbade her to wade out to it — they were worried she would inflict very bad luck on their family by bringing something that had been lost at sea into their home.

Ingaborg plunged in anyway. She describes herself wading valiantly into the crashing waves, choking on mouthfuls of salty water, her legs throbbing with cold. She was determined to collect her gift from the sea gods — a baby turtle, a wee seahorse, or perhaps a mermaid child or even a tiny dragon of her very own. She drags the tale out, building suspense and humour, until finally she gets to the part when she's looks into the barrel, sees Hannah and shouts: "It's a girl! The whales have brought me a little sister!" Uncle Olav laughs uproariously at this ending, his eyes watery. Ingaborg beams proudly when he tells her she has a true gift for telling stories.

"Just like you, Uncle," she says.

Hannah is warming to the old fellow — he is not so scary, not like Ingaborg's father, Gustaf. It prompts her to think about how it felt when her father praised her and she's suddenly overtaken by sadness. She retreats inside herself and sits quietly. Ingaborg, however, is squirming with excitement.

"Uncle Olaf, will you tell the story of great great uncle Nicolai for Hannah? It's my most favourite story and I know she'll love it."

The old man grins at her fondly, revealing a set of surprisingly near-perfect teeth. He sits forward in his chair and launches into a suspenseful yarn, clearly crafted by repeated telling.

Nicolai was a renowned Viking whaling captain in the 1700s. During a ferocious storm off the coast of Scotland, he heroically climbed the mast of his whaling ship to untangle a critical rope. A gigantic gust of wind tore him from the mast and cast him into the sea.

Nearly drowned, he was saved by the very whale he was trying to kill. It carried him to the shore, where he was found by a beautiful Scottish witch named Moragh. She nursed him to health, they fell in love and had a son. He was never able to kill another whale after having been saved by one.

Alas, two years later, Nicolai was summoned to Norway to aid his ailing father with the family herring business. It was another two years before he could return to his love and their child in Scotland. When he finally reached the cottage on the cliff, he instead found a pile of still-smouldering ashes. When Nicolai looked up, he saw the spirits of his beloved Moragh and his son in the sky far above, holding hands, smiling and sending their love down to him.

Nicolai waged a war of revenge upon the perpetrators of this atrocity, slaying priests, religious zealots and government-appointed witch killers — all told he killed 20 men. It was a woman who took him down with a butcher knife to his back, felling the magnificent Viking warrior like an oak tree. His spirit did not hesitate to leave — it rose and joined those of his wife and son, and together they journeyed to Valhalla, the resting place of the great God Odin's chosen warriors and heroes.

Uncle Olaf smiles to see the rapt expressions on the faces of the two little girls. Telling stories gives him joy.

I'm reaching out for my spirit line again, hurling it into the future.

~ ~ ~

Images of brilliant northern lights through a small, frosty window — blues, greens and purples. I see Ingaborg and Hannah huddled beneath a quilt on a lumpy woolen mattress on the floor of their cold attic room. They press their feet around clay bricks that have been warmed on the hearth. There are horrible noises coming from below — Ingaborg's father rants angrily and her mother tries to calm him, then the sound of blows and slaps, crying and, finally, the murmur of praying.

I leave the girls drifting off to sleep, tucked together for comfort. Again, I cast forward.

~ ~ ~

It's a sparse room with simple plank benches for pews and an ornate cross at the front. Norwegians seem to love starkness — especially the people of this remote colony, who follow a particularly strict interpretation of their faith.

The church congregation is singing *O Holy Night* but Hannah's voice soars distinct from all the others. One by one, the other voices stop, except for Hannah's. Everyone is looking at her like she's someone special. Her last sweet, pure notes ring brightly in the room.

Ingaborg's parents, the Kleppens, look proud. Hannah wonders if they believe they are earning some bonus points with God for saving her.

The service is over, and as they walk away from the church, Ingaborg bumps Hannah playfully — they often do that, it's a little game between them. They giggle and begin to run. Hannah is relieved that Ingaborg isn't upset that she drew so much attention for her singing. Poor Ingaborg rarely gets noticed, except when she does something wrong.

They duck off the path and behind a tree — they are supposed to go directly home after church, but the Kleppens are staying on to attend a community meeting, so of course they doddle.

Ingaborg tells Hannah that one day she too will make beautiful music, but her family has no money for an instrument or lessons. One day before Hannah came, she says, a visiting missionary was tuning the old piano in the church. Ingaborg was there to clean, a chore the women of the colony do by turns. She was so entranced with the sound of the instrument, the man allowed her to watch him work.

She describes the row of taut steel strings in the back of the piano and the heavenly sounds they made when she strummed them. She says Hannah is lucky that her voice is her instrument and it travels with her everywhere.

Hannah is hiding on the stairs, listening to Ingaborg's parents talking. Gustaf is complaining — he has been making attempts to report to the authorities about Hannah being found alive. He had sent a message to the shipping agency in Holland months ago, and at long last received a reply saying that he should have contacted the passenger agency in Scotland, because that's where the ship was registered. After all this time, they are no further ahead. Their plan is now to contact agencies in both Scotland and Holland, as the child may have relatives in either. She doesn't know the surname of her mother's sister in Scotland but at least it is a lead they can pursue.

Hannah creeps back up the stairs and crawls in bed with Ingaborg. Holland no longer exists, she thinks.

~ ~ ~

I see seasons passing, like a living slide show. The winters are long and dark — maybe three of them in all. One winter day it is so cold and there is so much snow that the family are trapped in the house for what seems like forever.

The two girls are drawing pictures at the big kitchen table when Mr. Kleppen comes in and looms over them. He jabs a finger at Ingaborg's sketch. It's the Norwegian god, Odin, but she has depicted him in feminine form — a fierce, curvaceous god with blonde curls dancing like a dervish beneath a lush and heavily fruited tree.

"You godless, heathen little witch child, I will send you to God himself for reckoning," he rants, taking up the fire bellows and beating Ingaborg with it again and again. She does not cower or cry but her face is red and set with anger and determination. Ingaborg's mother and her sisters sit rigidly, wishing Ingaborg would cry, apologize or pray. They pretend not to see the violence, not to hear, for fear of drawing his ire. Then Hannah begins to sing a hymn, her voice strong and clear.

When Gustaf hears her, he stops, hurls the bellows to the floor and leaves the house. After he is gone, Ingaborg's mother scolds Hannah, telling her she risked being beaten herself. She sends the girls to bed, but first she lets her hand rest briefly on Hannah's head, as if to transmit her unspoken thanks.

As terrible and foreign as this violence is to Hannah, she has become accustomed to it in a way — she seems to have fallen into the pattern of being the witness and the comforter. She accepts the good and the bad of this family, grateful to them for saving her life. On this night, she snuggles in closer to Ingaborg and holds her tightly, remembering the safe feeling of her mother's arms when she woke from a bad dream.

~ ~ ~

Oline and Alexandria are teaching Hannah and Ingaborg to make leftsa, a potato pancake rolled up with cinnamon and sugar. The older sisters snap bossily and walk them through the steps, expertly producing precise, perfect rolls.

The younger girls start off cooperating, but soon their playful nature takes over and they begin forming the dough into snakes. Ingaborg, relishing the annoyance she's causing her prissy sisters, feeds Hannah a whole spoonful of cinnamon sugar. Oline and Alexandria flounce off in frustration and Hilde steps in to chide Ingaborg for her behaviour. As a punishment, Ingaborg must clean the soot off the fireplace.

Of course Hannah offers to help Ingaborg with the chore and as they set to work, she tells her friend that she never knew how awful sisters could be and that she can't believe she used to want one of her own. "I'm glad I have you as the sister who found me."

"Oline, Alexandria and I aren't the Norn sisters, it's true," Ingaborg giggles. Hannah looks querulous.

"They're the weavers of fate! Uncle Olaf has a book about them. They are three angelic sisters who live at the foot of the Ygdrasill, the tree of life. Their main job is to keep the tree alive with a magic potion made of mud and water." She is scrubbing the hearth and black water flows down her arm into her sleeve, but she doesn't care.

"The eldest Norn sister is Urd. When a baby is born, she begins to weave a tapestry for it, tying in all the things the little baby's soul brings into this life. When the baby gets older, Verdani, the second sister, appears. She draws all the threads together and adds colours and textures — things that make each person's tapestry unique.

"Skuld, the third Norn sister, appears at the time of death." This she says in a low, spooky voice and moves in close to Hannah's face. She feigns fear and they giggle.

"What does she do?" Hannah asks.

"She makes sure the tapestry is finished so it can be woven into the future, to become a part of the Wyrd."

"The what?" Hannah is confused.

"It's everybody's stories all put together. Uncle Olaf calls it the fabric of existence."

This is a big notion for these two wide-eyed girls.

Ingaborg's expression turns serious. "Uncle Olav told me I mustn't ever talk about this in front of the rest of her family, because it's from the pagan times. It would make Papa very mad. He thinks the old ways are evil."

Hannah nods in understanding. "I like this story. It tries to make sense of the world."

"I like the idea that the world is much larger than this sad little island, with its big mean God and my horrible Papa making everybody as miserable as he is."

They are sitting side by side, leaning towards one another.

Hannah smiles dreamily. "Maybe one day we can explore the world together."

~ ~ ~

The mood is merry and Oline and Alexandra are lighting candles — it must be Christmas. They gather around the warmth of the fire, drinking mulled apple cider as a treat — all of them except Mr. Kleppen, who sits on a kitchen chair at the window, smoking his pipe.

Hannah tells Hilde and her daughters about Hanukkah, the celebration of light. She draws a picture of a menorah and explains the meaning of each of the eight candles.

In Holland, she explains, it's a tradition to have yearly visits from Sinterklass, a white-bearded, red-suited man. On Sinterklass eve, children leave their wooden shoes by the door filled with carrots for his white horse. In the morning, the carrots are magically gone, and they find small gifts in their place.

Hannah's eyes become teary as she tells of the time she and Finn secretly left their clogs on the doorstep, even though it wasn't really a tradition for her Jewish family. When they rushed outside upon waking, they found a lovely set of silver bells in each shoe. She'll never forget the look of joy on Finn's face.

"That's like one of our traditions — well, not for us, but for some families," Oline exclaims. "Here, people leave a bowl of porridge on the hearth and an elf named Nisse comes in the night, gobbles it up and leaves a gift."

All of a sudden, Mr. Kleppen rises, knocking his chair over as he comes toward them.

"My daughters and your greedy, stupid talk of gifts and magic. Christmas marks the birth of our lord Jesus Christ, God's son, who died to save us from our sins," he shouts. He stands above them scowling, looking down on their shocked and frightened faces — and then he turns and goes out into the snow, cursing and slamming the door behind him.

~ ~ ~

There's a swirl of blue and I see the family on Christmas morning, thrilled to find their bowls of porridge have been transformed into four pairs of red mittens on the hearth. This is the first year that Nisse has visited the Kleppen home, Ingaborg tells Hannah in an excited whisper.

Gustaf casts a stern glance at his downtrodden wife, who looks at him innocently. A moment later, though, he puts his arm around her shoulders as the girls hold up their brightly clad hands. "Perhaps if their hands are warm, they won't be so slow to bring in the wood for the fire," he mutters.

~ ~ ~

Warm weather finally arrives, and in contrast to the darkness of winter, the summer days are never-endingly light.

Ingaborg and Hannah enjoy hours of freedom when they're sent down to the shore to gather firewood for winter. They scour the beach, gathering shells, driftwood and odd things, which they bury in a secret spot at the foot of the cliff. When Oline and Alexandria aren't looking, they shed their outer clothes and wade into the frigid water, bravely ducking their whole bodies in.

Laughing, they scatter bits of bread they've sneaked from the kitchen to feed the birds, crustaceans and small fish that scoot through the shallows.

Now they hear the birds calling — they circle over their heads and dive, squawking competitively, for the treats. At first, the birds startle Hannah and remind her of her terrifying ordeal in the barrel, but she soon finds herself just as fascinated with them as Ingaborg. There is a profuse variety of ducks, gannets and gulls. Large grey-blue wading birds with purple beaks stride in the shallows, little brown birds flit through the foliage and splendid white birds with blue feet stand like clowns on the beach, unconcerned by the activity around them. Then there are the chattering black birds with orange feet that come very close and chitter and fight over the crumbs.

~ ~ ~

A neighbour arrives and spreads an intricate, hand drawn map of Europe on the Kleppen's table. Hannah excitedly shows Ingaborg where she came from. With her finger, she draws a line across the expanse of blue sea and follows Denmark's jagged coastline to where they now live on Lunde Island — which is hard to distinguish on the map, being so small. She looks at the enormous island that is Great Britain and wonders how that fated ship managed to go so far astray that she would land in this distant place.

The Kleppens tell the neighbour they have finally made contact with the authorities in Holland. Hannah secretly prays no one will claim her. As far as she knows she has no remaining relatives there and it would be so sad to go back to a home without her family.

Now the adults are talking about the school that will soon start up in the community, something the island has never had. The girls are excited at the thought of going to school together. Mr. Kleppen gruffly says he's not convinced it's something that he wants for Ingaborg, given her rebellious nature. Hannah watches her friend grow pale, her happy mood and hopes crushed.

~ ~ ~

A young man and his parents have come to the Kleppens's home to arrange for his marriage to Alexandria. It's an occasion that should be joyful, but instead it's enormously awkward. The Kleppens and their guests sit rigidly at the table. Gustaf is clearly uncomfortable but trying to appear welcoming and generous.

Alexandria is visibly nervous, tittering and glancing at the young boy, whose name is Erik. Oline is keenly interested in the proceedings — she's hoping she'll also be married one day soon.

The dowry has already been negotiated, so the elders are attempting to begin planning the ceremony and the feast. Since neither family has much money, they are wary of committing too much. As it is, the young couple will live in a tiny house on his parent's small farm and have few prospects for ever having their own land.

Hannah and Ingaborg have been instructed to prepare tea. They are twelve and thirteen, and Hilde thinks it's time for them to take more responsibility in the kitchen. Ingaborg is sullen. She bangs the kettle loudly on the hearth. Hannah takes it from her, giving her a questioning look.

"It's ridiculous," Ingaborg says, too loudly. Hannah shushes her.

"She's never even spoken to that boy. Anyone can see he's an idiot."

Hannah stands back in shock, then reaches for Ingaborg's arm, but she pulls away.

"You will not see me marrying one of these village oafs just to escape this dreary house!" She spits the words, then thumps up the stairs.

Gustaf glowers menacingly at Hannah as she sets the tea on the table.

Oline sniffs and breaks the silence: "I believe our Ingaborg is jealous of Alexandria's good fortune."

There's an awkward moment before the group seems to accept her interpretation. Slowly, the conversation resumes.

It's clear to Hannah that Mr. Kleppen is barely controlling his rage. His face is red and his hands are vibrating, waiting to strike a blow. She knows Ingaborg will pay for her outburst when these people leave.

I'm remembering how I felt as a child, scared of my own father and what he might do. I want to come back to the present, but I don't want to leave the girls alone with that man.

"I know, my time travelling friend," Celeste's voice intones. "But Hannah will be fine — what's happened is in the past and you've shown you can will yourself to return whenever you want. They will be safe until you come back.

"Climb the stairs and join me in the present. Counting as you climb from one, two, three, follow your path to the present...four, five, six...breathing deeply...seven, eight, nine, ten. Open your eyes feeling fresh and relaxed.

"Welcome back. You've had quite the journey over several years of Hannah's life," Celeste says gently.

"I know, it's just so compelling. This family totally resonates with me, Celeste. I don't know if I've made up this story based on my ancestors or if I've actually visited them. It sure feels real, though. My father's family, the Kleppens, came from Norway — he never lived there himself and he's never talked about his family history. The only real reference I can remember was when he used to tease me that he wanted to name me Ingaborg because it was an old family name. Mom wouldn't let him.

"It's a crazy coincidence that the two stories of Hannah and the Kleppens would come together like this!"

"Perhaps it's not a coincidence. Your intuition took you to Hannah for a reason. Maybe you were searching for your family stories."

Liv tilts her head and smiles at this idea.

"Liv, when you were in hypnosis, you said you didn't want to leave Hannah because you were remembering how it felt to be afraid of your own father? Do you feel like talking about that?"

"I think so. It's something I recognized all too well — that cloud of anxiety that keeps Hilde and those girls walking on eggshells around their angry father. You see, my dad was an abusive drunk, so my brothers and I, and especially our Mom, had to be careful to avoid setting him off."

"Ah. Your nightmare is beginning to make sense to me now. We should talk more about this."

"Yes, I guess that *is* a part of my life I should revisit at some point, as much as I just want to forget it."

Walking slowly home to meet the school bus, Liv swings a fabric bag containing two gleaming jars of freshly made raspberry jam protectively wrapped in large chard leaves from Celeste's garden. *Just like Celeste to give me so much of her time, and then give me her delicious jam too, expecting nothing in return.* Liv ponders her next hypnotherapy session. *Am I ready to go back to my childhood?* It will take a great deal of trust to talk about the things she's never told anyone. No one would be a gentler or a more supportive listener than Celeste.

Liv rounds the corner on the path, giving her a view of the road. She can see the yellow and black school bus in the far distance, with many stops yet to make.

This experience with Hannah confirms for me that life is just one big interlocking puzzle. One piece leads to another. Even the way we came to Little Mountain took place because of a mystical string of events, and meeting Celeste was part of it.

She and Ross had been living in Twin Rivers and were planning to take in the Pumpkin Hoot, a backwoods music festival they'd heard about north of the city. At the last minute, Ross was summoned to the college to deal with some union emergency. Liv was disappointed, and determined to go anyway. So she drove up on her own with two-year-old Leah.

Just south of Little Mountain, where the highway drops down and follows the wide, glistening river, she saw up ahead a curtain of misty water pouring from a low-lying cloud just up the valley. She slowed the car as she drove into it, and then slowed further to a crawl, stunned by the force of the rain pounding loudly on the windshield. Leah woke in her car seat and looked alarmed. And then, suddenly, it was over. They carried on, turned a corner and were treated to the sight of a rainbow that spanned the whole valley. She stopped the car to take a photo, finding herself at the driveway of a small farm. It was the quintessential homestead — two meadows dotted with daisies, separated by a stand of tall trees. The quaint little farmhouse was nicely fixed up, with pots of geraniums on the porch. The river slid lazily past, its banks lined by enormous cottonwoods, the whole idyllic scene framed perfectly within the brilliant rainbow. And there was a "For Sale" sign. She was entranced and for the rest of the journey, daydreamed herself and her little family there with their own cows, horses, pigs, lambs, dogs, cats and an organic garden patch.

Entering the festival grounds, Liv skirted puddles, lifting Leah over the muddy patches. Her white, gauzy peasant dress barely concealed her huge, pregnant belly. Just in front of a row of artisan booths, her foot slipped in the ooze and she landed on her side in a cold, slimy puddle. A woman ran to help her up and took her to the booth where she was selling her stained glass and jewellery. It was Celeste.

Seeing how rattled Liv was from her fall, she encouraged her to sit a while and drink some herbal tea. Celeste had a natural way with children and kept Leah occupied with her first taste of homemade strawberry fruit leather.

The sun came out and with the help of a gentle breeze, Liv's dress dried as the women got to know each other. The harmonious music of Pied Pumpkin carried over the crowd and completed the festive, happy, hippie mood. The two women recognized each other instantly as friends and knew intuitively they would meet again.

The next weekend, she and Ross went to see the property. As they walked the land together, he was quick to see its charms and to share her vision. Other than being just off the highway, it was like a storybook farm, with an angle-roofed barn, a paddock with a rail fence, fruit trees, a big vegetable garden and a bright red tractor. The defining moment was when they came to a charming little bridge a previous owner had built to a small island in the river. They were sold by the notion of owning their own island.

It hadn't taken long to run into Celeste again the following spring when they moved to the farm — she and Jacques were their closest neighbours. The two women quickly and happily insinuated themselves into each other's lives forever. Still, even after all these years of friendship, there are things that Liv has never told Celeste, or anyone.

I've been guarding my secrets, keeping them on a dusty shelf in my mind and not even daring to look at them. It isn't going to be easy to share these brutal truths, but I know now I must. With Celeste's help, maybe I can let the puzzle pieces fall into place and be able to move forward with my life.

She leaves her jars of jam on the porch and strolls up the driveway, smiling and waving, just as the school bus screeches to a halt. The door opens, revealing two smiley, gap-toothed girls swinging their My Little Pony lunch kits. Following behind them is a tired, crabby looking kindergarten boy, slamming his Spiderman lunch kit against the bus door on his way out. The bus driver, Mr. Kinney, sits draped over the steering wheel. He points at Micah, scowls and gives a shake of his fist. Clearly, her son has run afoul of the rules again. Liv gives the bus driver an apologetic smile and shrugs her shoulders.

"Who needs a hug?" she calls.

"Grumpy Mr. Kinney, not me," says Micah with a pout. But he runs to her anyway.

6

~ Disclosure ~

Session No. 4 transcript, Sept. 21, 1987
Little Liv, 1961

"I'm right here with you, Liv. Hold the soapstone and trust me to lead you to a safe place, knowing that you can return at any time. Counting down from ten, moving past the trees, breathing evenly and deeply, you walk down the path toward the ocean…nine, eight… down the stairs, one by one. The ocean is now in view, the golden sun illuminating the water…seven, six…choose the path slightly to your left, breathing in the salty air, listening to the gulls overhead…five, four… deepening your connection…three, two, one. There you are. Let's begin with a sweet memory from your childhood."

There I am, a little girl running and skipping on a breezy ocean beach. The thread between us is thick and bright, pulsing like a living umbilical cord. It joins our hearts — the energy she projects is strong. I resist merging with her, imagining myself as this younger version of me and feeling also like she is not me, not who I am now.

It's White Rock beach, near where I grew up. I see the big white, painted and repainted rock.

This was my favourite place in all the world when I was a girl. I loved having the freedom to explore and discover the treasures that washed up on the beach. The rock was the biggest one I had ever seen, a graffiti rock since the 1920's. I loved reading all the words and seeing the hearts, names and swear words that would appear each year, before they repainted it white again in spring. No matter how far I'd wander out in the shallow tidal pools, I wouldn't get lost because I could always count on being able to see that rock and figure out where my family was in relation to it.

She's six years old, wearing a red bathing suit with a white ruffle, like a skirt, below the waist. God, she looks so much like my little Molly!

Dreamily, I float and hover very close to my little self. I can see silver glints in the distance as the salty sea breeze gusts and blows her blonde puppy dog tails loose and strands of hair brush across her freckled nose.

Her small footprints in the sand fill in with water and are erased and absorbed by the beach. They're tentative prints — she dances lightly and gingerly around the bubbling holes in the dark grey, wet sand, not wishing to disturb the clams, sand dollars and tiny crabs below. Delighting at the sensation but worrying about the responsibility.

Art, my oldest brother, catches up and grabs little Liv by the arms and twirls her around in the shallow, warm tidal pool. Her laughter bubbles up straight from her belly and touches my adult heart with such a happy jolt that I can no longer resist joining her and being one with her.

Quickly, though, my laughter turns to shrill screams as Lee and Gord, seven and twelve years old, pick up bullwhips — those long strappy, olive-coloured strings of bulbous kelp — and swing them at Art and me, whipping our legs! The salty brine stings my eyes as it splashes up. Art says, "Bug off!" and they run away, flinging sand at each other.

There's Mom, down the beach, calling us to come and have some fish and chips on the logs. We run.

My baby brother, Alex, is fast asleep in a buggy upholstered in faded teal vinyl beside Mom. His black hair is shiny and thick and his chubby cheeks are rosy, like baby Snow White.

Mom hands out the fish and chips, bundled in newspaper — little me delights in the mouthwatering crunch of golden-brown crispy fish with a splash of sour, malty vinegar and unpeeled potato fries smothered in dark red ketchup. Root beer in beer bottles from home are uncapped by Gordon and passed around. Froth foams down the sides, as they have been shaken.

Dad is sitting off to one side with his sunglasses on, drinking a bottle of real beer, the one with the green and red label with cowboys and Indians on it. He smiles toward our mother and motions her to bring him his fish and chips. It isn't the drunk smile I spent my childhood running from. It looks real. When we're finished eating, Mom asks Dad to help us build a sandcastle and, to my surprise, he gets up willingly.

We have one large orange plastic sand pail — an empty Neapolitan *No Name* brand ice-cream bucket — and two red plastic shovels, as well as some wooden pixie stick spoons. We each have a job. Mine is to fill the bucket with sand. Art and Gord take turns dumping it and shaping the mounds into a castle, while Lee takes a shovel and begins to dig a trench all the way around. Dad has some good ideas about making moats and bridges using driftwood and explains that this is because he's worked as a bridge builder. I tell him that he's a good builder. My six-year-old heart is soaring and I am feeling like I'm in an episode of Father Knows Best or Leave it to Beaver — I like to imagine belonging to families like them. The sand castle is spectacular! No one is fighting or yelling or crying.

Art and Gord run down the beach in search of a piece of driftwood to serve as a drawbridge and Lee heads to the picnic basket for a drink.

Dad picks up his beer and downs the last mouthful, looks at me with this funny, sort of twisted smile and then he touches my leg, up high beneath the white skirt of my bathing suit. I flinch and freeze, bracing for more, terrified that someone will see. Quite suddenly my sandy legs are covered in goose-bumps and I can't stop shivering. He moves his hand away.

Oh god, I don't want to remember what my dad did to me. But I want to spend more time with my family and with little Liv.

"It's okay. Take a deep breath and just go a little further, to where you're feeling safe...."

Mom calls to me. "Honey, you look cold! Come and get a towel."

Relieved, I run to her. She's moved Alex closer to where we built the castle — he's awake now and splashing in the shallows and shoving sand in this mouth. She pulls me into her lap, wraps me in a towel and gives me a warming snuggle. She's wearing red lipstick and her hair is dark red and done in pin-curls — the kind where you roll little bunches of your hair around your finger up to your scalp, then fix them with two bobby pins in the shape of an X. I notice she's forgotten to take out one of the bobby pins.

Wrapped up on her lap, I feel so warm and safe. I recognize the perfume she always wore — White Shoulders, kind of like flowers and sweet spice mixed together. I touch her skirt, it's soft cotton, a tropical print in shades of green and purple. Then I reach up to touch the stiff collar of her loose-fitting white shirt — a man's shirt, my Dad's. I see the outline of her white bra.

Looking up into my Mom's jade green eyes I see the reflection of the sun and the sea. I suddenly realize that had had my mother known my dad was sexually abusing me, she would have protected me. My mother most certainly loved me. My brothers weren't monsters. My father was sometimes an okay dad. There must have been other times like this.

In the distance, across the bay towards Point Roberts, I see a flash of fin and a silver splash — a whale is breaching and it takes my breath away. I jump out of Mom's lap, run to one of the great driftwood logs and clamber up, hoping to see more of the whale. It breeches again and, against a watery field of shimmering blue, I see its magnificent body rise up and arch over, creating a powerful splash. As its tail sinks tantalizingly out of sight, I reach my arms up in the air and breach my back like the whale. I jump down off the log and run across the sand, feeling freedom in my limbs. Carefree!

Breaking away from little Liv, I leave her in this beautiful state of childish wonder — she's down at the waterline, playing a game with the ocean, chasing the waves as they retreat and trying to evade them when they rush to shore. She's revelling in the sensations of being alive — the wind in her hair, the sun on her skin, the yielding sand beneath her feet.

As I retreat, I can't take my eyes off her — she's a splash of red and white engaged in a private dance with the ceaseless ocean. I'm struck by the metallic reflection of the sky on the tips of the waves, and then the light kind of lifts off the water and gathers around her like a living aura. With her every movement it follows her, wavering and glowing.

I whisper a promise to her that I'll keep her safely in my heart and I'll tell her story if she wants me to. And I want to.

Celeste waits through several seconds of silence, and then speaks in a gentle, soothing voice.

"Liv, I'm right here. Join me in the present." Liv opens her eyes and meets Celeste's gaze with a look of utter sadness, then closes them again.

"You can tell me. You're no longer in hypnosis, but I'll leave the recorder on if you like and you can tell me."

"Okay." Her voice is very soft.

"In my tiny bedroom, I would lay awake, listening. I could often hear mice scurrying around inside the walls, a sound that didn't faze me. My imagination worked frantically to create stories about the families of mice. They would lead me into their world. The water stains on my ceiling became constellations of stars. The stars would become dolphins and swim in the sea with mermaids and starfish and the mice would be on little boats made of matchstick boxes, bravely trying to stay afloat."

Liv's voice grows louder and more sure as the words, long unspoken, are set free.

"As his footsteps crept down the hall I shut my eyes tight and pulled the blankets over my head. I couldn't bear to see the last vestige of light from the moon disappear when he quietly closed the door behind him. My stomach would begin to churn. My heart would beat faster. It was then that my imagination couldn't take me far enough away. Even the mice ran into their dark holes. There was no hiding. It was a little bit like the hypnotic state I'm learning about with you, except I wasn't in control. As my father came closer to me and pulled my covers down, I gave up and became a witness to what was happening to me. I realize now that was when Hannah's spirit would come to me. I'm sure of that now. I sensed her presence. She would take my hand and we would bond, just as we have in our sessions.

"Moments ago, in hypnosis, with little Liv on the beach, I felt Hannah was with me again. When my father touched my leg, I sensed her rushing to my rescue. When times got rough, she would be with me and together we would roll into the deep waves, knowing we could tumble and bruise, but we could never fall in and drown, no matter how stormy it got.

"We were like two pirate princesses in a glass bottle, in our own world of make-believe. I was never truly alone. Her eyes would reassure me that I would survive the rough waves, rough hands, the bitter smell of tobacco mixed with alcohol and spit... my stolen childhood."

Celeste shifts over onto the couch beside her. She reaches for the ever-present box of tissues, hands several to Liv, and takes a few for herself.

"Oh Celeste, thank you for being you and for not being freaked out by my past. I've never told anyone about the abuse, because the last thing I ever wanted was for people to pity me or even to feel hatred towards my dad."

"Liv, I sit in honour of you, and in rage about the sexual abuse you suffered as a child. I didn't know. I'm so sorry for what you went through."

Celeste pauses for a few moments and wraps Celeste in a warm embrace.

"There is no need for you to relive that, Liv — we won't use hypnosis to return to that time again. It was never, ever your fault or your responsibility."

"I know. I know that now. But Celeste, I think I need to tell you about what my father did to me. Are you okay with that?"

"Whatever you need to say, I am able to hear."

"My memories of the abuse are strong and some are very detailed and disturbing. But I couldn't tell you how often it happened. I think it started when I was very small, three or four years old, maybe earlier, but it's definitely tied in with my earliest memories.

"I know it was happening before I started school because it was when I had an orange cat named Penny. Our cats weren't allowed indoors but some nights I sneaked her in through my bedroom window and she would gratefully curl up on my pillow, and her purring in my ear would finally lull me to sleep. One night she came in with a tiny newborn kitten in her mouth. She dropped it onto my pillow then pounced out the window to retrieve three more mewling kittens. I stayed awake all night, watching them in awe and afraid if I fell asleep they would disappear.

"A few days later, looking out my bedroom window I saw my dad pushing a burlap sack into a bucket full of water. He held it there for several minutes, long enough for him to smoke a cigarette, and then he threw the sack in the fire barrel by the garage. I couldn't bear to look. I knew it was the kittens."

"Your father betrayed you in so many ways, my friend."

"After that, when my dad would come into my room and shove Penny off the bed, I felt less in a dream state, but instead more alert, afraid and angry. How could he do that to her? How could he do this to me? Before then, I hadn't known what to feel.

"Penny was hit by a car and killed when I was in grade one, so the abuse was happening when I was five, and even younger."

"Oh, poor Liv. Penny was a comfort to you and then she was gone."

"It always happened when he was drunk and that was either when he was out of work or during the weekend. When he was sober, he was the quietest man, usually pretty negative and critical, but he never raised his voice. We all lived in fear of him when he was drinking. One time, he was out of his mind on what Mom called "moonshine." Mom knew he was going to get violent when he started shouting, calling her terrible names. She quickly herded us into the boy's bedroom and we pushed with all our might against the door as Dad was bashing his body against it, trying to get in and shouting horrible things. Finally, Mom yelled at him to stop and said she would come out and they could talk. She told him to sit down at the kitchen table and calm down. But when she went out he must've hit her in the face because we heard a loud crack and then she shouted that her glasses were broken and there was no money to buy new ones because he was a 'useless piece of shit.' Then we heard breaking plates and the front door slammed, the car started and peeled down the long gravel driveway so fast the rocks sprayed the bedroom window.

"He would hurt my brothers in different ways. It would usually start with him demanding they do something, and if they didn't cower or appease him to his satisfaction, he would call them names or lash out and slap them or kick them.

"My brothers saw me as the favoured child because Dad didn't yell at me or hit me like he did them — they didn't know my abuse was secret, carried out in the middle of the night.

"I'm sure my mother never knew what he did to me. She would have left him, for sure. Or would she? She didn't leave when he struck her and belittled her and my brothers. As an adult with kids of my own now I see that at night, she was probably exhausted from looking after us, trying to make ends meet on no money, and grateful when he passed out in his chair rather than joining her in their bed. Their room was at the opposite end of the small house and the TV was always blaring until after the 11:00 news was over, so she wouldn't have heard anything from her bedroom. She also took pills to help her sleep. Mother's Little Helpers, like the Rolling Stones song....

"I was so young, I wouldn't have had words to describe what he was doing to me. But somehow I knew it was wrong and dirty — my mom had taught us not to talk about our private parts or anybody else's. I didn't want to be wrong or dirty. I wanted to be a good girl."

"It wasn't your fault or your choice, Liv. You were a good girl."

"What he did — it wasn't intercourse. I guess you'd call it molestation. He would pull my pajama bottoms down and rub my vagina and stick his fingers inside with one hand. I would hear the sound of his pants zipper coming undone. With his other hand he touched himself and I imagine he ejaculated into a wad of toilet paper he would take out of his pocket. I remember the sound of the paper and the smell of his hands and his breath. There were no words from him, only 'shhhh' if he sensed I was waking up — but for the most part, I kept my eyes tightly closed and pretended to be asleep. Somehow, I knew I had to do that. I have a vague memory of him putting his hand over my mouth and nose to stop me from talking or crying or asking questions. I think it would have been intercourse eventually, like he was grooming me for it. He put my hand on his penis when I was a bit older, nine or ten, wanting me to rub it I guess, but I continued to pretend I was asleep.

"From preschool age onward, I got terrible yeast infections and stomach aches. Mom took me to the doctor several times, and even to the hospital on a few occasions. The pain in my abdomen was so bad once, and the infection count so high in my blood, that the surgeon was about to remove my appendix. A last-minute urine test confirmed it was a severe urinary tract infection, so the surgery was called off. Soon after, our doctor told me I had to clean myself more thoroughly and gave my mom a talking to about keeping the bathroom clean — he assumed it wasn't being kept clean enough with seven people sharing one toilet, the boys peeing on the seat, and so on. Of course, all I heard was that I was dirty. So, I started to clean myself all the time, trying to clean my disgusting body, rubbing and rubbing, using lots of soap, especially on the mornings after my father's visits to my bedroom. I got so sore.

"I remember my mom giving me heck for using too much toilet paper. She told me not to wipe myself so much. She got a huge box of cornstarch — I called it my rooster powder because it had a picture of a rooster on the box. I remember crying in pain in the morning after peeing, blood on the toilet paper, running to my mom to tell her, 'I need my rooster powder.' She'd make a paste and put it on my vagina to soothe the flaming skin. When I got to be a bit older, I put it on myself."

"What was that doctor thinking?" Celeste's voice is incredulous. "You would think he would suspect that a little girl whose vagina is being rubbed raw is being interfered with."

"I know, Celeste. I sometimes wonder that too."

"I guess things were different then. Sexual abuse was a hidden, unacknowledged phenomenon, but it existed all the same. Now we know how common it is — there are statistics showing that one in three girls and one in six boys are sexually abused. Nobody knew that then and nobody talked about it. I am so glad that even in elementary schools now, they teach kids that it's okay to talk about this stuff and to ask for help."

"Yeah, there wasn't anything like a Children's Help Line I could have called back then. There were some kind people who knew our family was struggling and they kept an eye out for us kids, but I never considered telling them about the abuse. Pop, for instance, the dairy farmer next door. He must have known something was off with our family. He hired me for twenty-five cents a day to help him round up the cows every afternoon. I reveled in our calm, gentle control of the cows as we clapped our hands and yelled 'come-on ladies' and marched them up the hill.

"There were other 'earth angels', like Miss Rose, my grade two teacher, who told me I was a great story writer. She entered my poetry and stories into the Fall Fair and I won first prize. Our Brownie or Scout leaders would sometimes take my brothers or me aside and ask how things were.

"People probably don't even realize how important it is to be kind to all children. We never know what kids might be going through. I always lied when I was asked and said things were fine, but I actually think it helped just knowing someone saw us and cared.

"Dad never touched me sexually again after he joined AA and quit drinking when I was 12. He stopped physically hurting my mom and my brothers. He got a decent job working on a bridge building crew and worked his way up to being foreman. He did relapse occasionally. Mom told me later he quit because he had begun peeing blood, which scared the shit out of him. The doctor did some tests and told him that he would die if he didn't stop.

"Mom joined Al-Anon and I joined Ala-teen. It made a huge difference to me to be with people who understood — to be told that my dad's drinking wasn't my fault and that I couldn't control or fix it. I felt like I could be myself. The other kids were kind of cool. I remember entertaining them with my stories about secretly pouring bottles of booze down the drain, thinking it would solve the problem.

All it did was cause Dad to visit the local bootlegger, get higher than ever on 150-proof alcohol and put the family even deeper in debt.

"Mom used to make us dress up in our Sunday best for Dad's AA birthday celebrations. You should see the awkward family photos from those times!

"My brothers and I had grown up very fast out of necessity, and there was no way to turn back the clock, and to become regular, playful children once our problems were apparently gone. They were never really gone, I guess. They were a part of us.

"My father came from a messed-up place, Celeste — not to give him excuses for what he did. He never talked about his childhood, but over the years my mother pieced together a vague picture of his early life from talking to other family members and from things he said during his drunken rants.

"My dad's aunt Bertha — she's dead now — was able to tell me his story in far more detail, when I was a teen. She says my grandfather Jorgen, my dad's father, emigrated from Norway to be a prairie farmer in the early 1900s with his young Lutheran bride.

"Things didn't go well for them — the farm was unproductive, probably because he was always drinking. Jorgen became cruel and bitter as he realized that life in Canada was no better for him than Norway had been. He beat his sons — my father, Hans, and his brothers — with barbed wire and nearly killed them on several occasions. My father has nasty, jagged scars on his back and his legs. He would never tell us how he got them.

"When my dad was eleven, his mother died because Jorgen refused to get her medical help when she became gravely ill with mastoiditis. She might have died anyway, as there were no good antibiotics at that time, but he refused to get the doctor to even see what was wrong. He has one photograph of his mom, my grandmother, and I look exactly like her.

"Dad's sister Pearl ran away when she was fourteen — Aunt Bertha said some people speculated that her father had been 'using her as a wife.' When I first heard that I thought it meant he made her cook and clean, but now I realize what that meant.

"The following year, Jorgen blew his own brains out with a shotgun. My dad, who was twelve at the time, found his father's bloody, faceless body in the barn when he went to milk the cows."

"Oh my God," Celeste says, wide-eyed. "The level of trauma that family experienced."

"I know! So, then Dad and his brothers were sent to live with an elderly aunt and uncle who had a farm south of Edmonton, where they were treated like farm hands. He and his brothers started smoking and drinking when they were twelve or thirteen. When Dad was sixteen, he and his brothers joined the army — and that was the last Aunt Bertha knew of them until now, except she heard later Pearl was a prostitute in Winnipeg until she died of a venereal disease in her twenties.

"With this history, while not an excuse in any way, it's not surprising that my dad became an abusive alcoholic. Mom told me he was a wonderful guy when she first met him and the first couple of years of their marriage were happy — she didn't know what prompted him to start drinking excessively and get abusive back then. She thought it was the war. I don't think she understood alcoholism until she went to Al-Anon.

"We were proud of Dad for quitting drinking, and I guess we all put the violence and the poverty into the locked cupboards of our minds and left it there."

"Liv, I wish I didn't have to ask this, but do you want to press charges against him? As your therapist, my main concern is you, but I also need to consider whether any other children are at risk from your dad now."

Liv shakes her head. "At this point, as you know, he's dying from lung and liver cancer. He's at home, but in a hospital bed and not even able to get up to the bathroom. He has to wear a diaper. He can't drink alcohol and he can't hurt anyone. I can't muster up the strength, the anger or the need for justice twenty years later. I would never leave my kids alone with him, though, ever!"

Liv is silent for several minutes, aside from deep, wracking breaths. She looks up and sees Celeste gazing at her, her amber eyes red and puffy. Liv realizes her friend has been absorbing all the emotion seeping through her words.

Celeste gently touches Liv's arm and speaks softly, "Thank you for sharing this with me."

"Does this help us figure out where we need to go with the therapy, or am I completely lost, damaged beyond help?"

"Oh, my incredible friend, you are not beyond help at all! I am so sorry for your family's tragedy and pain — and also so impressed that you've had the courage to unearth this abuse at a time when you're dealing with so much. I need you to know that I believe you and I believe in you. Imagine bringing the raw trauma of so many past generations into your lifetime, and still being able to give your children healthy, happy lives and be the kind of friend, neighbour and human you are! You are not only amazing, you are healing from this and you're breaking this terrible cycle of abuse.

"We can't leave off like this, with such an emotionally wrenching experience. I'd like to hypnotize you again, but this time I'm going to help you restore that piece of yourself that was lost. Can I do that for you?" She knows her friend is likely to gloss over her inner thoughts and feelings if she's not encouraged to process it now.

"Okay," says Liv. "I've come this far, there's no point putting off the healing part!"

This time the hypnosis session has a dreamlike quality — the sensations are peaceful and there are no encounters with demons from her past. There is warmth and comfort. When Celeste calls her back, Liv awakens effortlessly, refreshed. She takes a huge breath and releases it.

"I feel like you've taken out poison and replaced it with calm. I feel so much lighter and stronger. All this turmoil is better out than in."

"I'm so glad," Celeste smiles. "My adopted grandmother, who lived to be ninety-nine, used to say, 'Handing someone a cheese sandwich does a lot more good than offering up words of pity or advice.' She volunteered helping the homeless and hungry during the Great Depression. Sometimes words just don't cut it, Liv. Before you go, help me eat some of the banana cranberry muffins I made this morning?"

7

~ *Dissonance* ~

Walking home, Liv has lots of time, so she stops at the paddock to visit Majic, her gentle grey gelding. He sees her coming and canters toward her, chuffing. He sidles in and places his velvet muzzle into her hands, looking for treats. She brushes her cheek against his smooth head, breathing in that deeply herbal horsey smell. He's getting fat, she notices, and feels a flush of guilt. Nobody has ridden him for weeks, so it might be challenging to get a saddle on his back. She makes a mental note to not allow the children to try to mount him until she rides him a few times first, to remind him of his manners. Majic follows her to the paddock gate. She scoops up a handful of the succulent alfalfa growing wild along the fence and feeds it to him. He nickers in appreciation.

As she negotiates the path through the trees, she finds it blocked by dead birch branches that have fallen from a mature clump. She begins gathering them up —the mornings are growing colder, and there hasn't been any kindling to start a fire to take the chill off. As she nears the house she becomes aware of the rhythmic thump of music from within, growing louder. She recognizes the jarring, jazzy dissonance of Dave Brubeck. That music is always unsettling to her. Ross is home. She'd gotten used to not expecting him, and now he's here. Her heart begins to thud and she stops.

There's no alternative. She has to go home because the school bus will drop off the kids in about half an hour. *Be brave*, she tells herself.

Then she sees him, sitting on the rocking chair on the porch with his rifle. *What the hell is he doing? Has he completely lost his mind?*

She's approaching from the side, so he hasn't seen her yet. She stops in her tracks, puts down her bundle of twigs and watches for a moment as he points the rifle toward something in the field. A wild animal? She realizes he's set up some sort of target and that's what he is aiming at. She approaches a little closer, but carefully, as she finds the look on Ross' face disturbing. His face is intensely scrunched and his chin is down, his wire framed glasses near the tip of his nose. She tries to make out what he's using for a target and realizes it's a photo of Chairman Mao Tse Tung — the cover of an old Macleans Magazine. Ross fires and hits the dictator right between the eyes. Liv jumps at the sudden BOOM and the visual of the paper target exploding into the air. She's conflicted — should she run, or try to confront him? Then there's a whirl of blue in her mind and a sense of calm settles over her. She needs to manage Ross and somehow divert the kids away from this scene.

"Ross, what are you doing?" His head snaps in her direction. His eyes are strangely unfocused. He doesn't answer. She climbs the steps onto the porch. Ruby sits in attendance at his side, her ears perked, tongue lolling.

"I see you got her a new bike," he says, smiling oddly. Liv can't tell if it's an apologetic gesture or a sneery one. "I was trying to teach her something, you know."

"I thought she'd learned enough from the experience. What are you doing?"

He jumps up, leaving the gun on the porch, takes her arm and hustles her inside. He brings his face very close to hers. She has to force herself not to draw away — she doesn't want to spook him by seeming not to trust him. Liv sees true concern in his eyes.

"I need to practice," he says, "In case they come."

"Who?"

"Oh, you know who I mean. They've been here before and this time they could really hurt us and the kids, Liv."

"I don't know who you mean, Ross."

"Those men — they're from the government, the *other* government that's really in charge. The Nazis of the New Age. They've been following me since college. They're the antithesis of everything I believe in. They know I'm a sociologist, and they think that means I'm a communist. They've been trying to get to me for months now. "

Liv's head pounds with alarm and mixed emotions — she feels sympathy for him, and yet she's repulsed and nervous, which makes her feel guilty. Most of all, she fears for the kids' safety. The bus will be here in fifteen minutes, she calculates. If she can get away and intercept it she can take the kids somewhere else.

"Ross, I'm worried about you. I don't think there are spies after you. I think you should go lie down. Ruby will bark if anyone comes."

He wavers on his feet and his eyes close briefly — he seems to respond to the idea of rest — so she puts her arm around his shoulders and guides him to the sofa. He's suddenly passive. She calls Ruby and makes her lie on the floor beside him.

"You rest. Everything's fine. But just in case I'm going to go get the kids so I know they're safe."

There's a flicker of belligerence in his eyes — is he wondering if she's tricking him? He looks at her closely — she can smell whiskey and body odor and his pupils are dilated.

"Yeah, you go get the kids. I can protect you better when we're all together." He's absolutely serious.

Driving away, she knows she won't be returning home tonight with the kids. She'll phone later with an excuse as to why they're staying at a friend's house. Maybe she'll play along with his delusion that the government men are after him and tell him it's for the children's safety. As disturbing as this realization is for Liv, it sets her on a clear path.

Ross is mentally ill. It explains his decline, his lethargy and his rapid swings of temper, even the affair. It's up to me now.

8

~ Regret ~

The next morning, Liv wakes pinned down by the soggy weight of a five-year-old's leg across her chest. She had tossed and turned all night, trying to get comfortable, unaccustomed to sharing a king-sized bed with her three restless and upset children. They're at the home of a good friend, Mo, who happens to be the doctor in the nearby town of Cutter's Gorge. She'd gone to Celeste's first, but she wasn't home and Liv thought that would be the first place Ross would look for her anyway.

As soon as the kids were settled in having supper, she called one of her neighbours, Rob, and quickly explained what had happened with Ross. Rob was a friend — he and Ross were actually partners in adventure at times, going off on fishing and ATV trips, always with plenty of alcohol.

All Rob said was, "Oh man," several times. She asked him to go check to see if Ross was okay.

"But don't tell him where we are. If he asks, just tell him I had to go into the city because one of the kids is sick — tell him Micah has another really bad ear infection. And Rob? Can you call me back at Mo's and let me know?"

Several hours later, Rob called to report that he'd found Ross asleep on the sofa.

"He said he just had a bad headache. I talked him into locking the gun up. We had a few drinks. He didn't talk much. Then he passed out again, so I came home."

"Thanks for doing that. Just so we have our stories straight, did you tell him we'd gone into Cutter's Gorge?"

"He didn't ask."

The morning routine is totally thrown off. The kids are cranky and confused to be at Dr. Mo's. No one has slept well. "Come on, my bunnies. Gotta get ready for school." Liv hears the forced gaiety in her own voice.

"What about my birds, Mom?" cries Leah. Part of her morning routine is lifting the cover and feeding the cheerful little finches in their wicker cage.

"I'll go home and look after everybody once you get on the bus, don't worry."

"I don't have any clean clothes to wear," pouts Molly. Mo comes to the rescue with a creative wardrobe fix — a fine pink cashmere sweater she never wears fits Molly as a dress, with the sleeves rolled up. Molly is thrilled, as she loves the softness and the colour.

Micah is outside playing with an axe by the time Liv gets the girls dressed and downstairs. She strides out and takes the axe away, then in one motion swings it and buries it deep into the chopping block with a force that surprises her and impresses her feisty son so much that he forgets to protest.

With Mo's help, she gets the kids fed a pancake breakfast and ready for school, lunches in hand. Mo has also contacted the bus driver to pick the children up at her house. She'll call later about where to drop them off.

Though she is trying hard to be happy and reassuring with them, Liv is certain that Leah and Molly can see right through her. Micah probably can as well. His behaviour has always been sort of an emotional thermometer in their family. The more out of sorts everyone else is, the more out of control he will be. Walking to the bus, Micah falls on a wooden plank cattle bridge, gets a giant sliver in his knee and has a complete meltdown when Liv pulls it out, screaming, "I want my Daddy." She raises her voice in frustration, "Your Daddy is crazy," and instantly regret pounds in her head. She's able to soothe Micah with a Batman Band-Aid Mo has on hand to cover his splinter wound, as well as the promise of an afterschool trip to the candy store.

Liv is near collapsing and feeling like the shittiest parent ever when the bus finally roars off. But now she can pick Mo's doctor brain.

She had told Mo some of what had happened the night before, but now her friend wants to hear the full story. Coincidentally, she's been studying to specialize in psychiatry and recognizes the earmarks of paranoia immediately.

"Aw, Liv. I knew from talking to you that he was struggling. I don't want to alarm you, but his behaviour indicates serious mental illness — it sounds like bipolar disorder to me. And if he's been self-medicating with alcohol and drugs to try to deal with the headaches, that's probably contributed to the problem."

"Bipolar disorder? That sounds pretty heavy. You don't think he's just an arrogant, alcoholic A-hole going through a mid-life crisis?"

Mo smiles, "Sounds like more than that to me."

"You know, it's weird. His headaches were always manageable until he lost that damn nomination last fall."

"I heard he campaigned for that and I was surprised he didn't win. I would have thought he'd be a great candidate."

"He was! He's an amazing speaker and he can really rouse a crowd. He even convinced me that we could move to Ottawa for a few years. As the campaign went on it seemed like he got higher and higher with the idea of being a politician —it scared me. He was so invested in winning. He was devastated when he lost. That's when he crashed — but who could blame him? The headaches got out of control, and his drinking and dependence on prescription pills got way worse."

Mo nods in agreement. "Yes, come to think of it, the last time I saw him was right at that time. He tried to get me to renew his painkiller prescription, but I could see he'd recently filled it. He was so angry that I wouldn't give him more. And I haven't seen him as a patient or at any community events since."

"Yeah, he switched doctors pretty fast when he couldn't get the pills from you. I figured you were onto him but I didn't think it was my place to say anything at the time. He always says he could stop the alcohol and the pills if he wanted to. He just doesn't want to."

"Do you believe that, Liv?"

"No, just the part about him not wanting to," she smiles sadly. "I don't even know if I believe myself. If I'm really honest, I think there have been signs of this since I first knew Ross. My Grandma used to say, 'believe only half of what people say but everything they do.' Ross' actions have not matched his words for a long time. He says he loves me and the kids but he only shows it after he's had his fill of alcohol, tobacco, or whatever else he's using. Throw in a mental illness and does that mean even his actions aren't true?"

"It's pretty impossible to sort it all out yourself. My best advice for you would be try and get him to go to the hospital for a psychiatric assessment. At the very least, he needs to go to a treatment centre to deal with his drinking and his prescription drug abuse. He's out of control. You shouldn't go back there until he's rational. You understand that, don't you, Liv? You can stay here as long as you need to."

"I know Mo, thank you so much for all of this. I know I have to try to convince him to get help. I just want our old life back. I think."

Then Mo gives her an empathetic hug and heads off to her office.

Liv slows and pulls over onto the shoulder as she approaches her driveway, craning her neck to see whether Ross' car is in the yard.

No. He's gone. She's thankful today will not be the day they have "The Talk." Although she feels much more confident, she's still gathering the courage.

As she enters she can hear the finches chirping, so she deals with them first — she cleans their cage, gives them fresh food and water and has a little chat with them. She washes up the few dirty dishes in the sink — it looks like Ross found the left-over chili. He must have taken Ruby with him, which is a bit worrying with the mood he's in. She hopes he looks after her.

Heading outside to see whether the cows are all accounted for and the sheep haven't gotten into the wrong field again, Liv has a sudden revelation. Everything she can see, they built together. Ross was as good with his hands as he was with his brains. He had boundless energy and had done much of the building himself over two years, hiring local guys and contractors to help when needed. She recalls standing, with Ross hugging her from behind, laughing and celebrating their final decision on the spot they had decided to build their home, a gentle slope with a beautiful view of the river and the mountains. "Perfect," they had both exclaimed at the same time. She had loved designing their home, filling it with colour and practical touches. They had been so proud of what they had accomplished.

And now it's all in jeopardy, falling apart.

All this time, she's been thinking he betrayed her, but really, his mind has betrayed them both. She feels some forgiveness for him, now that she's able to attribute the affair and the harshness he has shown towards her and the kids to the illness, over which he has no control.

She grabs a tub of garden compost and two slop buckets from beside the barn. She fills the pails half full with powdered grain and adds water from the hose to make a mush. The three half-grown pigs snort from their pen in eager anticipation of food. The buckets are heavy and Liv groans as she lifts them one at a time over the fence. She doesn't feel like joining them in the pen today — although it's fun to play, she ends up smelling like a pig pen!

Now to her favourite farm creature. Majic has been watching her from the paddock. He pines for the apples, but can't access the tree from his field, so she picks a few for him. He comes right up to her, even though she has grabbed a curry comb and he knows he's in for some unwanted attention as well.

As she brushes the horse's tangled silver mane, Liv scolds him, "How did you get so tangled up? You walked through burrs, didn't you?" He flinches a little as she pulls a burr from his forelock. "That's okay, Majic. So did I, so did I," she reassures him.

She needs to untangle her feelings, both bad and good, before she can consider whether to even try to weave her marriage back together.

For all their recent troubles, there have been wonderful times with Ross. *I miss how it used to be.* A nostalgic home movie begins to play in her mind. Newly in love, walking the wild beaches on

Maui. Dipping little Leah's toddler body into the warm sea for the first time, each holding one of her hands and loving the sound of her happy squeals. Family camping trips and boisterous gourmet feasts with their friends — Ross would cook and preside front and centre, instigating political rants, entertaining all and making everyone laugh. It's been about a year since Ross cooked one of his famous meals. They have so many friends — college profs, students, draft dodgers, cowboys, farmers, musicians, artists and First Nations chiefs. Never a weekend would go by where there wasn't some amazing social event happening.

Liv laughs to herself as she runs her fingers through Majic's now tangle-free mane and moves on to his tattered tail.

There was a time when Ross would do anything to please her. The lobster incident comes to mind. The previous summer, she and her friends had worked for months to organize The Octopus' Garden Children's Festival in Little Mountain. They fundraised and got the schools and everyone in the community involved and pulled together a wonderful day full of artistic activities and professional entertainers. It went beautifully. When she arrived home with the kids, she found the whole crew there, in her yard.

Ross had been working on a little project of his own, a surprise for Liv and everyone who had created this monumental children's day. He had secretly ordered a hundred live lobsters from Prince Edward Island and prepared a feast at their farm after the festival. It was all great until Liv realized the lobsters were to be dropped live into pots of boiling water. "That's horrible, Ross. I'm not eating tortured animals!" With a mischievous smile, he ran into the house and brought back half a dozen bottles of Chardonnay, which he poured over the frantic, clattering lobsters in the salt water tank. Friends gathered around and watched as the lobsters took in the white wine. It was not until their movements slowed to more of a slow dance, and they seemed drunk, that Ross dropped them into the steaming pot. "See Liv, they're happy!" Ross exclaimed as he took her by the waist and swung her around, "I'd do anything for you, Liv. Anything." The ill-fated lobsters emitted only the smallest whistling wheezes and by the time they were served up with fresh butter and lemon, Liv had to admit they were delicious. His was a brilliant gesture, for show but also just for her and typical of Ross — until recently.

Liv summons more images — like she's trying to soften her heart against its will when all it really wants to do is harden. In a rollercoaster of memories, she sees Molly riding on Ross' shoulders, giggling and happy.

Casting back to their sixth anniversary, she recalls she and Ross paddling effortlessly downstream in their forest green canoe, toasting their happy lives with chilled champagne, laughing, passing the bottle back and forth, nearly tipping the canoe. Liv realizes she had kept the good part of that memory and forgotten the rest. Until now. When they got home and sent the babysitter off, Ross decided he had to go to town to buy more alcohol. He never did come home that night and she can't recall why. *How many times have I suppressed the bad memories? My eyes are open now and I won't close them again.*

The hazy memory disappears, making room for a miserable flashback of the last time she had tried to initiate sex with Ross, a few months earlier. It's now been nearly a year since they've had sex. Reaching over to his side of the bed, she had massaged his thigh and he seemed receptive so she reached up and touched his face and kissed his lips. He rolled away from her. Ignoring the sting of that, reaching over his back, taking his penis in her hand, thinking a blow job might bring her the intimacy she was craving, Liv was shocked to discover his penis covered in ointment of some sort. She hadn't let herself suspect for a moment that his penis had been busy elsewhere.

"I have some kind of rash," he lamely explained, and she rolled as far as she could, to the far side of the bed and didn't sleep. *I knew. I knew then our marriage was in trouble but I just couldn't bring it to the surface.*

Day-dreaming and "day-maring" over, animals and home looked after, Liv is finally ready to head over to Celeste's. Passing through the mud room, she remembers to take the clean clothes out of the dryer and throw them into a basket to bring to Mo's house. Then she hears a car pull in and a door slam. From the half window in the utility room door she sees Ruby scrambling up the stairs and Liv's heart thuds and her face flushes at the realization that Ross is home.

She's used to having some pretty intense feelings about Ross, but fear has never been one of them, until now.

Liv reflects on yesterday's event on the porch. *I can handle this.* She opens the door to the scruffy, unshaven, red-eyed version of her husband.

"Hi Ross."

He steps inside and she takes a step backwards but they remain facing each other.

"Liv, I don't know what's going on, but I feel like my head is going to explode."

"Oh Ross, I'm so sorry this is happening to you, to us."

"What are you talking about? It's what's happening to the world." His eyes flash with rage. He bellows, "Look at the big picture, Liv! Not our insignificant little lives. We mean nothing."

Liv fights back tears, fights the feeling that his words are about her not being good enough, smart enough, important enough. She instinctively backs away from him, gathering the courage to speak.

"Ross, you aren't well. Can you hear me out? You need to see a doctor and find out what it is. You seem to have some kind of illness," she says carefully, knowing this will be treading on thin ice. "I don't know what to expect from you next. You've been staying away from home for days on end, you had an affair, you think people are out to get you. You get drunk and high every single day. You haven't been acting like you."

"Haven't I, Liv? Maybe I have. Maybe this is the real me." Ross reaches into his pocket and pulls out a joint and lights it up.

"Mo thinks the highs and lows you're experiencing might even be bipolar disorder. It might be why your headaches are worse too."

"Oh, you would see it as a disease, something wrong with me, something that can't be fixed. Maybe a lobotomy is the answer," Ross sneers at the idea and laughs hollowly. "Wouldn't they love that, destroying my Commie brain, all in the name of medicine? Turn me into a zombie with no thoughts at all."

"Ross…," Liv attempts to interject, but he goes on.

"You're either with me or against me, Liv. I know you're angry because I screwed around, but if you're in on this, you better tell me now."

"I'm not your enemy. Yes, I'm angry, but I love you and the kids love you. You need to get help for yourself, for our marriage, for the kids. We're all scared right now."

Ross comes even closer and says, incredulously, "Scared of me?"

She can't back up any further into the utility room because the clothes dryer is in the way, so she freezes as Ross flings the remainder of the burning joint out the door and grabs her by the shoulders, squeezing hard, his narrowed, bloodshot grey eyes only inches from hers.

"And I think you've signed on with *them*. Don't even pretend you haven't. I'm outta here. You don't have to be scared of big bad Ross anymore. I won't be back."

"If you do come back and you're like this, I'll have to call the police. I don't feel safe with you."

He tears off, leaving Ruby at home and Liv to contemplate what just happened.

Did he just leave me? Did I send him away?

She closes the door, and, with a shaky hand, locks it.

9

~ Disorder ~

Feeling anxious in her own home, Liv starts off early to Celeste's for her ten o'clock appointment. The birch and willow leaves, yellow now as October quickly approaches, stir in the breeze and the odd red maple leaf flutters to the ground. *It seems too sudden for all this change.*

Celeste listens to her friend's account of the bizarre target-shooting incident on the porch the previous day with expressions of surprise and horror, occasionally interjecting to ask a question and reassuring her that she handled it all really well.

"Yeah, I think I did. There was a moment there where I was freaking out, just about to panic. And then my mind cleared — I think it was Hannah's influence, the way she handles Ingaborg's father. I just knew what I had to do — humour him, make him feel secure, and then get me and the kids out of there."

"Then he showed up again this morning, when you were about to leave?"

"Yes, I don't think I handled that quite as well. He got pretty angry when I suggested he might have bipolar disorder. For the first time ever, he was rough with me. It wasn't really painful but he squeezed my shoulders and said he thought I was against him. He had no right to lay a hand on me."

"Are you worried about your safety, and about the kids? Do we need to call the police?"

"No, when I ran over here I was feeling a little scared but I'm calmer now and he's gone into town to stay for a while. His friend Mel called me yesterday and he even admitted he is worried about Ross. At least it's out in the open now. Mel and his wife Sandy are going to encourage Ross to stay with them for a few days, get him to stay off the booze and see a doctor if they can."

"Maybe he'll listen to a friend."

They sit for a few moments, absorbing the implications of this new chapter in Liv's marriage. Her troubles churn in her mind as though they're in a Mixmaster.

"It feels like all the compartments in my mind that I've been keeping neatly shut have opened up and I'm having a terrible time sorting them. Part of me wants to run."

Celeste nods to encourage Liv to keep talking.

"You know, Celeste, when I was five or six I ran away from home. It was after one of the nights my dad had been in my bedroom. The sun was barely up, but I was an early riser. I was wearing a light grey velvet dress with fabric-covered buttons up the back — I'd worn it so much that it was torn at the waistline. I went into my brother's bedroom to ask if someone could help do up my buttons. They told me to piss off. It wasn't even light yet."

"Brothers," Celeste interjects with a smile.

"Angry and rejected, I decided to run away from home and gathered a few belongings in an old kerchief and tied it on the end of a stick, like I'd seen Pebbles do in an episode of The Flintstones.

As I walked down the highway, my tears had dried, my anger had dissolved and I had faith that I was going towards something safe and better. I remember the feeling so well. I wasn't afraid at all, in fact I was excited.

"My brothers realized I had gone and caught up with me on their bikes after about half an hour — no doubt terrified I was going to be hit by a car. I told them I was going to White Rock beach. Gord apologized for not doing my buttons up and Arty let me ride on his handlebars all the way home. I was mad they'd shown up and interrupted my plan.

"You were an incredibly strong little girl, Liv. It must have felt like you had nobody on your side," Celeste says. "I can see you gathering up your internal and external resources now, rather than staying in a bad situation or running blindly towards the unknown. Do you think we should we slow down on our sessions for a while, Liv? You're going through so much right now."

"No, I want to keep going. It feels like my past lives are leading me places I need to go to sort out my heart and mind. They're all part of my resource team, so to speak."

Celeste nods in agreement as she passes Liv a piece of paper etched with *Twin Rivers Sexual Assault Centre, 604 472 3141* in her tidy, flowing script.

"You've begun some important work here Liv. You can always talk to me about anything under the sun, moon and stars, but sexual abuse isn't my area of expertise. These people will be able to help you. Promise me you'll go?"

"I will. The world didn't end when I told you and I realize I haven't even begun to deal with the abuse. God, I was just a wee girl! Saying those things out loud to you and visiting little me in that last session really made me realize I need to give a voice to her. Thanks,

Celeste. You know, I think looking back at my childhood and allowing myself to feel some anger actually helped me when I was confronting Ross yesterday on the porch. My need to protect myself and my kids was far stronger than my need to be 'the perfect wife.' I stood up for little Liv, as well as Leah, Molly and Micah. It was new for me but it felt good. I'm looking forward to today's session."

"Where would you like to go now?"

"Oh, I'd love to go back in time and see if there is another person in my past who can teach me a thing or two."

"Well, let's see if we can make that happen."

10

~ *Spirit Friend* ~

Session No. 5 transcript, Sept. 24, 1987
Moragh of Pine Glen, 1745

The luminous blue line that seems to guide me to my past lives leads me across a tumultuous sea, up a craggy cliff to a green mountaintop meadow and into a cottage made of stones and bark. With a powerful whoosh, I catch up with my astral body and my senses clarify. I'm overwhelmed by the distinct scents of eucalyptus, lemon and lavender.

The lazy wisps of fragrant steam mingle and dance with the brilliant blue thread and pull my spirit, fully and willingly, into that of an enchanting auburn-haired woman who is tending a blackened cast iron pot over an open flame.

She raises her head and glances around the room expectantly, as if she can feel the stirring of my presence.

"Failty dhachaidh! Mo cridhe…Welcome home. How are you, my friend, my spirit from afar."

"She's speaking to me. She knows I'm here!"

"Ciamar a ta Moragh…My name is Moragh. Whaur ar ya frae? Methinks the future me? We are in for a wee bit of a journey together, are we?"

"Hello Moragh. I am indeed your soul from the future and have come to explore this earlier life."

"Tis a fine treat for such a day. It so happens at this minute that my spirit is low and I am feeling both defeated and angry but getting stronger as I inhale this dreamy steam and meet the likes of you. Show yourself that I may know ye."

Just as it was with Hannah, I understand Moragh's lovely lilting Gaelic speech, although I have to pay close attention so I can translate as I speak.

By envisioning my own life and what's in my heart, I project images to Moragh so she can see who I am, who I love, and how our spirits have been tied all these years. She sees my past connection from my Norwegian ancestors and how the line runs all the way to my present life in Little Mountain. She sees into my heart. She nods and smiles with recognition. I conjure images of my three children and she gasps.

"The wee one is the perfect likeness of my Nic! It's as if he sprung from me. I love that he lives on, as do I through you."

She resumes stirring the concoction in her kettle. I'm loving being joined with this vibrant young woman. I can tell she's very strong and not afraid of anything. I wonder what could have happened to upset her.

"Treachery, my spirit friend. Eucalyptus, cinnamon and turmeric from Spain — it was not worth it, Mo Cridhe, not at all. That cursed snaggle-toothed thief, Christo Mirabella. I shouldn't ever have trusted that he wanted to do a straight trade of coin for goods."

Moragh shows me the events of the day as if she's playing a film for me: I see her holding out her hand in this very kitchen to pay a nasty looking man in a fancy black cloak for a small sack of herbs and spices. He snatches the coins and puts them in his pocket, then suddenly grabs Moragh, causing her to drop the sack. The herbs and spices scatter, green and red powders spread across the stone floor. He roughly pulls her toward him as if to kiss her. His breath is rotten and foul. Moragh slaps his pocky face and turns to run, but he lunges and clutches her, tearing the bodice of her dress nearly in half, exposing her breasts. Moragh's fierce green eyes flash, not with fear but strength as she fights him, pounding furiously on his back and thick head. In spite of her strength, he throws her on the ground and my spirit rages in commiseration with her.

As they grapple on the floor, he drops one hand down to open his trousers. She's able to jerk her knee up and land one well-placed blow to his groin. That sets him back. His face a mask of red-pained fury, he throws his substantial weight against her again. Reaching into her apron pocket, she retrieves her small knife, the one she uses for snipping plants. She jabs the blade deep into his thigh.

He withdraws with a scream. "You witching whore, you'll pay for this," and he jumps up, sweeping through her cottage, smashing things to the floor, searching for her stash of coins. His attention diverted, Moragh takes the opportunity to grab a small, cloth-wrapped sachet from the top shelf of her cupboard and sneak it into the pocket of his heavy black cloak.

"A keepsake, so to speak," Moragh explains to me, with a wry smile. "I merely wounded him, so sadly he will live to spread his deceitful tales and his wicked deeds, but I did feel the need for some retribution. The potion within will cause Mirabella some anguish, which he richly deserves."

As we've been talking, she's been tending the pot, adding fuel to the fire and stirring it occasionally. Now she selects three jars from a set of shelves in the corner and adds a pinch each of penny royal and black cohosh and a healthy dollop of pine oil into the brew. Then she pulls out a vial and drizzles a thin stream of thick amber substance across the bubbling surface. A stringent, fresh fragrance immediately lifts into the air, somehow so familiar!

"It's Balm of Gilead," she says. "A very precious resin that speeds emotional and physical healing." A little more than necessary, she judges, but she feels the need to cleanse not only her battered, bruised body but also her tiny home of the evil that beastly man brought in.

"It bothers me sorely that I am a target simply because of my sex and my standing in life," she tells me. "But at least I can feel fortunate because, unlike most women of my time, I know independence and I know love. Most women are chattel, rape is all too common."

"Still to this day, Moragh," I say out loud, and she raises her brows in surprise.

Moragh vows to herself that she will never lift her guard with a man she doesn't know and trust ever again and she will always have her knife on hand! "And so should you, Liv from the future! With my man gone to Norway, I am vulnerable. I must be my own protector."

Now Moragh reaches up to pull a necklace over her head. She holds it out so I can see the black, crescent moon-shaped pendant on the chain and takes a deep and mournful breath.

"This pendant was my grandmother's, and before that, her great grandmother's. It's made of obsidian. It carries the strength of the hardest stone into loving human hearts — not to harden the person, but to make their hearts stronger than flesh and blood. It's said to ward off darkness by taking it in and transforming it into light."

I'm entranced as Moragh continues, her voice deep with emotion. "My Grandmother Fee and her beloved Gwynneth burned to death while sleeping in the small wooden cottage they shared over the hill from this one of mine."

My sadness combined with Moragh's is overwhelming. I must take a moment to collect myself.

"It was rumoured the fire was set on purpose in retribution — the two women had long been suspected of not only practicing witchcraft, but of sharing a love considered unnatural.

"They judge it a crime for two women to live together and never take husbands, but my dear grandmother and her friend loved each other perfectly and if that is wrong, so be it," she declares. I can feel her probing me for a reaction.

"Yes, so be it," I emphatically respond.

Moragh smiles slightly as she takes the pot off the flame and sets it on the stone floor to cool. Aromatic steam rises and she breathes it in — there is a sensation of clearing, as if my senses have become sharper.

She takes off her torn dress and stands in her cotton shift. She's tall and slender, yet her limbs and back are muscular. Her lively eyes are sea green and she has light freckles on her nose. She gathers her wild-looking thatch of auburn hair and twists it into a knot at the nape of her neck, then collects a small basket and takes a seat on the hearth. She inspects the tear, then pulls out a needle and thread to mend it.

"Grandmother Fee made this for me. She spun the wool herself and dyed it this mossy green with sorrel root. It's my only frock. My dear bairn will soon be home an' it's best he not see the damage to the dress — or to his mother."

At twenty-four years of age, her hands are reddened from hard work and weather, but she sews nimbly.

"My parents died of influenza when I was six, so it was Grandmother Fee and Gwynneth who raised me. They taught me all they knew of herbs, potions and magic, life and love. Together, we gathered botanicals for their healing qualities, while they patiently instructed me on their names, the particulars of collection and their uses. Every leaf, root and berry, it seems, has some dedicated power, even the lichen that clings to the stones."

Moragh pictures the land for my benefit — rolling green hills strewn with boulders, pastoral and lovely, yet stark and forlorn at the same time. They had to wander far and wide across the highlands to gather enough good for their healing arts. At sixteen, the women felt Moragh was ready to move into her own place and begin her own life as a woman. The property with the two wee huts had passed down to Grandmother Fee from her great grandfather Fergus, although many locals felt it was wrong to have passed property to a female.

"Had I not moved into my own cottage at 16, I would have burned to death with my Grandmother and Gwynneth," Moragh exclaims.

She finishes her sewing, breaks the thread with her teeth and then holds the garment up — the mended tear is visible, but at least her skin won't be. She rises, takes a cloth and begins to wash herself with the warm, fragrant water from the pot.

"It was I who discovered their bodies together in the dying grime of the fire, although I could scarcely believe it until I found my grandmother's obsidian necklace on her poor burned body."

I feel a lightness, as if I'm being lifted by an invisible force. Moragh says she's taking me along on a memory to show me how she became the person she is.

I see her forlorn figure kneeling, hunched over, in the midst of the charred ruins of the cottage. She's exhausted from hours of crying — for her loss, but also out of despair. She knows her beloved guardians have been murdered and there's no point in trying to prove it.

When she finally rises, she's determined. She will honour the two women by living true to herself, to the land and the sea. She will continue their healing work and perpetuate the knowledge of the mystical powers of plants for future generations.

But first she needs to say farewell to her grandmother and Gwynneth in the old way, as she has been taught. She gathers armfuls of tall, dry, fragrant grass, twisted branches of juniper and whatever wildflowers she can forage from the surrounding fields to build a pyre on the bodies of the women.

Although she hasn't spoken to anyone of the tragedy, a handful of people appear, walking silently through the dusk. They gather around her to help usher the two beautiful, wise souls on their journey back to the earth. As the moon rises, a man comes forth and hands Moragh a torch, which she uses to light the pyre.

Standing at the centre of the circle and lit by the bright flames, Moragh places the obsidian moon around her neck, as her Grandmother had instructed her to do in the event of her passing. As the chain settles around her throat, Moragh feels her heart throb and expand; her mind suddenly tingles with neural connections. She feels her spirit brighten like an ember fanned by the wind. She is energized by a surge of love, an awakening of wisdom — all of it bequeathed to her by her beloved grandmother.

One by one, the people come forward to pay their respects to Moragh, then move off toward their own homes, until she is alone.

She stays by the fire all through the night, and in the morning, she gathers handfuls of ash and scatters them in each of the four directions. They fall from her outstretched hand and are taken by the wind. She imagines each particle touching down on the earth like droplets of pure, healing love.

~ ~ ~

We're back in Moragh's present again. She puts her dress on and finds that the bodice fits her more tightly because of the mending. Her full breasts bulge out of the neckline in a more pronounced way.

"Through the ceremony, it was as if I was imbued with all their healing knowledge an' it was made stronger through magic. It is a daunting responsibility. To be a healer is a blessing and a curse. It's a useful skill that I trade to make my living — along with raising a few chickens and sheep and what food I can grow. But 'tis also a dangerous legacy, for some consider it a dark art."

She wished she had been forewarned that one day she would carry this burden alone — perhaps then she would have been more attentive to their teachings. But now she would need to learn how to harness this power and use it with wisdom to heal and do good for the earth. Fearful she would forget, she began to make a record of all the plants and their uses, laboriously sketching every detail of her specimens with charcoal on parchment.

"I don't know everything, but I must! Our ways cannot die," Moragh tells me. "What is remembered lives! You remember, Liv from the future, you remember these things if I'm to die."

In the lonely days of mourning, Moragh took stock of the herbs and remedies, experimented and helped many of her country men and women with their ailments. One day, a hopeless young widow came to Moragh and begged for a cure for her loneliness. Her Grandmother's teasing words sprang to mind, "Moragh you are sixteen now, we've a good mind to make you a little love potion … rose petals, spearmint, cardamom, cinnamon, basil and a strong wish for love ought to do the trick." Moragh had retorted, "Ewwwh, I do not need any such potion Grandmother!" But as she brewed and blessed these ingredients for the widow, she couldn't help but think of her own loneliness and desire for a good man, being eighteen years of age now. Tasting a fair bit of the tincture herself, she wished hard and had a sudden urge. "I must go to the sea!" It was like a powerful itch deep within her. Giving the widow instructions and bidding her goodbye and good luck, Moragh quickly gathered her cloak around her shoulders and clambered down the rocky path to the sea.

An enormous grey whale appeared in the shallows, closer to shore than she had ever seen. Moragh stared with fascination as the great grey creature ponderously manoeuvred its body around and plunged back into the deep. Then she noticed a dark, heavy bulk being jostled in the surf on the wave-tossed beach. She ran to investigate and found the half-drowned body of a man.

Even under hypnosis, Liv can't contain her excitement and blurts out "This must be Nicolai, from the tale that Uncle Olav told Hannah and Ingaborg!" She laughs at her own outburst and then urges Moragh to continue sharing this memory.

"Aye, his name was Nicolai. He was cold as the dead. I had never seen such a man — unnaturally tall, lean and muscular, his hair near white-blond, with the chiselled face of a God. I fashioned a litter of driftwood and sea kelp and rolled his poor broken body on it and with every bit of might and maybe a little help from my Grandmother on the other side, I was able to haul my unconscious patient up the trail to my cottage."

From his sodden clothing, she deduced that he was a seaman, probably a whaler. "The style was unfamiliar, being made of leather with unusual fastenings. He was from across the sea, a foreigner. Maybe Norse."

She was attracted to him at once, even before it became clear that he would live.

"I watched him through the first night and in the morning he began to rouse. I fed him broth." As he regained his strength, they awkwardly began to learn to communicate.

"Before we knew one another's minds, we discovered the joy of our bodies," she says with a chuckle. Whoa! Moragh is sharing some pretty steamy images!

Now she goes to the cupboard and pulls out a batch of dough wrapped in damp fabric. She shapes it into four small round loaves and places them on the embers in the hearth.

"Me bairn, little Nic, will soon be home for his sup."

She reflects on the trauma of her day, then surprises me with an ironic smile.

"I must tell you, my spirit friend. That nasty Mirabella will suffer with that little bit of a curse I slipped in his pocket. The day will dawn that his despicable penis will be rendered limp for at least a fortnight!"

Her concoction, she tells me, contained the red berries of the chaste tree — an ingredient long known to discourage the male libido. Ironically, the same substance is used with good success to enhance fertility in women. She makes a mental note to replenish her supply of the berries, just in case she should need them for more positive potions in the future.

A raven caws outside and Moragh shudders with a premonition.

"Faith protect me — I shouldn't have plied my magic for revenge. This was one of Grandmother Fee's most fervent instructions — that magic should only be used for good, not for ill."

Images of Mirabella's grimacing face and putrid teeth flash through her mind again, but she willfully banishes his vile spirit from her thoughts, seizes her cloak and goes outside into the dusky red autumn afternoon. She ambles through the mossy meadow to a stand of brilliantly coloured oak trees and looks to the south across the moor, watching for her son. She begins to softly sing a Celtic song her grandmother taught her.

Cauldron of changes
Feather on the bone
Arch of eternity
Ring around the stone

Moragh breathes in deeply, replenishing her heart with the wonder of nature, and gazes out toward the horizon again. She spies a small figure running toward her. His face is beaming as he nears and he leaps into her arms for a hug. Her heart melts at the sight of her boisterous, bright-eyed five-year-old Nicolai.

My heart and spirit soar with recognition — this towheaded boy could be Micah's twin! He smells like the earth after a rain and his blue-green eyes twinkle with mischief.

Back at the cottage, Moragh passes her son a piece of potato cake warm from the fire, and he launches into a lively description of the day's escapades with his friend Fiona. They found magic stones, climbed trees and helped Fiona's grandfather gather the sheep to be sheared. This sturdy lad with his flowing Gaelic chatter is bewitching. Clearly, he effects his mother the same way — she drapes herself over him and kisses his cheek.

He leans into her and enjoys her warmth, then looks up into her eyes, "I gave Fiona the holy stones I found by the sea," he went on with a faraway look in his eyes, "So she can look through and see the fae folks when I'm no longer..." Moragh takes his small face tenderly in her hands, her face pale, but says nothing.

Sensing her fear, he adds, "Tha mi ag iondrainn papa — I miss Papa.'

"Soon we will be together again, my bonnie bairn. Soon, I promise."

Spurred by her son's request, Moragh indulges in thoughts of her beloved Nicolai. Who would have dreamed that she would fall in love with a man who made his living slaughtering whales — creatures she had revered since childhood? The mere sighting of a whale was a supernatural experience for her. Mind you, when she told him she believed the very whale he and his crew had been hunting had safely brought his wrecked body to shore to be rescued, he made a promise to himself, to her, and to the sea, that he would never harm another whale.

Moragh bids me along on a journey into her past and conjures up her favourite image of Nicolai — he's holding their son for the first time, cupping the tiny baby in his strong hands, tears of joy in his sky-blue eyes, his tangled flaxen curls framing his beckoning smile. "I am the most fortunate man in the world," he says, beaming.

Moragh begins to project episodes of her life with Nicolai, clearly wanting me to understand the depth of their commitment. I see them working together, tilling the soil by hand and trying to coax food from the rocky land. They harvest the stones to build an enclosure for the gentle brown-eyed milk cow Nicolai brought home for his growing son. They acquire a few lambs and some more chickens. Moragh's meagre living was needfully enhanced by this energetic, hard-working man.

Just watching them, I can see their fascination is mutual and profound.

"Ach, my spirit friend. Our lives were inspired by love. Our bodies seemed to fit together like a puzzle and when he whispered words of love and desire into the hollow of my throat, the real magic began.

"For nearly three years we lived in a state of wonder that such bliss was possible. My fair man loved to tease me and call me his Wild Celt. He praised his good fortune to have found a passionate woman, so unlike the cold, pious women in his home country. He is larger than life and he *is* my life.

"But all of a sudden, Nicolai was summoned home. It was a matter of family honour — his father was ill and his rivals were luring his crew away and impinging on his whaling and fishing territory."

I see an image of Moragh and Niclolai, with little Nic on his shoulders, standing on a long pier, their hooded garments whipping in the chilly wind. When it's time to board the ship, Moragh has to wrench the clinging child down into her arms. It's heartbreaking to see him struggle, his pudgy toddler arms reaching for his father.

A huge part of Nicolai's heart stayed in Scotland, and an equally huge part of Moragh's sailed away that day. He stayed true to his promise to Moragh that he would never hunt another whale. He dismantled his father's whaling business in favour of the herring hunt and cared for his father and supported his mother as was expected of him.

"And what of you, my friend, and the lot of women in your time? I sense your man, the father of your bonnie bairns, is not your match. I fear your safety if you stay with him. I sense a shadow all around him."

"You're right Moragh. It's why I'm here. The lot of women has not improved much in all this time, and even though I feel betrayed and unloved by him, it's hard for me to break away. I've been harmed in this life because I'm a woman and I need to gather my strength to talk about it and to be part of changing it along with others, past and present and future."

"Break away you must, Mo Cridhe. Have courage."

"Thank you so much, Moragh. I will leave you here, content that you are safe with your son — although I have a strong sense of foreboding for us both. But I will return another day, if I am welcome."

"Indeed you are, my spirit friend. Always."

"Celeste? Are you there?"

"Take my hand, Liv, and I will walk you back."

11

~ Lemon Balm ~

Sleep would've been nice, especially since Liv finally has the bed to herself. But it isn't meant to be. She is tossing and turning, unable to sleep, when she hears a rustling in the kid's room around two a.m. She pads downstairs and finds Leah, curled up in bed, determined tears in her eyes, snuggling a little bat, which is moments away from death.

"Oh Leah, who is this little creature?" Liv whispers.

Tearfully, Leah replies, "Mom, it's a tiny baby bat I found last night and I've tried to take care of it but I think it's really sick." Liv moves onto the bed and takes the bat, now still and cold, in her hands.

"Somehow this little fellow got really hurt, Leah. But you know what, you kept it warm and safe and comfy for its last hours, and now it isn't in pain anymore. I'm just going to put him in a special box, and we can bury him in the yard tomorrow."

"Oh Mom, baby animals shouldn't die."

"I know, Sweetheart. It's not fair. I'm glad you helped him, though." She strokes Leah's forehead and she soon falls fast asleep.

Liv lays the dead bat to rest in an empty chocolate box, and no sooner does she get her own tired body back to bed when she hears a loud cry from downstairs. She thinks at first it's Leah, upset about the bat, but soon realizes it's Molly having one of her night terrors. She finds her standing beside her bed, staring at the bookshelf, her eyes wide and her forehead sweaty despite the chill in the room.

"The books are falling. I didn't do it, I didn't do it." Her voice is panicked and she's shaking. Liv reaches out to embrace and comfort her, but she stiffens and pulls away.

Liv speaks softly, "It's okay, Molly, the books are okay. See? There they are on the shelves." No response. Molly's eyes seem to stare blindly, as if she's in a trance. This isn't the first time this had happened. Molly has been having episodes of night terrors since she was about five. Dr. Mo says they can be caused by stress or lack of sleep.

God knows poor Molly has been through enough lately.

But what to do with her poor scared, unresponsive daughter, stuck in a nightmare?

"Lemon balm and lavender to ease the nerves and bring on slumber," she hears Moragh's advice echoing softly in her mind. Fortunately, both happen to be in a vase with wild roses she'd made into a fragrant bouquet in the kitchen. Liv wraps the herbs in a facecloth and wets it with tepid water and coaxes her sobbing daughter to lie down. She snuggles beside her and places the soothing poultice on her forehead. Instantly she's cooled and calmed.

Crowded but cozy on the single bed with the Care Bear quilt that Grandma Hazel made for her Christmas gift last year, Liv and Molly fall asleep before they're able to name all of the Care Bears: Love-a-Lot Bear, Cheer Bear, Friend Bear, Good Luck Bear, Bedtime Bear… they sleep curled into each other until the dastardly rooster crows at 5:30 a.m.

Liv manages to organize breakfast: granola with milk, toast, jam and strawberries. Everyone but Micah is sleepy and quiet. Micah is in full form, taking baking soda out of the cupboard and adding vinegar, to try to make an explosion. All he makes is a gigantic mess.

Ross comes home in the mid-morning, looking haggard after a week of sleeping on Mel's sofa bed. His attitude is apologetic and he seems sober.

"Liv, I'm sorry. I should have called. I know you've been left holding the bag here, looking after everybody."

"Does this mean you're ready to talk about our marriage, Ross? Are you ready to see a psychiatrist?"

"I don't think I can survive this life without you and the kids, Liv. I did see the doctor — he gave me some new painkillers for this interminable headache."

"What about Anya?"

"That was a mistake. It's run its course."

"I need to know that you're willing to work to repair our marriage, and to get help. And you need to stay off the booze, Ross. I can't have you here if you upset the kids."

"I just need to rest."

She doesn't have the heart to send him away.

The following day when she finally has a chance to call Celeste, she tells her, "I think he's trying to get back on track. He was cheerful and fun with the kids this morning and left for work in good spirits. He says he went to see his doctor in Twin Rivers and got some new painkillers, but I think he's doubled the dose and he still complains of terrible migraine pain. He hasn't seen a psychiatrist."

"Do you feel safe when he's there, Liv?"

"I'm OK. He's been pleasant and attentive for the most part. He told the kids he wants to take all of us to Disneyland — including my mom, and he doesn't even like her! I don't know what he's thinking. We can't afford a trip. It seems destined to be a broken promise to the kids and that makes me mad. He is still sidestepping any talk about our marriage or his mental health."

"Sounds like you're both reverting to your patterns in some ways, but at least you're setting some clear boundaries and able to speak your mind."

"Yes, I am, but I also realize it's just a matter of time before there's another incident. Who needs Disneyland when your life is such a rollercoaster? I feel like one day I want to help him through this, and the next I don't. I'm getting stronger and more confident, but I feel I need to go deeper to figure out why I have made the choices I have in this life. I really hope we can revisit Moragh's story today."

"I suspect we will. One never knows exactly where hypnosis will take you, if anywhere," her friend replies. "But together, we seem to have found a way to manoeuvre very well within it."

"See you in an hour!"

Just as Liv arrives at Celeste's, the phone rings. It's her daughter Rebecca, who has some urgent issue regarding her application for Master's studies. Celeste signals to Liv to make herself at home and attends to the call.

Liv pours two cups of rose-hip tea and hands one to Celeste at the kitchen table with a smile of understanding. She's looking forward to the day when her own children are grown and successful and seeking her advice on such important life decisions. Liv takes her own tea and moves to the living room, where she relaxes into the serenity of her surroundings. She pauses once again to admire the rich jewel colours of the stained-glass Buddha and then reclines on the sofa and closes her eyes. She's so tired from her sleepless night and she can hear Celeste's animated voice and laughter in the next room, and it lulls her into a pleasant, meditative state.

An iridescent fog passes across her eyelids and she has the sensation of utter weightlessness now so familiar to her from her sessions in this room. She directs her thoughts to a question: *What did I see in him in the beginning?*

A memory comes to her — the moment nine years ago when she first saw Ross. She was a student sitting in one of the cramped desks in her first Sociology 101 class, waiting for the professor to appear. On the whiteboard in bold red letters someone had written: GOD IS DEAD.

Liv and the students around her were shocked that anyone would have the nerve to walk up to the board and write that. One girl who was particularly offended had just risen to go up and erase it when Ross sauntered in, looking amused and confident. He was handsome in a distinguished way, sort of like Donald Sutherland with a touch of George Carlin. His greying hair was pulled back in a ponytail with an accompanying short-styled beard and moustache — a look reserved only for the very cool in the '70s. His grey eyes sparkled with amusement as he observed his students' reactions to the words on the board.

"I just committed a taboo by trashing a powerful social belief. Even those of you who don't believe in God were outraged by this statement."

His voice was as compelling as his words. It was deep, mellow and commanding — she found out later that he put himself through university by working as a radio news announcer.

He challenged the class to acknowledge what had just happened re: the God is dead supposition. From there he segued into a discussion of how the colonizing Europeans had destroyed the indigenous people they encountered. The introduction of new technology and food, coupled with devastating epidemics and an aggressive campaign of assimilation, violence and abuse, decimated their population and undermined their cultural beliefs. He listed other countries where this had happened — was still happening.

"Really bad shit happens when you deny people the things that hold their culture together," he said, now leaning back in his chair with his feet crossed on the desk, lighting up his second cigarette. Liv was fascinated at his ability to look so elegant while smoking and ranting. Throughout his lecture, he'd been blowing smoke rings and drinking coffee — or more likely something even more potent — from a large red mug.

He concluded the class by saying he would prefer to teach only those bold enough and tough enough to learn some truths and have a good hard look at themselves as part of a really fucked-up society.

"And, by the way, I'm happy to lose the Christian zealots and the Barbie and Ken dolls who just signed up for this class thinking it would be an easy A."

Some of her fellow students were rapt with interest and enthused by this performance, while others were outraged. None walked out, though.

Liv was definitely in the first category. She emerged determined to show this brilliant, intimidating, arrogant man that she was absolutely not one of the Barbie dolls.

She smiles to herself in her semi-hypnotic state and allows Ross' seductive smoke rings to summon memories from the early months of their relationship — images that bring a blush to her face.

Dancing to a slow country song, deliberately brushing against him and brazenly gazing into his eyes.

She was drawn to him in a way she had never experienced before and she pursued him without shame. She gained access to the group of student activist types he hung out with. A few weeks after classes began, she contrived to join them at Joe's Cabaret on a Friday night. She drank way too much. She enticed him onto the dance floor and held him close as they waltzed to Don't It Make My Brown Eyes Blue. Later, in the parking lot, she kissed him for so long she nearly fainted, breathless. They left together that night in his little Alpha Romeo sports car, to drive to his rustic cabin on a lake, twenty kilometres out of town.

With Ross she felt exceptional, as if she were somehow endowed with some of his brilliance. She was entranced by his intelligence and insight into things she had never even thought about.

She didn't give the negatives a thought — the age difference of nineteen years, his brash self-confidence, his drinking, chain-smoking, the fact he'd been married three times previously. None of that mattered to her. Not then. He wrote eloquent love poems and painted extraordinary watercolours expressing his love and admiration of her.

She got pregnant accidently, spurring a shotgun wedding. Her unimpressed parents and her bewildered brothers attended the tiny event at city hall. Liv smiles as she recalls the family photo taken that day — the entourage are all trying to look happy, but the only joyous ones are she and Ross, beaming in the centre of the shot.

They lived in the city for a while, their lives full of friends, parties, romantic dinners, picnics, holidays to Tofino, California, Ottawa, and

Mexico — memories of their enviable, fulfilling life ripple through Liv's mind. It feels good to remember this part of her marriage. In all the turmoil, she'd forgotten the love that started it all and the immense pride she felt whenever she was with Ross. She'd felt like a better person for being with him. She felt in control and safe. *What changed?*

Celeste wraps up her phone call with her daughter and enters the room, rousing Liv from her reverie.

"Did you and Rebecca get everything sorted out?"

"Yeah, she just needed someone to go over her research hypothesis with her. Sorry to make you wait."

"Oh, don't worry about it. I occupied myself by reminiscing about when Ross and I met — how attracted I was to his mind and his incredible charisma in the classroom. His unconventional techniques and the joy he took in pushing the boundaries made him pretty irresistible to me then because I trusted his judgement. But now..."

"I can see how you'd be concerned his mental illness might cause him to jeopardize his teaching career, let alone your marriage," says Celeste.

"For sure! The guy is pretty well always in shit with the dean for something! He revels in pushing the boundaries. And there have been a few really dicey episodes in the past. About five years ago, he had a really outstanding seminar group — these students were really brilliant, in fact, three of them went on to do grad studies.

"Anyway, in one of their seminar sessions, Ross challenged them to consider what it would take for them to revolt. One of them said the parking situation at the college made them want to take up arms and they laughed, but then they started riffing on that idea. One of them came up with the name for their guerrilla group — the Parking Liberation Organization, or PLO."

"Oh, that's too funny," Celeste says, chuckling.

"Celeste, they actually went through with it. One night, under the cover of darkness, they removed all the signs on the college grounds that designated where students could park. The next morning, they showed up at all the road entrances in masks and told the students driving in they could park anywhere they wanted — so they parked in staff parking, on the sidewalk in front of the administration building, even on the lawns."

"Parking pandemonium!"

"No kidding. And even though Ross had told them he couldn't have anything to do with it, the word got out that his seminar group was responsible and he very nearly lost his job."

"What about the students?"

"Oh, the administration crushed them. Within hours they'd identified them and threatened immediate expulsion if the signs weren't returned by a certain deadline. They gave in immediately and dug up the signs, which they'd buried in the bark mulch in the gardens. They didn't get expelled, but each one had a nasty letter on their file."

"I see what you mean — that was a pretty risky thing to put in motion with the whole PLO terrorist craze at the time! Hard to see the point of it."

"Well, that's the irony of the whole thing. Just last spring, I ran into one of those students — she has her PhD now and she's working as a sessional with Ross' department. She told me the PLO incident was a defining moment for her — it taught her never to pursue a cause she isn't ready to die for; to choose her comrades carefully; and that for any act of rebellion, one should expect a swift, decisive and devastating overreaction from the status quo."

"So, there was a method to his madness...sorry! A poor choice of words, considering his current mental state."

Liv gives a little chuckle, amused in spite of herself by Celeste's faux pas.

"OK, enough of Ross. Let's see what Moragh is up to."

12

~ *Defiance* ~

Session No. 6 transcript, Sept. 27, 1987
Moragh of Pine Glen, 1745

I call a greeting to Moragh and hear her welcoming laughter as I ride the trail of blue light to her door. We join at once, our spirits joyful at the reunion.

She's at her son's bedside, looking fondly down at his angelic face as he sleeps. The light is dim — it's early in the morning. She quietly dons her cloak and steps outside her door.

Plump rainclouds are gathering in the sky. Carrying a wide basket with the handle over her crooked arm, Moragh makes her way along the hillside, stopping now and then to collect some of the useful herbs she will need to attend to her fellow country-folk over the coming months — comfrey, St. John's Wort, borage, milk-thistle — each with their own purpose. She visualizes her medicine cupboard, trying to remember what items are running low.

Despite the impending rain, it's a glorious day. The sun has yet to be engulfed in clouds and it warms her face as she walks, holding up the hem of her long green dress as she wends her way amongst the heather and waving grasses. Her bright auburn hair, long and loose around her shoulders, is fanned by the billowing wind.

She spots some raspberry leaf and dandelion in the distance, and while keenly aware she's wandering far from her sleeping son, she climbs quickly to the top of the hill to gather these needed herbs. She pulls out her small knife and quickly harvests a few raspberry stems with healthy leaves, then bends and uses it to loosen the soil around the dandelions, trying to get the roots as well. As she rises and turns back toward the cottage, she sees a group of people approaching and a dark fear creeps over her.

They walk toward her purposefully — there's no point hiding, they've clearly spotted her. Five men, followed by another two on horseback, stomp through the heather. They're not farmers — they wear tall boots and dark cloaks, except for one who wears long black robes and the white collar of a priest. Witch hunters. Possibly the same ones who torched Grandmother Fee's cottage. Two dogs burst into sight and lope toward her. It's then Moragh recognizes the cursed figure of Christo Mirabella amongst them and she knows it's he who has brought the men here.

"Fie on him! May my curse forever plague his pathetic member!" She mutters to me.

Like a trapped wild animal, Moragh looks for a direction to run. The men block her path to return to little Nicolai — besides, if she were to run to him it would only put him in more danger.

She considers running in the opposite direction to lead them away, like a sandpiper will do to protect its nest. But no. There are far too many of them, and they are far too close. She must face these evil men, and all she has to defend herself is the small knife she uses for cutting stems.

My heart is pounding along with Moragh's and I desperately wish there was something I could do to help, but there isn't. I am merely a spirit, along for the fated ride.

"Liv," Moragh calls me by name for the first time. "This is surely my last day in this lifetime. I'll not have you harmed, but I'd have you be my witness. Take to the sky, cast your spirit line to that rosy thrush in that tree there. See and remember — because what is remembered, lives."

I already know from the story told by Uncle Olav in Norway this does not end well, but I can give her some comfort by imparting one bit of information.

"Moragh, be assured that whatever happens, your Nicolai will avenge your death tenfold and join you and Nic in the hereafter. Your spirits will live on together."

"This fortifies me, my spirit friend. Now go, for they are almost upon us."

I cast my glowing blue thread at the thrush, unsure whether it will accept the intrusion.

~ ~ ~

Suddenly, there is silence. All I am is one bright eye, looking down from the branch of a tree and viewing the scene as if through a spyglass.

Moragh stands proudly, ready to face them. She looks so strong and determined, for a moment I wonder if she can fend them all off with her knife. I can still hear her thoughts.

"I honestly wish I did have the powers these horrible men believe I have. I would make myself invisible and fly off with my child. I would kill them first to put an end to their murderous rampage. Yet the wise part of me knows there would be others who would gladly take up their cause."

The hunters form a circle around Moragh and their large salivating shepherd dogs jump on her and knock her to the ground — but then begin to lick her face. The dogs know she's a threat to no one. She struggles to her feet, stands erect and looks into the eyes of each and every one of the men, even the two on horseback — and detects varying degrees of hatred, fear, self-righteousness and lust in each of them. Not an ounce of shame or compassion. When her eyes land on Mirabella, he leers at her, thinking he's won.

"A curse to last a lifetime, you dirty cur," she sneers.

His eyes widen.

Moragh's composure belies her inner terror. She's thinking only of her son. She knows she's strong enough to face her own death, but the thought of his suffering is too much to bear. The only small chance she has is to find a way to outsmart these men. It looks to me as if she's trying to reduce their bloodlust by exuding calm. It's not working. They will frenzy until she cowers.

The largest man, a portly fellow with a red leathery face, saggy bags under his eyes and a bloated nose, asks her name.

"I am Moragh Shannon of Pine Glenn."

"You have been accused of causing grave damage to this man," he says, indicating towards Christo Mirabella.

"Aye, I arranged to purchase some herbs and spices from this man, and in return he attempted to rape me, ransacked my home and stole my money."

One of the men strides to her and grabs her by the arm, forcing her roughly to her knees.

"You can't rape a whore, witch."

His company snickers.

"Moragh Shannon of Pine Glen, we charge you with witchery and attempted murder by way of a lethal potion. These crimes are punishable by death."

These words pierce my heart. I lose my connection briefly — my companion, the thrush, is startled and takes off, me with it. From a dizzying height, I watch Moragh being dragged through the field, which from here looks like a flowing sea of waving green grass studded by islands of mauve-blooming heather and lavender. The thread that bonds me to her spirit has become tenuous, but I can still feel Moragh's strong presence.

Desperate to follow the action, I cast my spirit line toward her once again, but I remain with the mindless thrush. Perhaps she's blocking my soul from re-joining hers? But, maybe as a result of my efforts, the bird coasts above the humans and I am able to watch from above.

The hunters have their prey and are satisfied now that she is fearful and subdued. They bind her hands and begin to shove her back and forth between them, groping her. They make their way to the edge of the cliff and then prod her down the path to the sea. Now the storm is upon us — the thrush, buffeted by the gusting wind, shapes herself into a bullet and plummets down to the branch of a gnarled, storm-twisted tree. Huge, icy drops of rain pelt down, driven nearly horizontal by the mounting wind.

I realize there will be no trial — or at least not in a court. They plan to throw Moragh into the very sea that she loves and that has sustained her. I've heard of this archaic test for witches — if she doesn't drown it will prove without a doubt that she's a witch and then she'll be burned. If she does drown, it'll mean she's not a witch — but by then it won't matter.

When they reach a point on a rocky ledge overlooking the roiling sea, they bind Moragh from neck to feet with an old, prickly rope taken from a dinghy lashed to the rocks below. A few people from her nearby village have gathered, attracted by the commotion. Someone shouts, "Kill the witch!" But most of the onlookers are clearly horrified to see their neighbour, their healer, in such peril. Moragh meets their eyes, wordlessly thanking them and cautioning them not to step forward, for there's nothing to be gained except more trouble, hate and horror.

Her fear has been replaced by defiance. She looks up at my terrified spirit cowering on the tree branch and silently communicates to me: "No matter what happens, by flesh or by spirit, help me to be with my child, Liv. I must be with him at the end."

The clergyman stands over Moragh. His white collar is stained with sweat and his drenched cassock flaps wetly around his stumpy, somewhat bowed legs.

"Moragh of Pine Glen, I declare you a heretic, the devil's gateway, who has come to poison God's kingdom. In God's name, you will be cast out, subject to His judgement."

Four men spin Moragh around until she's dizzy and disoriented and then hurl her over the rocky ledge into the sea below.

Thankfully, she's been thrown with such force that she doesn't hit any of the rocks on the way down. Silvery white flashes cut lines in the sea, streaks that race to meet Moragh as she falls through the air. Watching her descend, I leave the thrush behind me as I instinctively reach out to her, and this time my spirit thread connects with hers. As she hits the water, I am with her once more.

Moragh has the presence of mind to fill her lungs with air during her fall, but the shock of impact and the cold water almost make her exhale. She relaxes her body as she sinks, and as she starts to rise, she kicks her bound legs together, like a mermaid, propelling herself away from shore. I feel myself kicking along with her — kicking out the injustice, hatred and fear and pushing powerfully with the water and praying for a miracle.

"These waves could dash me on the rocks," she thinks. I marvel at her fearsome will to live. But her breath is running out — she begins letting bubbles of air escape from her mouth to make it last as long as possible. She squints through the salty water at the silver sky, aching for air, but stays submerged, fearful that she'll be seen. Suddenly, from out of the depths, two ghostly white figures flash into view — Hannah's splendid belugas! They swirl effortlessly beneath her and, cradling her body with theirs, propel her through the water at great speed. They pop her up to the surface, out of sight, in a shallow bay she doesn't recognize. As her head breaks the surface of the water, Moragh gasps for air. The whales circle around her as if in encouragement before scooting back into the satin darkness.

I urge Moragh to shore — she's limp with exhaustion, but she must keep moving. Somehow the rope that bound her has frayed and broken. She rips it off and hobbles over the pebble beach to the shelter of a rock overhang. She's breathless and shivering. I'm relieved, but fearful of what might happen next. I feel compelled to feed her tired spirit.

"Moragh! Your strength astounds me. You survived."

"Aye, my sister soul. But my son is still in danger."

Her breath returning, she sheds her sodden dress, leaving only her light cotton shift. She appears to have lost her shoes to the ocean. She cautiously begins to explore, looking for a route back up the cliffs. She finds a trail that looks promising and begins to climb, her strong body negotiating the hazards of the path by instinct rather than thought. Her mind is churning with fear for Nic.

"For the first time in my child's young life, I wish I had not borne him to this world. I cannot bear the thought that his life may be taken for reason of being my son — the son of a witch."

She is staggering by the time she reaches the top of the cliff, where her trail meets another that runs north and south along the crest. She crouches low to make sure it's safe to proceed. In this pause, she addresses me in her mind.

"Thanks be that you are with me," then her deep, now hoarse voice calls,

"East, give me Air so that I may breathe,

South, bring me Fire, so that my strength will be forged like an arrow

West, bring me Water, so that I may bathe in love

North, let my hands touch fertile Earth that I may dig for wisdom."

I feel Moragh regaining her strength and summoning her resolve. She rises and begins to walk quickly along the trail, ever watchful.

"Mo cridhe," she says to me in a loud whisper. "There has always been, in the back of my mind, a strong feeling that my little Nic would not be with me for a long time, at least not in this lifetime. This premonition always damped the joy I felt at bringing him into the world and loving him more than I ever thought it possible to love another. I must get to him."

She seems unaware of being drenched and cold. Her feet are bare and bleeding, her hair dripping and matted. She pushes on, moving at a brisk walk and breaking into a run for brief periods, until her heart begins to thud dangerously.

Her mind is thundering with horrible images — her worst imaginings. She consciously pushes them away, distracting herself by singing a song Grandmother Fee taught her. She sings it silently in her mind and imagines she can hear that dear woman's husky voice singing along.

Back to the river, back to the sea

Back to the ocean, one with thee

Back to the forest, back to the fields

Back to the mountains, her body revealed

Back to my bones, back to my skin

Back to my spirit, the fire within

As she nears the crest of the hill overlooking her cottage, her pace quickens. Finally, she reaches a point where she can see her home — a sweet, welcome sight — on the opposing hillside. But as she stands there looking, she's alarmed to see a wisp of smoke rising at the roofline, then a flash of white flame at its base.

Moragh races down the hill and across the meadow. Her mind is teeming. She had been hoping the witch-hunters, having fulfilled their angry mission by tossing her into the sea, wouldn't bother to return to her cottage and her sleeping son. She grasps at the possibilities — perhaps Nic woke up and escaped to the safety of the neighbour's, or maybe one of them, aware of her capture, ventured to the cottage to rescue him. But she knows he's probably inside.

She reaches an oak tree near the cottage and hides behind its trunk to take stock of the situation. The men are on the far side of the cottage, stomping on her garden and celebrating loudly. The flames are building from the foundation, licking up the walls of her home.

She cannot wait for a safe moment — she must rescue Nic — so she scurries to the door and opens it. Smoke billows and then is sucked inside as the fire gasps for fresh air. She plunges in and shuts the door behind her. Despite the thick haze, she can see that Nic is not in the room.

"Nic?" She speaks in a normal voice, so as not to startle him — although she's aware of the irony. She hugs the floor and searches the small space, lifting blankets and looking under and behind the scant furniture. She scrambles to her herb cupboard and reaches behind into Nic's favourite hiding spot — her hand touches his solid, unconscious form.

She pulls him out and gathers him in her arms, murmuring his name. He stirs weakly.

"Mathair!" It is an exhalation.

"Ah, my wee bairn."

With tears in her eyes, she lays him tenderly on the floor where the smoke is thinnest and nestles beside him, touching his face and whispering reassuring words. But she can see he's fading away. The men still rant outside, fortunately unaware of her presence inside the house.

There is no escape. There is no magic to break the evil that has been set upon them. Moragh clutches Grandmother Fee's pendant, hoping to access some of the wisdom it contains. Her mind clears and she makes a decision.

"Wait for me, leanabh mo chridhe. I will come with ye." She rises and selects two bottles from the shelf, one a tonic for pain and the other belladonna. She empties the vial of powdered root into the thick liquid, recorks it and shakes it as she sinks to her knees at her son's side.

"Nicolai." His deep blue eyes open and strain to focus on his mother's lovely face.

"Drink, my son. Your pain will away." She tips the vial to his perfect mouth and lets several drops fall onto his tongue. Then she tilts the bottle to her own lips and drains it.

She lies down beside him, wraps him in her arms and nuzzles his ear, telling him she loves him and they'll always be together.

They glow with an eerie, opalescent light.

Our connection is growing hazy. It's as if I'm spinning around them but it's Moragh and Nic who break away and begin to flow upwards, as if they've been turned to pearly smoke. Holding hands, their spirits lift together and rise above the cottage. They pause and look down for a moment on their earthly bodies, emitting love and light to those who have loved them. Then they are swept away like dust out to sea. And I am alone.

"Come back to the present now, Liv. Slowly waking up to your current life...ten, nine, eight...letting go of the trauma of this past life ...seven, six, five, four...holding onto the knowledge, insights, wisdom and love that you gained...three, two, one. Here you are. Breathe, relax and re-enter, feeling refreshed, safe and well."

Liv opens her eyes to see her friend's face etched with concern.

"Oh, my dear friend, what a tumultuous path your soul has traveled. Poor Moragh. Take a moment to get yourself back to this century."

Liv gazes around her, marveling at the almost surreal clarity of seeing through her own eyes as opposed to those of Moragh, her brave sister soul.

Liv suddenly remembers a moment several years ago when she visited a psychic while pregnant with Micah. It was kind of a lark — she went with Kat, just for fun. The thing was, she didn't know she was pregnant yet. Ross had had a vasectomy three months earlier and they'd only had sex maybe once or twice after that. She didn't know that unless a man frequently ejaculates, it takes time to diminish the little swimmers. So, although she was having a few pregnancy symptoms, like sore nipples and a bit of nausea, it didn't even occur to her that she could be pregnant.

The psychic told her she would be having a son who had also been her son in a previous life. She said they'd lived by the sea in Scotland and had been burned to death together in a fire. At the time, she found it amusing but hadn't taken it seriously.

When Liv found out a few weeks later that she was indeed pregnant, the emotional chaos that ensued was unbearable. Ross accused her of cheating on him and she was so hurt and angry, they had a huge fight. She threatened to leave him. He didn't seem very upset at the thought, which made her even crazier. In the end they sorted it out, but it was the first time she had any sense that their marriage wasn't perfect — that he wasn't perfect and neither was she. She began to question him more. He seemed to trust her a little less. It was as if they had both been knocked off the pedestal they had placed each other on, and the only place to go was down.

It's funny, even though I didn't pay any heed to what the psychic told me, when Micah was born I did feel a strong sense of recognition, a sort of feeling that we'd done this before. It's always seemed like we had an unusual connection — the way we share insight into each other's thoughts and moods. Sometimes he'll surprise me by saying exactly what I've been thinking. And this prevailing fear that I'll lose

Micah — that he'll die. Did I inherit that memory, that intense fear, from Moragh?

Liv turns toward Celeste and quietly speaks, "Remember that time when we had the bonfire at the skating pond and Micah tripped on a rock and nearly fell into the flames? He missed by millimetres and got through it with just a small gash on his forehead. I freaked out, took the kids and left because I could see him burned and dead and I couldn't get that image out of my head."

"I remember how scared you were that night. But I also know you have done an amazing job of protecting Micah. He can be a really scary little dude with his love of heights, power tools, fire and speed! There's a certain amount of protective mama bear in all of us, but it does seem that yours is excessive — it could've lingered in you because of Moragh."

"You're right. Hopefully, now that I know that, I can overcome it. And if I inherited her fears, maybe her strength and wisdom were also passed on to me.

"There's a reason I survived *my* childhood, Celeste. I think it's because I've always carried Moragh's strong and wise spirit with me. And Hannah's indomitable one as well…and perhaps others I have yet to meet."

13

~ Gravity ~

"Where are you, Ross? I can hardly hear you!"

"China. I have to go to China — there's some really bad shit about to go down and I have to stop it."

"China? Seriously? I don't understand. Why would you do that? What can you do about something that's happening in China? Are you telling me you're a secret agent or something?"

"Funny, Liv, but it isn't a joke. In a way *I am* an agent. Liv, can I trust you? Can you take the earpiece off the phone to check and make sure there are no bugging devices, please?"

"What? No! You're talking crazy."

"You're the only person I can trust. They'll kill me if they find out I know what they're up to."

"Kill you? I don't understand any of this. Are you really going to China? Is this real, or are you drunk or having some kind of breakdown?"

"LIV, you have to listen to me! This is real. We are running out of time here. I need you to believe me. I'm going to tell you what I know so far: Hu Yaobang has been disgraced and now Peng Zhen is trying to challenge Zeng's authority and primacy. This is a major threat to the balance of power, not to mention the interference of Russia. There are Nazis in China, Liv and they're taking over the Communist Party, and the German Nazis leftover from World War II are there and Gorbachev is in there like a dirty bastard and World War Three is about to happen!" He's talking very fast and so loudly that Liv has to hold the receiver away from her ear.

"Ross, you're scaring me. Come home right now. Please? You need some help."

"Oh fuck! Here they come, they've got guns. I have to go, Liv. I love you."

There's a click and the line goes dead. Liv stands stunned for a moment. Here she is with three sick kids and a farm to manage, and her husband is in crisis in an unknown location.

"Liv, come in, come in, I've missed you! How are the kids? Chickenpox — what the hell! All three at once, and Ross off on some wild trip to China?"

Liv relays the whole story, at least what she knows of it. Ross is home now. Liv spent the previous week trying to track him down, in between caring for her three poxy children. Molly suffered with high fevers and lots of spots. Micah and Leah had a slightly gentler version and the homemade calendula lotion Celeste had sent over helped a great deal with the itch. The kids slept a lot, so Liv got on the phone with friends in Vancouver and with Mastercard to do some investigating as to the whereabouts of her husband. Friends were no help, as they hadn't seen him, but a helpful Mastercard representative told her there had indeed been a charge for a return ticket to China. Other recent purchases were for alcohol, cash and restaurants in Vancouver. She needed to know if he was holed up with Anya, or if he'd actually flown to China. She couldn't tell from the charges if the meals were for two or not. That wouldn't be proof anyway — he could be with anyone. All scenarios were equally terrible to her, including the one where he had simply lost his mind. When he finally arrived home, he looked like a bedraggled homeless person. In contrast to his look, he had a new car — a ridiculously impractical luxury Thunderbird sedan — and a debt of $8,000.

"I told Ross that's exactly what a person with bi-polar disorder would do, but he ignored me. He won't talk about China, Vancouver or the car. He took to our bed without even asking about the kids or noticing that he'd missed both Thanksgiving and my birthday. That isn't like him.

"By the way, Celeste, thanks for the moon earrings — my best birthday gift. My only one, actually. I love them — they remind me of Moragh."

"You're welcome, Liv. Sorry I didn't deliver them myself, but I had the house full of family and I've never had chickenpox so I didn't want to risk it. I felt so bad missing your birthday — your thirtieth is a landmark. Our gang has rescheduled your birthday bash for two weeks from now, so make sure you get a sitter."

Liv takes a seat on Celeste's sofa in anticipation. But Celeste isn't ready yet.

"Do you know what you're going to do from here, Liv?"

"Not really. When Ross was gone, his faculty head, Fielding, kept calling from the university because he missed a whole week of classes and a bunch of important meetings — they're in the midst of faculty and institutional evaluations to do with accreditation. Fielding appealed to me as if I had some kind of influence over my husband's behaviour and he couldn't seem to accept that I have none. Finally, I was so worried that he might be fired that I lied and told him Ross was home, but sick in bed with the chickenpox!"

"Protecting him."

"Yes, even though I really wanted to hex him with a virulent pox curse for real! I can't help but feel some compassion for him. I get that he's not doing these things to hurt me. Why can't he just stay home, let me take care of him and help him get better, so the kids can have their dad back, and so I can try to love him again?"

Celeste's expression is serious. "Liv, it sounds to me as though he's in the manic phase of bipolar disorder. I've been reading up on it. It all fits — the affair, delusions about saving the world, paranoia, the headaches and the crashing depression. Wow!"

"I have no idea what to do. He's so exhausted, Celeste. He didn't have any classes today so I told him I was going out so that if he needed to he could sleep all day. I don't know how much he's drinking or how many pills he's taking, but I know it's a lot more than usual. I called his doctor in Twin Rivers, but he couldn't tell me anything confidential. He did say Ross was there two weeks ago, before China, and that my concerns were valid and if he got worse, I should take him to the hospital. He's willing to refer Ross to a psychiatrist, but it takes months to get an appointment. When I suggested that Ross probably would never agree to take medicine or to stop drinking, his doctor agreed, so that told me a lot, without telling me anything for sure."

"He needs to deal with this, Liv. It's not your responsibility to see that he gets help. You have no control over that. You can only encourage him and hope that he follows through. You need to set the boundary and get you and the kids out of there if he crosses it."

"You're right, Celeste. I hate conflict, but I have to take control, for all our sakes. We can't go on like this."

"Do you feel up to a session today?"

There is firmness in Liv's voice, but exhaustion in her face. "Yes, I don't want to be home today, not with Ross like he is. I don't want to let go of that blue thread. Maybe this next life we look at won't be as harrowing as Moragh and Hannah's... or this one!"

"I'm so happy if this is helping you. You do have the strength and wisdom of Moragh and the resilience and adventurous spirit of Hannah and I know you will get through to the other side of all that's happening in your life right now. Are you comfortable? Ready to start?"

Liv relaxes into the spongy cushions of the couch and nods.

"I want to go somewhere exotic and warm."

"Okay, slow even breaths...here we go down the path, through the trees...ten, nine, eight, seven...counting down the stairs toward the sea...six, five, four... through the mist...three, two, one. Reaching the sands of time and following your soul's thread to wherever it leads you today...."

14

~ *Peaceful Resistance* ~

Session No. 7 transcript, Oct. 17, 1987
Veda, 1918

I descend down the stairs that curve around immense, majestic cedars to the ocean's edge. My glowing thread beckons me out and across the sea and I thrill at the sensation of floating over the water to a much warmer place. The humidity grows stifling as I pass over the sandy shoreline and look down on a hilly, lushly vegetated terrain. I dive and weave amongst laden mango trees, groves of tamarind and coconut palms, inhaling their exotic aromas. My spirit line swirls and turns to dance around an Indian elephant who is gracefully pulling down a tall palm frond with her trunk. She bellows softly — perhaps she's communicating with the little one playing near her feet, but it sounds to my ears like a warm greeting to my spirit.

Now I'm travelling over an arid grassland dotted with scrub and bush, toward a settlement. Oh! Quite suddenly it's become dark — I can't see a thing.

I remember to look up. My grandmother once told me if I ever got lost at night, I could get my bearings from the night sky. The waxing moon and the Southern Cross constellation share some silver light with me. I've steadied myself. There's my spirit line. It's leading me toward a woman wearing a dark green sari with a tattered shawl covering her head and face. She's moving as quickly as she can along a well-worn path, her range of motion limited by her narrow skirt. The blue cord is dancing toward the tiny bundle she holds tightly to her chest. The dwelling place of my spirit in this time appears to be the tiny brown-skinned baby in her arms.

I'm hoping my spirit hasn't chosen to enter this perfect little body only to be snuffed out a few moments later. The mother's emotional state suggests the infant is in grave danger. This wee one's spirit is barely a glowing ember, unsure whether it wants to stay in this world or not. I hesitate to join with her because she seems so frail, yet she is the carrier of my soul from many years ago and I want her to live and carry on.

Celeste gently speaks, "Go with her, Liv. If your connection is strong, you'll still be able to engage without fully entering her fragile body."

"You're right, Celeste. The infant's soul is speaking to me. The story is coming to me as if it's one I have always known."

She is wrapped in a threadbare scarf and only a shock of her wispy coal black hair can be seen. The woman carrying her is weeping, her mouth twisting in anguish. She's exhausted and in terrible pain, having just given birth. Blood soaks through the front of her sari, staining it a dark brown. Her heart is pounding as she considers what her next move should be.

Had she given birth to a son, her labouring pain might have been transformed into pride and gratitude, but alas, the child is a girl. Her first daughter was allowed to live, but the second was killed and the same would have happened to this child. Even though her baby is barely six hours old, she is already considered a worthless mouth to feed. Had she stayed, her husband's brother would have come and taken the child, smothered her and buried her beneath a tree, as is custom in their village.

So, her mother has fled, hoping to give her away and save her life. Failing that, she will take her child's life mercifully, with her own hands.

She doesn't give a thought to her own safety — if she is caught, her husband's family, with whom she lives, will kill her.

Desperation is the prevailing emotion I'm sensing. Darkness is turning to dawn and there is music coming from the larger road that intersects the narrow red dirt path we're on. The mother is trying to decide if she should avoid this sound, as someone she knows might see her and report back to her family.

She strains to see more now. A large procession of what seems like hundreds of people comes into view, led by a man wearing a white sarong. They're singing and chanting Satyagraha, rejoicing in the power of truth.

Raghupati Raghav Raja Ram
Patita Pavan Sitaram
Sitaram, Sitaram,
Bhaj Pyare Mana Sitaram
Raghupati Raghav Raja Ram
Patita Pavan Sitaram...

Now a chorus of voices is calling for the man in white to speak. "Mahatma Gandhi, Mahatma Gandhi," the people chant.

The man is small and thin with wire-framed glasses. He stands before the crowd and smiles and it seems as if he's beaming that smile to each person individually. My spirit soars with shock at first, like I've just won the lottery, and then immediately my disbelief transforms into humble honour, being in the presence of such an admirable, spiritual, important person in the history of our world. The energy of his spirit is so powerful and gentle that I sense all will be well — this child of my soul's past will be allowed to live her life.

"The only devils are the ones running around in our own hearts," Gandhi begins, and goes on to say, "An eye for an eye will make the whole world blind." He explains how each of us must first take responsibility for our own pain, our own problems and our own suffering — only then can we gain the strength to stand up for what is right, and only then can we do this with a peaceful mind and in a way that truly benefits the world.

He talks about the futility of war and says, "The only way to conquer one's opponent is with love." He says all people are born equal and deserve to be treated with kindness and respect. He speaks about the caste system and the salt tax and unfairness — how this unjust tax is causing the poor people in this country to starve and turn against each other. He speaks of the need to band together and show the government they are strong, united and peaceful. He bids his followers to join him on his walk to the sea.

"We are the salt of the earth and we have traditionally made the salt from the earth and the sea," the great man says.

When the speech is over, the woman weaves her way through the crowd and I follow, invisible. Some of the people smile at her and nod their approval at the tiny bundle in her arms. She speaks to a group of women, asking them if there might be anyone who would save the life of her baby daughter. Hushed voices carry her request from woman to woman, sharing the plea. Every one of them knows this heartbreak and is aware of the huge risk she's taken by fleeing, much less trusting her secret with strangers.

My spirit cord suddenly throbs with energy and splits into two distinct, bright threads. One still binds me to the baby and her mother, while the other twists about and extends toward another woman who's standing nearby. She's perhaps forty years old, dressed in a simple white tunic, and her head is shaven, making her brown, angular face seem especially small and delicate.

I'm able to read this woman's thoughts as clearly as if she was telling me her story. She's a widow who has no children of her own. When her husband died, she refused to follow him into death by throwing herself on his funeral pyre, as is the custom, so she was shunned by her family and the entire village. She doesn't want — nor is she allowed — to remarry, so she's lost her chance to bear a child of her own. With Gandhi, she found acceptance. She follows him because she shares his belief in equality for men and women, for children and all religions and for the abolishment of the caste system.

Her smile is wide and warm. Surrounding her is an aura of intense azure blue and as she moves closer I can see her light expand and mingle with the thread that connects this infant to me.

This woman gently lifts the scarf covering the baby's face and looks deep into her amber eyes.

"Welcome to my life, little one."

It's as though she's been eagerly expecting this child for years. Tears of joy run down her face. She turns to the birth mother, whose face is haggard with grief and pain. As their eyes meet, the young woman manages a weak smile, "Please have these two gold bracelets in gratitude for saving my baby daughter."

146

"No," says the woman, knowing there would be severe consequences to the mother if it were ever discovered she had given away her only gold possessions. "What do I need gold for? You are giving me the most precious gift I could imagine. My name is Suraya. I will care for this child as if my own."

My spirit is awash with the emotions charging between these two courageous, beautiful women.

"My name is Puja," the exhausted mother tells the woman. "Thank you for your kindness. I hope we might meet again one day when it is safe."

"Puja...meaning prayer. You are aptly named, and you have answered my prayers by finding me. I can see you are a devout woman who seeks to do what is right. Will you join me in prayer?"

Puja nods and the two women intone together.

Asato ma sad gamaya

tamaso ma jyotir gamaya

ma amrtam gamayathe

From what is not, lead me to what is

From darkness, lead me to light

From death, lead me to what is undying

"I have named my daughter Veda. It's the only thing I can give her," the young mother says.

Suraya nods, her eyes full of empathy. "It's a good name, full of promise."

Then little Veda is gently separated from her mother's rapid heartbeat, only to be held close to another heart that beats with a calm, strong rhythm.

"What will you do?" the elder woman asks.

"The woman who attended to me is a good friend. She told my husband's family that the baby was a sickly girl who died shortly after birth and that, in my shame and grief, I have gone to bury her."

Puja tearfully looks down on her child for the last time. She raises her eyes to Suraya's and the two women stand close together, facing one another, with the child warm between them and the red dirt road beneath their bare feet. Then the young mother turns away and disappears into the throng.

I feel so loved and so fortunate to witness this piece of my soul's history. The threads of life are tangled, but not broken, yet I feel suddenly adrift.

"Come back to your time, Liv. Climb the stairs back to the present...one, two, three, four...returning to safety with me...five, six, seven...feeling rested and calm...eight, nine, ten."

Liv and Celeste are both spellbound by this virtual experience of life as a girl in India in the 1920's.

"That country holds an exotic magic, while at the same time being horrific and cruel," Celeste says. "Imagine being cast away for being born a girl."

"Ha, yes I sure can now. And it still happens today, apparently," Liv sadly shakes her head in empathy. "I have to tell you — when I was fourteen, I learned about Gandhi from reading an article in National Geographic and I chose to do a school project about him in grade nine — that was in 1969. I think even my teacher thought I was pretty weird. All the other kids were writing about sports stars or Elvis Presley or the Beatles. I was in love with Gandhi's belief that it was possible to create change in the world through peaceful protest. His story inspired me to become a bit of an activist. My mother drew the line when I announced that, in solidarity with Gandhi, I would only wear handmade cloth and that I wanted to fast in protest of the slaughter of baby seals."

"At least you drew the line at shaving your head and wearing a loincloth!"

"I compromised by refusing to eat meat and tie-dying my brothers' old undershirts and sewing long, flowery skirts made from curtains. I joined Greenpeace, marched and collected names on petitions. Armed with my passion, naiveté and good intentions, I worked hard for the sea mammals, old growth forests and against the war in Vietnam. These were my teenage causes and I imagined I was just as impassioned as Gandhi and his followers."

"I can see that in you," Celeste says fondly. "Choosing Gandhi as a guiding mentor in your teens seems a whole lot healthier than what most of us did by choosing Mick Jagger or the Grateful Dead," she laughs.

"I've never told you about my near claim to fame with the infamous environmental activist Paul Watson?"

"Well. I'm impressed! Do tell!"

"I met him at an anti-Vietnam war protest at the Peace Arch border crossing. He was handing out petitions to ban the baby seal slaughter on the east coast."

"I remember that era. Didn't he spray paint the seals green, so their coats would be worthless and they wouldn't be killed?"

"Yep, he was my hero. So, a few months later he came to my high school in his funky orange VW bus to pick up my signed petitions. I was giddy and nervous, dressed in my favourite faded bellbottoms and blue peasant blouse. I'd even ironed by curly locks, in an effort to look more like Joni Mitchell and less like the Sunbeam bread girl everyone always said I looked like."

Celeste laughs as she imagines this scene.

"I was so inspired by his passion for the cause and somewhat convinced he would fall instantly in love with me and scoop me up and away from my mundane life, to join his band of ocean saving pirates.

"What he saw was a grade nine girl, star-struck, wordless and sweaty. He took the paper from my outstretched hand and said, 'I thank you and the seals thank you.' And with that he flashed a peace sign to me and the other students who were gathering nearby, handed some new petitions to all of us, and beetled off in his bus."

"Awwh, what a let-down, but I'm glad to hear he didn't take advantage of you. Imagine if you had gone off with him!"

"I eventually lost my crush on my favourite celebrity activist." Liv demurs.

"But you never lost your passion for environmental and social justice causes," Celeste says, then adds with a laugh, "Not too shabby for a near claim to fame, Liv. Would you like to return to Veda next time? There's sure to be a lot more to her story."

"Absolutely. I'm curious to see whether Gandhi played any kind of role in her life and I'm spellbound, yet not entirely surprised, to see that my spirit once resided in a South Asian child.

"Oh, and before I forget I wanted to tell you this weird thing that happened yesterday afternoon. I took the kids to the thrift store — they love poking around looking for treasures and I thought I might find something to spark an idea for our Halloween costumes. So Micah was sifting through the bins of children's toys and games, and he found an old wooden abacus. Its red, blue and yellow counting beads were very faded and the metal rods a little rusted in spots, but Micah smiled and shouted 'This is mine from when I had brown skin! I helped my dad in a store, counting money with this.'

"I was utterly speechless. He's five years old — how would he know about an abacus?"

"That is so cool! I can see Micah as a little Chinese boy! Maybe not a Buddhist, though, since he's incapable of sitting still. Ha! I believe all of us are born into the world remembering our past lives, and then as time goes by, we slowly forget, or learn to dismiss it as nonsense."

"Hmmm, kind of like me having little memory flashes from Hannah and Moragh's lives. I guess that makes sense if one believes in reincarnation, which apparently I do now."

Celeste jumps up and scans the massive cornucopia of books on her lending shelf in the corner of the living room. She finds the one she was looking for and hands it to Liv.

"It's all about a team of Tibetan monks who go around trying to find the reincarnated souls of Buddhist monks to initiate them as candidates for becoming lamas. They have a series of tests and questions they ask young children who have shown signs of remembering past lives. They've recorded some amazing answers and test results."

"So, they're building a record of solid evidence that past lives exist. Can I borrow this?"

"For sure, Liv."

15

~ Grounding ~

The October sun shines brightly on the fading green hayfield. Clumps of dried yellow sunflowers stand rakishly against the fence. Liv throws the chickens their wheat scratch and takes a moment to breathe in the cool fresh air. She spies four jiggly pink pig bottoms, curly tails up and waddling past the barn. Snorting in their piggy way, they stop to chomp on the fallen crab apples under the ancient tree. Liv runs to shut the driveway gate so they can't get out to the highway. Later she will have to find a way to entice them back into their rickety pen. For now, she lets them enjoy their freedom. She gathers a few apples and rolls them through the fence to Majic, who whinnies in appreciation. His coat is getting furry like a teddy bear, ready for winter. *God, I wish I was ready for winter*, she thinks. He sidles over to the timber frame barn and saws himself back and forth, scratching an itch.

Distant laughter alerts Liv to her children's approach. She can see Ruby's black tail wagging as she herds her pack of kids. The quintessential family dog, Ruby is her children's guardian and enthusiastic playmate — they have as endless an ability to throw sticks as she does to retrieve them.

They've been for a picnic to Leah Mountain (a hill on their farm, named by Leah when she was three years old), and now here they come home again, happily chattering with their lunch pails in hand — getting along, thankfully. Her children's solo hikes usually involve a short, meandering walk before they scarf down their snacks of cheese and crackers, ants on a log (celery sticks spread with peanut butter with raisins on top), dill pickles and chocolate chip cookies. Then they come home.

Watching them, Liv realizes she hasn't been there for them of late. She's been so into the drama of her marriage and her past life explorations, she hasn't been in the present moment with her kids. She's been there physically, but she's just been going through the motions making food, cleaning, reading stories and putting Band-Aids on knees.

At least I'm here, which is more than Ross can say.

This weekend Ross' excuse for not being home was that he was going to help their friend campaign for the provincial election, but she doesn't believe him.

He just wants to keep on with the crazy life he's living, and not even try to make changes or keep our family together. It feels like we're already leading separate lives.

She hopes her children can be resilient and have the ability to forgive. That moment when children realize their parents aren't perfect is bound to come soon, if it hasn't already.

She plunks herself down on the front porch step and watches them drop their lunch pails and begin chasing each other, playing tag. Poor Micah is always "It" — he hasn't a chance of keeping up with his sisters. But one day, she suspects, he'll surpass them in strength, stamina and maybe even stubbornness. Liv smiles, imagining her daughters' dismay the day he outruns and out-jumps them. Molly and Leah tell Micah he is now the monster and he has to catch them to turn them into monsters. "Don't make Micah always be the monster," Liv shouts at them, secretly worried that a monster can be created that way.

It's a perfect, crisp autumn Sunday. Liv has always had an issue with Sundays. It's no wonder. Growing up with an alcoholic father, Sunday was the day he was either really hungover, sick, nasty and out of booze. Or he'd get his hands on some moonshine and become a crazed drunk, wreaking havoc and varied abuses on the family. As an adult, without being aware of the reason, Liv feels the need to have plans that take her out of the house on Sundays.

Restlessly looking around her, Liv has to acknowledge how much she loves her beautiful home on the river, her prolific vegetable garden, her animals. This is the life she wanted. She's most comfortable in her faded denim overalls and gumboots. It all seems so tenuous now.

What would my life be like without this place? My god, I'd miss the people, so much.

They're the kind of people who are there for you through everything. Fun, smart, down-to-earth, creative, inspiring people. Some are back-to-the-landers, some forever ranchers whose families homesteaded here a hundred and fifty years ago. There are the right-wing, gun-toting rednecks; the draft dodgers who never left even when they could have; pot-growers; urban professionals, like Ross, who want to live two lives and are willing to commute 100 kilometres each way. Then there are the people who don't fit in anywhere else, who live here for the cheap rent and to stay off the radar. It's an odd mix, but it has its magic. Someone's barn burns down and the town not only raises money to replace it, but everybody pitches in to rebuild it. If one of your neighbours is sick, people drop by with casseroles to fill their fridge until they're well again. When the little school needed a playground, the whole town, young and old, came together and built one. Nobody bothers to gripe that the government should make things happen — people around here just get things done.

This is my town. I don't want to think about leaving it. But I am.

Her children have chased each other to exhaustion and now lie in the tall, golden grass, gazing at the clouds above and trying to spot animals in their wispy shapes. Liv calls them over and wraps them up together in a hug. It's far too nice a day to go inside or do chores.

"Let's go play at the river!" Liv exclaims with such enthusiasm Micah jumps up and down and screams, "Yes, yes, yes!" Molly rolls her eyes at him and Leah runs to gather up the buckets and shovels from the sandbox.

Towels and lemonade in a rainbow-striped beach bag, they're off down the grassy hill, past the grazing cows and through the golden poplars to the river's edge. The silver sand beach is expansive, as it's been a long, hot summer and the water level is low. Soon, an elaborate miniature water system is under construction. A series of ponds and channels lead to the river's edge where the children have dug a lake, which they call Pirate Lake. The sand is fine — dry and white on top, moist and brown underneath, perfect for digging. There are fine flakes of mica in the mix that glitter in the sun. Molly investigates and declares them to be genuine flakes of gold and runs to Liv for confirmation.

"They do look like something precious, don't they? But I think it's mica. It's a mineral, sweetie."

"Micah? Did you name Micah after a mineral?"

Liv laughs. "No! I just thought of it and your dad and I both liked the sound of it. It was different."

Molly prances over and dances around Micah, who is engineering a driftwood bridge over one of the rivers. "You are a mineral! You are a mineral!"

He tries to ignore her but is soon flinging sand in her direction.

"Mom!"

"Hey, Molly, don't you think the sparkly bits would be perfect pirate treasure? We can bring down a tin to use as a treasure chest."

All three kids get down on their hands and knees and search for larger flakes. Liv strolls along the shore, looking for the glint of mica in the shallows. The water is crystal clear — which only happens in the fall and winter in this river. The rest of the year it's milky with silt. Today it's a shiny, jade green — a smooth, gliding surface. The beach is littered with bright yellow poplar leaves and the occasional scarlet maple leaf.

There is a certainty to fall, Liv thinks. *Things will die, winter will come. Everything will lie dormant, resting. And in the spring, the river will be swollen with melting snow. All will be a tangle of growth and change.* Opening to the inevitability of change in her own life, Liv feels a bit of joy bubbling up inside her heart as she watches her kids at the river.

The following morning, Liv bids farewell to her giggling horde. Ross has spent the night in Twin Rivers again. He seems to be back to his new normal and able to maintain a sleep and work routine, even though his alcohol and prescription drug use seems really excessive to Liv. He has an appointment with a psychiatrist in two months and has promised her he will keep it. He seems to have an amazing ability to control his mood when he feels he must. But Liv has a sense that he is hanging on by his fingernails, for her benefit, to prove he doesn't need psychiatric help.

Liv reflects on the fact that mornings are much easier when Ross isn't there as she pops into the barn, determined to hop onto Majic's back and ride over to Celeste's so she can continue her past life adventures with Veda. She ladles a scoop of oats into a bucket and drizzles molasses over them. She rattles the bucket temptingly as she walks toward the paddock. She's thrilled when Majic falls for her ploy — he perks his ears and trots right to her. She lets him enjoy the oats as she saddles him up.

As Liv hoists herself up and over Majic's back, he turns his head and gives her the horse's version of a mischievous look, then dances sideways out of the barn into the green field. Pulling him back sternly, Liv tells him to mind his manners. She bids him to go around in small circles to remind him to listen. On the seventh turn, he begins to settle down and submit to her pace, so, with a gentle pressure of the reins, she steers him toward the river and they trot along the river trail. Her view of the jade green river is truncated by silver birch trunks, their brilliant yellow leaves spectacular with a blue-sky backdrop. Majic's hooves crunch through drying poplar leaves that give scent to the air. They reach their destination far too quickly.

"Hi Celeste. Can I tether him in the clover patch here?" she calls to her friend, who is crouched in the garden harvesting carrots.

"Sure! He's looking so furry and fine!" she says as she feeds a handful of fresh, crunchy carrots into the horse's velvet muzzle.

16

~ *Salt* ~

Session No. 8 transcript, Oct. 26, 1987
Veda Part 2, 1918

I fall into step beside Suraya once more. The procession has been walking long days and into the night. We make our way through dusty villages and vast wasteland, dotted with the odd signs of human and animal life. I can hear Suraya speaking about the salt tax imposed by the British Government and how it's causing so much poverty and death for the Indian people. She says softly, as if to me, "Gandhi is leading us to the sea in Dandi where we will show the people that we can make our own salt from the sea and the British won't be able to tax it. We can share the wealth with the people who need it."

Veda is still an infant but a little rounder in the face. She's bound to Suraya's chest with the faded blue and red paisley scarf from Puja. Suraya has mended the torn bits with white thread. Veda dozes with the rocking movement of Suraya's body, but soon wakes and cries — her stomach is clenching with hunger.

The procession stops by a farmer's field and Suraya appeals to him for some yak milk for the child. He mutters something about hateful rebels and says he has no milk to spare, so they move on. Little Veda begins to cry frantically now. Suraya sways her as she walks and murmurs comforting words into her tiny ear.

The next farmer is friendly. He smiles and admits to Suraya that he secretly admires Gandhi and his mission to reclaim India from the British. He goes into his small mud and straw hut and returns with not only a small clay jug of yak milk, but also some lentils wrapped in fresh naan bread, which Suraya gladly accepts, blessing him humbly. Using a hollow reed like a straw, she dribbles milk into Veda's mouth. She eats a bit of the food and shares some with her fellow walkers. She takes the last piece of naan all the way to the front of the line to Gandhi and offers it to him. Gandhi gently refuses the nourishment — he is not taking food as part of his protest. He thanks Suraya and he asks if he can see the child she's carrying. Her face glows with pride as she lifts the scarf. Gandhi looks at the child and says that she is perfect, with a peaceful nature and an old soul. He touches her forehead.

Even though I'm just a spirit floating nearby, I feel his touch — it's as if he's blessed me for eternity. I've always touched my forehead in that exact spot when I'm trying to figure something out or calm myself. Sometimes, I press really hard, right where a person's third eye is meant to be. That's exactly where Gandhi touched Veda.

Images appear like a moving collage seen through a haze of red dust — walking and walking — sleeping huddled with other women and children in a barn or under the stars — vibrant flashes of red, blue, yellow, green, pink, purple and orange fabric, long dark braided hair — the view of a tiny baby surrounded by women.

~ ~ ~

I see Veda growing from a toddler to a little girl with long, black braids of her own. Suraya is always by her side, caring for her, feeding her, rubbing coconut oil into her hair and her feet after a long day of walking. They settle for months at a time at a riverside ashram Gandhi established for his followers, but they still embark on extended pilgrimages from time to time. Sometimes, they camp on a farm and work in the fields in exchange for food. I see Veda learning how to prepare meals over an open fire. She appears to be a cheerful girl, chatting with anyone and everyone, liked by the community of women and openly adored by Suraya.

~ ~ ~

I cast my blue thread into the future and find Suraya looking older and a little bent and Veda at maybe six or seven years of age, walking once more on a road swirling with dry dust, following closely behind Gandhi.

They march in silence in the stifling heat, accompanied only by their own measured breaths and the sound of hundreds of feet stepping on hard-packed earth. Occasionally their voices lift with a song or a chant and Veda's heart rises with the knowledge that she's part of something wonderful and meaningful.

The procession is passing through a village now. The market is buzzing with exotic smells, colourfully dressed people, laughter and good-natured bartering for goods. One young girl walking beside her mother pulls back to allow the walkers by — she is very thin and her clothes are ragged. Veda is drawn to her — she tries to catch the girl's eye but cannot. Loneliness floods over Veda's heart and I realize for the first time that there are very few children in the group she and Suraya travel with.

~ ~ ~

Forward again. A shimmer of blue light on water. Veda and Suraya are on a beach with a large gathering of devotees. I sense they have traveled far to reach this place. The crowd is noisy and jubilant, then there is a hush — Gandhi begins to speak.

But Veda is distracted — she's mesmerized by the sea, which she's never seen before. Far out on the glimmering horizon, she sees an enormous creature break the surface of the water — some kind of fabulous, gigantic fish! She thrills to the sight of it, awed in wonder.

I can see the luminous threads of hundreds of spirits, in all colours — everywhere. I feel a connection to everything — to the whales in the warm blue ocean, to those who walk on the dusty red earth with Gandhi and to the journeys of millions before and after.

Bound by a soul, Veda and I share this as one.

~ ~ ~

She's ten and has a friend now — a lively, bright-eyed boy named Anil. He and his father recently joined Gandhi's movement, shortly after Anil's mother died. His father bitterly blames the British salt tax for their poverty and his inability to afford treatment for his sick wife.

Veda is hastily tidying the cooking area after a meal, keenly aware of Anil, who waits for her in the shade nearby. Her chore complete, she appeals to Suraya, who swooshes her away, smiling. Veda and Anil set off at a run for the river, where they romp in the muddy water.

As I cast the thread forward, I see that Gandhi's vision, his voice and his message has grown stronger and more meaningful to Veda as she grows older. On this day, Veda and Anil are excited because Gandhi has called for all the children to gather. They love it when he does this.

To his fellow travellers, Gandhi speaks, "If we are to teach real peace in this world, and if we are to carry on a real war against war, we shall have to begin with the children."

Veda and Anil join the chattering group in the shade of a giant cashew tree, beside the Coca Cola-coloured Manori Creek, and soon Gandhi appears and sits cross-legged before them. The children are immediately attentive. The great man soon has them entranced with his fascinating stories, bringing to life the Hindu Gods like Hanuma the Monkey King and Veda's favourite, Ganesha the Elephant God, who has a mouse as a protector.

He smiles and looks into the face of every child, and each feels treasured. He tells them, in his level, quiet voice, the story of an Indian girl he met named Shanti Devi, who was a source of concern to her family because she did not speak until she was four years old. To her parent's surprise, when she finally did utter her first words, she spoke in full sentences and fervently insisted to her parents that she needed to return home to her husband and children in another town — a place they knew Shanti had never visited.

The little girl would not budge on her belief, and so her parents finally took her to the town. When they arrived, Shanti first recognized a man she knew as her brother–in–law — she called him by his name. Then she saw a man she knew as her husband and she ran to embrace him. As you can imagine, everyone was stunned by this, but they were even more surprised when Shanti, overjoyed to the point of weeping, set eyes on the very child she claimed she had died giving birth to.

Gandhi tells the children he met and spoke with Shanti some time afterward and found her to be a smart and honest little girl who earnestly answered his questions about her past life — answers no one else could have possibly known. For example, Shanti remembered having hidden money in a flower pot in her past life and indeed, she knew just where to go to find it.

The story of Shanti tells us much about reincarnation, Gandhi tells his young listeners. Sometime later, when Shanti Devi had clearly demonstrated her ability to remember the transference of consciousness and had also developed an ability to heal others through touch, she was declared a Hindu saint. Throughout her life, people went to her to be healed of their ailments.

"This tells us that it is ever so important to treat everyone with love and fairness in this life, because we have no idea where our karma may lead us or who we will become the next time around," Gandhi says.

Veda and all the children are wide-eyed at this thought. "Could we come back as a monkey or an elephant?" pipes Anil.

"Possibly," Gandhi answers softly. "But I hope you will come back as a person helping to change the world with your love and kindness."

I ride my glowing thread again into Veda's future.

She's twelve and standing in the crowd that has gathered to welcome Gandhi back from a trip to visit his wife Kasturba and their grown children in Pune, south of Mumbai. Veda is shocked to see how thin he is.

"He rarely eats but I don't understand how this helps the cause," she says to Suraya. "He thinks people will listen more if he denies himself food — but I'm not so sure about that."

Veda doesn't wait for Suraya's reply — she rises and timidly approaches Gandhi where he sits in a circle of elders. She asks if he will please eat the fresh banana she's picked for him. Gandhi gently tells her he will not break his fast. He asks her to remind him of her name and he bids her to sit beside him.

He tells her a story about a young girl from a wealthy family who went against her parents' wishes and became a teacher to the poorest children in the slums of Calcutta. This not only fed her own soul, but the souls of the children she taught.

"To follow your own path is the most important thing any of us can do. I am following my path and I am so happy that, for this portion of your journey, you are walking alongside me. I want you to eat this perfect banana you picked. Please do not worry about me."

As Veda walks away from this encounter, it's with a new understanding. There are different kinds of nourishment — the ones that feeds your soul are far more important than the ones that feed your belly.

~ ~ ~

Anil and Veda sit side-by-side under a baobab tree with Suraya, who is helping them with their reading. Veda is pleasantly aware of Anil's warm presence beside her. When it's his turn, he reads aloud a poem by the Sufi poet, Rumi.

This is love: to fly towards a secret sky,

to cause a hundred veils to fall each moment.

First to let go of life. Finally, to take a step without feet.

Veda is overcome by its beautiful simplicity, even more so because the words come to her through Anil's voice. Her eyes moisten. Suraya takes note and smiles at her.

"You are far too young to understand such thoughts. But your name does mean 'understanding', so perhaps you are capable of thoughts far beyond your years."

I toss the vibrant blue cord yet again, landing in a future where Veda is fifteen years old. She and Anil are walking along a Himalayan mountain-fed river that tumbles over rocks into a large pool. Veda is alert — she and Anil have been enlisted to take some of the children to the river for a cooling swim and she takes the responsibility seriously. They are nearly there and she's acutely aware of Anil, conscious of her body. She longs to plunge into the clear, cool pond with Anil, just like when they were children. Instead, she's preoccupied with being modest at all times, ensuring that her skin isn't exposed inappropriately.

Nearby, two elephants are tethered. They belong to the farmer, who uses them for logging the Sheesham trees, sold for making into furniture. They notice that one of the elephants is hunched with his head down and shuffling restlessly, and when they look closer they discover horrible sores on its feet from the chains. While Anil stands watch over the children, Veda runs back to the encampment and fetches some turmeric and almond oil. She gently rubs the orange salve into the sores and resolves to do it again every day until the poor elephant is relieved of its pain. She's become conscious of her own ability to show compassion and care.

Veda loves to hear Anil's laugh. He's reading aloud under the tree, and when he makes a mistake she teases him playfully. His laugh is the kind that comes from deep inside and she can't help but joyously laugh along.

She's distracted by the details of him — how perfect and strong his hands are, the interesting golden light in his eyes and the ease with which he moves through the world. He's just as captivated by her — he listens to her with such attention when she speaks, watching her eyes, fetching her fresh coconut oil and watching with rapt interest as she melts it in her fingers and runs her fingers through her hair before she braids it. When she shares some chapattis she's made herself, he declares they are tastier than any made by another hand.

~ ~ ~

There is a great crowd of people. My spirit line guides me to Veda, who is moving through the assembly with Anil. They look like a couple, maybe seventeen or eighteen years old. They have just arrived to the town square after a long train journey, to join a protest against British rule in defiance of the ban on public meetings. There's an air of expectation, a sense that they are gaining ground. The British are losing control of the Indian people and many say this is a direct result of Gandhi's tactics.

In addition to the protesters, many families have congregated here to celebrate the spring festival of Baisakhi. The heat is dry and suffocating, but the mood seems festive.

Veda and Anil join the gathering of protesters — she's apprehensive, but I can't tell why. Perhaps because Gandhi himself is not present. Neither is Suraya, as she is unwell and unable to travel. Veda senses danger and holds Anil's hand tightly, looking about for a safer place.

"Stay by my side, Anil," she pleads, and he squeezes her hand in reassurance.

At first, as the protesters sing Satygahra, the song for change, and all is peaceful. But suddenly, there's a commotion — British soldiers along with Indian men in uniform mounted on horseback are converging upon the crowds. They fire their rifles up into the air and then into the crowd. People panic and run, but the soldiers come from all sides and block their escape.

Veda's heart is pounding and she can't catch her breath. Anil grabs her arm and helps her climb down into a well to hide. There are others there, maybe about thirty people, crushed together and pressed against the walls. They wait, hoping to be overlooked. The terror is palpable. A few people sob quietly and are shushed. But then they see soldiers looking down, gun barrels pointing....

Liv has dropped the stone and is clenching her hands into fists, her thumbs tucked inside. Her face is drawn with anxiety.

Far, far away, she hears Celeste's voice, "Do you need to come back now?"

No, not just yet, I have to see it through.

Unconsciously, she takes the stone from Celeste and holds it in both hands, trying to breathe deeply and stay grounded.

Deafening blasts, screaming, the acrid, metallic smell of gunpowder, blood. Bullets are ricocheting off the stone walls, entering people's flesh and ending their lives just as surely as the ones fired directly at them. Veda and Anil, chests together, hearts pounding as one... the bullet enters through Anil's back and this is where....

I have to stop here! I know what happens. I remember this! I can't experience this death again.

"Leave that turbulent world, Liv. One, two, three, four, five … walk with me back to our time… six, seven eight… knowing you are safe…nine, ten."

Liv's eyes open, but she is pale.

"I might faint, Celeste. I was shot!"

"You're safe now, Liv. Hold steady, I'll be right back." Celeste returns quickly with a moist washcloth, which she applies to Liv's forehead.

"That feels great. Thank you." Liv sits back.

"Holy crap! What just happened?"

"I had the most intense sensation of confused memories — like a violent déjà vu!"

"This has happened to you before?"

"When I went travelling after high school, a friend and I visited a holy city in India called Amritsar. We went to this lovely brick-walled garden in the city centre called Jaillianwalla Bagh. There was a large, stone monument, but I didn't stop to read the plaque.

"I found myself drawn to an ancient well nearby, and as I walked around it I realized it was riddled with bullet holes… I was instantly overwhelmed with so much emotion that I fell to my knees. It felt like I'd been shot — I actually felt the pain in my chest! I covered my ears and closed my eyes. I could hear people screaming inside the well.

"My friend ran over and asked what the hell was wrong with me. I told her. She sat with me for a little while on the soft green grass so I could get myself together — I was shaking violently.

"Celeste, Veda was killed there, along with hundreds of others. That's why that place affected me so profoundly.

"That experience has always stayed with me. I've always known exactly what it would feel like to be shot, even though I never have been in this life. That bullet went right through Anil's back and as I held him up, it went through my heart. The sight and especially the sound of guns or explosives, even fireworks, the smell of blood — all of these things frighten me more than they should. Yet, I'm so drawn to politics and social equality and repelled by war. I think this story, this life as Veda is reminding me that as I go through this change in my life and my marriage, I need to find some kind of work where I can …without sounding too corny… 'be the change I want to see in the world'."

"That's remarkable, Liv! To have such an intense memory of something that happened in one of your previous lives — it's like Gandhi's story about Shanti Devi. Maybe now that you know where it comes from, it will be easier to let go of the fear. It isn't about this life, it's about that one. And, I think you're already on that path you talked about…making change in the world."

"Gandhi was a famous guy and all, and I do feel so honoured to have possibly been witness to his work, but what really stands out for me, in this life as well as in Moragh's life, is the love and acceptance from Suraya and the community of women who raised Veda. A throwaway girl, and yet, she grew up strong and confident.

"What I don't really understand is: why have my past lives been so full of tragedy? Did I do something to deserve it? Is it my karma?"

"You likely have had dozens of happy and uneventful lives, but your spirit line has led you to these because they are relevant to you now. You're choosing them."

169

"Okay, I think I get it. And honestly, I wouldn't change this story just because it ended tragically. I remember you saying that karma is the sum total of a person's actions, in this, and in past lives, which determines the next incarnation in the cycle of life, death and rebirth. It just doesn't make sense to me that if you lived some pretty good lives, like Hannah and Moragh and Veda, why don't you get to keep having better and better lives?"

"It doesn't seem to work that way. There doesn't seem to be an order. Somebody who's a saint in this life can be reborn as a mass murderer, or vice versa. It might be for their own spiritual development or for the karmic benefit of someone they don't even know. It seems to be all about the contracts made back in that library in the sky. But I have to say it's a sign of spiritual advancement that your soul spent time with Gandhi in a past life. That's where your peaceful and loving nature comes from, and you want to keep that."

"Thank you, Celeste. But something tells me I have at least one very dark past life left to explore."

They both laugh, but for Liv, it's a bit forced.

17

~ Unmasked ~

"Hey Liv, my witchy friend. You look fabulous — in spite of your green, warty skin and blacked-out teeth!" Faces glowing in the fire-light, Celeste and Liv have found each other at the Halloween bonfire at the Community Hall, coffee mugs in hand, watching the children gather around to see the fireworks display that's about to happen.

"Yeah, a witch for the third year running. This year I was tempted to be a beautiful witch like Moragh but for some reason I prefer the scary, ugly costumes for myself."

"It's good to take a break from being so gorgeous once in a while, I guess," Celeste laughs. She waves happily at some of their other friends, who are making their way toward them.

"Isn't Deanna hilarious in her belly dancing costume, with Ed following her around strapped to that skateboard as a legless beggar! And there's Mustang Sally in her cowgirl getup, with her long-awaited baby bump."

Liv sighs, "I've been so preoccupied, I've forgotten how much I need my circle of female friends."

Just then, Ross shows up and puts his arm around Liv. She isn't even sure it's him at first, but who else has a Ronald Reagan mask? He'd told her earlier in the day he probably couldn't make it to the bonfire, so she is taken aback.

Maybe it's her witch persona or Moragh's influence, but Liv suddenly feels an urgent need to be very clear with Ross.

She turns to him and says firmly, "Unless you can admit you are really not well and you follow through with seeing that psychiatrist, don't pretend we're a happy couple."

He takes his arm away, but stays pressed beside her. "Sure, Liv, if that's what you want."

He moves off and she can see him putting on the charm, entertaining their friends around the fire. Rob enlists him to help out with the fireworks.

Celeste has overheard their exchange and after Ross walks away she says, "Wow, sounds like he is still putting it all on you — like he doesn't even have a problem! Good for you for taking a stand, Liv. It must feel better to know you can."

"Yeah, I'm not going to pretend everything is normal anymore. I'm telling him it's his turn to sleep on the couch. I'm getting sick of not getting a decent sleep."

"Good for you, Liv."

Later that evening, when the kids are finally coming down off their sugar highs from all the Halloween candy and tucked into bed, Oliva hears Ross roar down the driveway to their home, in his fancy, new pig of a car. Still feeling irked about how he acted at the bonfire, she braces herself for an argument but hopes he will simply pass out.

He enters bright-eyed and animated, high as a kite on something, maybe just his own racing mind. He's carrying the ridiculous mask under his arm. Liv flashes back to a time in her childhood when she believed all adults wore masks — they might look happy and smiling but the face underneath could be angry, growling, hateful, dangerous. It occurs to her that in her life, alcohol, drugs, depression and insanity have been both the mask and the unmasking.

I won't be like my Mom and stick my head in the sand, she firmly tells herself. *I've seen the best and the worst masks and now I only want to see what's real.*

"Hey Liv, you'll never guess what." Ross is gesticulating wildly. "Those crazy fucking rocks were talking to me again. I had to pull over when I was right under Indian Head bluff. A rock fell down onto the hood of my car — nearly smashed the window."

"Really? Tell me about it."

"I don't know, Liv, you'll probably tell me I'm crazy. I'm not sure I can trust you anymore."

"I want to know what's going on with you, Ross. I can see you're struggling. I know the things you're seeing are real to you. Let me in on it, please?"

"Okay, so remember how I told you a while ago about how Chief Dan told me about what happened to him in the residential school."

"Yes, I remember. Horrific sexual and physical abuse."

"Criminal, and none of those bastards responsible — the church or the government — have had to account for any of it. Well, that's the message I got tonight at the bluff. There are dozens of stories like Dan's and that's just on their little reserve. Nobody's heard them. It's time for them to rise up and tell their stories. It's time to protest. We'll set tipis up at the city hall, bang drums, speak on loudspeakers, camp out for as long as it takes to get them heard and to get something done."

Ross' voice gets louder and faster as he carries on. "Do you know how many First Nations kids have graduated from Twin Rivers College? Exactly none! I'll set up a camp there too!"

Liv listens and agrees in principal with everything Ross is saying, but is alarmed at his assumption of leadership.

"Don't you think it'd be better if the people from the community did the leading, Ross? I know you want to do it for the right reasons and you're great at inspiring protests — I've seen that first hand. But are you just another white guy trying to speak for the native people? Might it be better to help from the sidelines?" Liv says, aware that she's challenging Ross' grandiose scheme.

"You don't believe in me anymore, Liv. I may as well give up. You're against everything I'm trying to do."

"No, Ross, I do believe in you and I believe it's time for you to help yourself instead of trying to save the world."

She has succeeded in derailing the plan. Suddenly he looks defeated. Moved by empathy, Liv tries to comfort him, but he waves her away, ashamed and embarrassed, and reaches for the liquor cabinet instead.

Wild November winds and freezing rain can't keep Liv from her session with Celeste the next morning. Somehow, Ross has managed to get himself up and off to work, even though she's pretty sure he didn't sleep, eat or shower.

She puts on her bright yellow raincoat and hat, her black rubber gumboots and she rushes through the farm chores, and arrives at Celeste's dripping wet with mucky boots. Shedding her gear just inside the door, she's thrilled to see Celeste meeting her with her usual smile and two cups of aromatically sensational Turkish coffee.

Celeste hands her one of the small cups. "There has to be something to look forward to, as the days get colder and shorter and bleak as hell. May as well be strong, expensive coffee!"

"I've been thinking, Celeste. Can we focus on my present life today? Veda's story has made me think a lot about the year I turned twenty. I don't need to be hypnotized to go back to that time, but I do feel I need to tell you about the changes I went through that year."

"Of course! I'm more than honoured to hear your stories, Liv. Do you want to record this?"

"Sure. We may as well."

Session No. 8 transcript, Nov. 3rd, 1987

That experience with Veda's death took me back to the period after high school when I was nineteen and travelling the world. It was a time when lots of young people were doing that, and the appeal for me was very strong. It was an excuse to get away from my family, to see amazing new places, cultures I'd only dreamed about, and most of all, to make friends and meet people who wouldn't know me as the shy girl from the poor family. I wanted to recreate myself and be a young free-spirited woman without the albatross of childhood poverty and abuse tying me down, making me feel confused and worthless. I wanted to find my voice.

She puts on her bright yellow raincoat, her hat and her black rubber gumboots and rushes through the farm chores. She arrives at Celeste's dripping wet, with mucky boots. I was oblivious to my parent's concerns for my safety. Seemed to me their concern was too little and too late — I was blissfully confident, aside from being a bit nervous about flying in an airplane.

When I look at the photos of my trip, I'm amused at what I captured through the lens of my camera. My first stop was Israel, where I worked on a kibbutz for a few weeks, then toured around the country. I was fascinated by the culture, extremely excited to be there, but shy at first. My first photos were of camels, children, shepherds and temples — all from a great distance, barely discernable. As my confidence grew, my photographs became closer up. I became bold enough to ask people for permission to take their photos. By the time I'd been travelling for a few weeks, my photos became more intimate — the timeworn face of an elderly rabbi, an Arabic man with his camel towering behind him, lovers embracing beneath a tree, even my own naked body lying in the warm golden sand on the shores of the Red Sea.

That photo was from a camping trip I went on with people from the kibbutz where I was staying. It was positively idyllic. People were playing flutes, guitars and drums. I remember watching my friend Maya dancing, with her sumptuous brown body and glistening black hair swirling down her back. She exuded the kind of sensual confidence I could only dream of and I wanted to be like her. The brilliant, painful burn I got reminded me that I wasn't like her in so many ways — I was naïve and tender and needed to find out what worked for me.

We drank wine and talked and danced and swam all day. At night, we watched the stars come out — totally different stars than we see in our northern sky. Our tents were full of sand by the end of the day and so we would have to shake them out before crawling into bed in the small hours of the morning.

It may sound cliché, but I really found myself on that trip. I met amazing people, immersed myself in totally unfamiliar situations and saw astounding things. I was free, uninhibited by my culture or my family.

When I went to India, it was different. I kept my body well covered, and avoided eye contact with men, other than travelers, as I'd been warned by my kibbutz friends in Israel to do so. I lived for two weeks at an ashram and learned a bit about meditation and Hinduism. I was drawn to these spiritual studies but too young and restless to stay longer. I left with a girl from California named Shelley who was also not ready to commit to the strict regime of the ashram.

Looking back, it seems as though it might have been a cult. We were probably very lucky to get out of there when we did. The leader was more than a little frightening, and we both wondered if he had motives beyond his desire to spread his vast spiritual knowledge. We'd noticed some of the young women and men who'd been there longer than us spending one-on-one time with him in his room and it didn't seem quite right to us. They would emerge with shaven heads and bewildered looks on their faces. Honestly, it had taken me years to grow my hair till it reached my bum and I was not about to let some old guy shave it off, no matter how enlightened he was.

We left to tour around India, and not long afterward I had the experience I told you about, at the well. I began to feel a bit nervous travelling in India. No denying that the soul, history and natural beauty of this country drew me to it, but the poverty was devastating, especially that of its women and children. It awakened my desire to help bring about some kind of change. I think that's the part of Veda's story that has really stayed with me through the lifetimes.

Shelley and I went our separate ways then. She headed south and I made my way west to the Greek Isles. I was staying in hostels, meeting other travelers from all over the world. We'd hang out and party and tour around together and they'd be like my new best friends, and then we'd move on. I worked my way up through Europe that way.

It was summer, so I decided to head to the Swiss Alps for some cooler air. Along the way I met a carefree, long-haired, twenty-four-year-old guy from Australia. Ian had the dark brown curls and attentive eyes of a Spaniel and that sexy Aussie accent I love to this day. We spent two glorious weeks hiking and camping, drinking rich coffee, eating homemade bread and cheese in the picturesque, storybook mountains of Switzerland.

I felt like a grown-up Heidi as we ran through fields of flowers with mountain goats and swam in the clearest, bluest, coldest lakes. He was chivalrous, even though that wasn't cool in the 70s — he carried my pack when my back was tired and wrote me poetry. To feel so cherished was such a new and wonderful experience.

When we mutually agreed to part at the end of two weeks, it was bittersweet for both of us. We felt we had discovered true love — but we were more committed to finding ourselves, and we knew we needed to do so independently. For many years afterward I wondered what ever happened to Ian Brown and what our lives might have been like had we stayed together.

After my time with Ian, I headed to Norway, thinking it would be interesting to visit my paternal ancestral homeland. This was an introspective time. I did a lot of soul searching and fervently wrote in my journal.

I kept to myself, pitching my tent in wild areas and eating simply. It was lonely, chilly and stark, like it seemed to Hannah when she first arrived. But wrapped in my famous blue sweater, I built my own campfires, brewed strong tea and felt stronger than I ever had. One afternoon I hiked to the top of a hill and came upon an abandoned cottage and was immediately overcome with an intense feeling of familiarity. I camped at a public park nearby for four nights, all the while imagining how my ancestors might have lived in that very spot many years before. Of course, it was probably just a creative musing — my family's ties to Norway had long been severed.

While I was there, I wrote pages and pages in my journal — details of my trip so far, friends and lovers I'd met but also about my relationships with my family. It seemed easier to have a more positive and forgiving perspective separated by such a great distance.

One day, I wandered into the village of Sognefjord, at the base of the green, daisy-dusted hill, and into the local library, hoping to find someone who spoke English who could help me trace my family name, but I had no luck. The librarian spoke only Norwegian.

I'd like to return to Norway when I've landed on my feet and the kids are older, now that historic records are more easily available. Maybe I can get more details about where and how they lived.

I was just getting ready to move on to Germany when I got a message to call home. My grandmother was in the hospital — she'd had a stroke. So, I returned after six months, instead of a year. I was out of money anyway, and Norway had been making me homesick.

"This was your mother's mom, Olive? You were so attached to her. Of course you needed to be there."

Celeste thinks a moment, then adds, "Isn't it fascinating where our choices lead us? Imagine if you'd stayed with Ian — you wouldn't even know Little Mountain existed! I'm just so impressed at your moxie to travel the world solo at such a young age. I'd love to see your photos."

"Yeah, well, they're stored away in a box, just like the ones from my childhood. And the journal is long gone — destroyed by a jealous boyfriend. He called it my 'book of zipless fucks,' like the Erica Jong book, Fear of Flying, which he also found so reprehensible and disgusting."

"You're doing great at opening these compartments in your mind, Liv. I know it isn't easy. But there are so many beautiful moments as well as the ones you've tried so hard to forget. Speaking of which, I'm wondering what happened when you got home from Norway?"

"A lot," Liv is suddenly flustered. "But I think I'd rather wait until next time for that. It's been fun to reminisce, though. Besides, I have to head out pretty quick to meet the school bus."

Outside, the rain has stopped and the world is cast in shades of grey — the bare branches of trees stand black in contrast to the sky, which looks like the inside of a clam shell — pure white, broken by whorls of grey and silver, lit from within. Lacking light to reflect, the river has lost its green hue. It slides by like a shiny black snake. Dry leaves crackle underfoot as Liv makes her way along the path. Even the ground is rigid and unyielding, beginning to freeze, but not yet covered with snow.

Despite the gloomy day, Liv feels uplifted as she walks home. She can see how it's cathartic for her to revisit the hard times in her life, just as the doldrums of winter are essential to the renewal of spring.

The only way I can dispel the shadows is to shed light on them. The more honest and open I can be about my feelings and my history, the stronger I am and ready to move forward.

Ross won't come home tonight, she thinks.

He's punishing me. But the truth is, I'm challenging that state of denial he's clinging to so desperately. He has no intention of changing.

There's nothing she can do about that. All she can do is look after her own welfare and that of her kids. She'll light a fire tonight — she'll create her own warmth, gather her children close and show them that, no matter what, she will always be there for them. Even without him, they are a family.

18

~ #MeToo ~

"So, Liv," Celeste begins at their next session, "The last time we talked, you told me you came home from Norway early because your grandmother was ill. Do you want to pick up where you left off? Was that when she passed away?"

"In some ways it would have been easier for her if she had died right then. It was so sad, Celeste. The stroke was severe. By the time I got home she was stable, but she was never really the same. She lost her ability to communicate. I could see in her eyes that she had things she desperately wanted to say.

"I visited her often, especially during the first few weeks. She'd been moved to a care facility. I'd take her hand and tell her stories about my travels or my day, and her eyes would fill with tears — so I know she heard me. She lived like that for two years.

"I got a job delivering mail that summer so I'd visit after work sometimes. In the fall I moved to Twin Rivers with my boyfriend, Vince, and started going to college. He was an elementary school teacher and got a job there."

"You never told me about him."

"We actually got engaged, but I broke it off. Nothing like a pregnancy scare to make you really examine your relationship! When I got my period, it was a second chance — I didn't love him and I was wasting both of our time. But then something happened to me that was so devastating, I just withdrew from everything."

A frown creases Celeste's brow, "Oh, my goodness. What?"

"Are you sure you want to hear about this? It happened about ten years ago and I've never told anyone…but it's been with me a lot since starting this therapy with you and it always haunts me around my birthday. The thing is, I don't want to go back there with hypnosis — it might feel like reliving it."

"I understand, Liv. If you hold the soapstone and focus on it while you tell me your story it'll help you stay grounded. I'm right here for you. Stop any time you need to. Do you want me to run the tape, or keep it off for now?"

"Yes, please put it on. I want to tell this. Just like I needed to let the sexual abuse rise to the surface, I need to let this come up as well. Somehow it's connected to me finding my way to move ahead in my life."

"Okay, Liv, we're going to do one other thing in preparation. Visualize your spirit line radiating around you, healing the trauma and preventing further harm from being done. Now let's connect that thread to others — let's call on the strength and courage of Hannah, Moragh, Veda and both of your grandmothers. Breathe in their love and their protection and know you're safe and cherished."

Both women breathe deeply. Then Liv speaks.

"I'm just going to say it. At my twentieth birthday party I was drugged and gang raped by a hockey team."

For a moment, Celeste bows her head, absorbing the impact of this stark statement. Then she takes one of Liv's hands in hers and looks up to meet her eyes, transmitting strength. Liv takes a deep, jagged breath and begins to speak, slowly at first, and with many pauses. She looks away from Celeste and focusses her eyes on the green angel hair fern on the coffee table, not wanting to be tempted to censor herself because of the pain or discomfort she might cause her friend.

Session No. 9 Transcript, Nov. 6, 1987

Vince and I had already broken up, but our friends in Portman had this party planned, so we sucked up our sad feelings and drove down together in my rusty little Volvo. Vince smoked pot continuously all the way — that was one of the things that turned me off about him, his heavy use of pot and alcohol. It felt like we were never on the same wavelength.

By the time we arrived at the party he was already quite out of it. We didn't see each other for the rest of the night.

The party was in a grungy old house on the outskirts of Portman, where four guys lived together. I remember it had this musty smell, like a combination of sweaty sports gear and rotting apples.

I grabbed a peach cider from the cooler we'd brought and drank it fast. I was both nervous and excited — lots of my high school friends were showing up and I really didn't feel like telling them what was going on with Vince. I went outside to the bonfire with my friend Lucy and we shared a joint. There were lots of people out there, some I hadn't seen in quite a while. I started to have fun. My friend Gene from the post office was strumming a Neil Young song on his twelve-string guitar.

I'd come a long way since high school, where I'd been fairly shy and quiet, with the exception of my small bouts of social activism. I was wearing a long, flowered peasant dress with a low top. I was the new me — the cool, seasoned traveller, now enrolled in a college in another city. Old friends exclaimed about my sun-bleached hair, my tan, my amber and silver jewellery from Greece.

When I went back into the house, someone had cranked the music up really loud — I remember the violent, jarring sound of Black Sabbath. The "cool" jocks from our high school had shown up and crashed the party. They were all part of the local hockey team — not a national-level team but the one that travels to other cities and provinces to play. They'd been doing everything as a pack, from playing sports to partying, since their early teens. These were the guys most girls wanted to be with — and most guys longed to be — in high school. Not me — even then I preferred the intelligent, artistic type.

But there was one of them that I had a serious crush on. Leif was Norwegian like me, and his smile was infectious. He looked like he would be nice, even though his group had a reputation for being a bunch of dickheads. My heart would skip a beat when he smiled at me as we passed in the hallway.

He was standing with a group of his friends, laughing and talking. When I saw him, I felt that same flutter of attraction again. He was talking with this Tim guy. I never liked him — he always had an arrogant smirk on his face, and you never saw him with the same girl twice. The two of them looked over toward me and exchanged glances. Suddenly I felt cold and nervous. I looked around the room — Vince was nowhere to be seen. I was annoyed by this and assumed he was smoking up with his friends or had already passed out.

I was heading outside again when Leif came over. We chatted a bit and he offered me a birthday drink, something mixed with orange juice. I drank some and noticed a bitter taste, but I didn't think much of it because I've never enjoyed the taste of hard liquor. We talked about what we'd been doing since graduation. He asked me about Europe but before I was able to answer, I began to feel very dizzy. The people surrounding me seemed to have auras — every colour of the spectrum. His was bright red with flashes of brown. He said, "You should come and lie down." Through my dense fog and growing unsteadiness he seemed like a bright haloed angel, leading me to safety. I trusted him completely.

He led me to a basement room and onto the bed. He began to take my clothes off, saying I would be more comfortable if I undressed. I said no, I was fine and just needed a nap, but he proceeded to lift my dress over my head. I remember feeling chilly and sweaty at the same time and asking him if he could turn off the black light in the corner of the room as the purple haze it was creating made me feel even more disoriented and strange. He said, "No, we like to see what we're doing." I didn't have any idea what he meant by that at the time, but a physical chill and fear permeated my body. I wondered if this was what it was like to die.

My limbs got heavier and heavier and it felt like my brain had turned into a stone. The room went a darker purple. I had no control of my limbs or my speech. The door opened and others came in, maybe eight or ten guys all together. As my eyes adjusted to the black light, I could see their shapes getting into position, surrounding me and guarding the door. Two of them were still wearing their hockey jerseys, red with white letters. Disembodied white teeth and numbers surrounded me. I heard one of them joke that he didn't score at the game but he was sure going to slam his puck into this hole.

I stopped breathing as they came closer to my body. I tried to scream "No," but nothing came out. They seemed to know exactly what position to take, just like they were playing a game, like they'd done this many times before. They held my arms and my legs and they took turns raping me. Brutally, forcefully.

Only one stood back. They called him Midget. He was smaller and shorter than the others. I tried to focus on the whites of his eyes his teeth and his t-shirt that had white letters that said *Led Zeppelin*. He made no move toward me — he was just looking at me, his expression sad and apologetic, sometimes twisting into anger. One of them noticed he was standing back and said, "Take your turn, Midget. What are you, a fag?" He looked at the guy and said "Fuck you," and I thought for a moment he might stop them or call the police — but he just stood there looking helpless.

At least he saw me. I've often felt that he shared that horrible experience with me and probably carries it, and many others like it, with him still.

The third or fourth guy ejaculated after only a couple of thrusts and the other guys jeered and teased him. Another guy right after that…I remember he had a buzz cut and a pock-marked face…he was the most cruel and violent. He bit my nipple and broke the skin — the pain tore through my nervous system, which otherwise seemed disabled.

One guy laughed, "Jesus man, you nearly bit her tit off, it's bleeding." I heard another one of them — I think it was Tim's voice — boasting that he lasted twenty thrusts before coming. The other guys cheered. "Hey somebody said it was her twentieth birthday, one for every year, eh?"

I remember thinking I was screaming but there was no volume — trying to fight but having no strength — trying to plead but having no words. Not even being able to cry. After the sixth or seventh guy, no one needed to hold me down. I was drifting in and out of my body.

Some came back for a second round. I recognized the guy who'd been jeered for coming so quickly and this time he was more brutal. He told the guys to let go of my arms and he turned me onto my stomach and raped me in my anus to a chorus of cheering and backslapping. My cowardly ally, Midget, had left the room at this point and I was completely alone. The ripping pain and terror, and maybe the drug they gave me, caused me to black out completely.

"Oh, my poor friend," Celeste says with compassion.

It's okay Celeste, it was really horrible, but this story is better out than in. Even in recounting it to you, it feels like it's losing some of its power over me.

When I woke up, I was alone in the same room. The house was quiet. My head pounded with pain. When I tried to stand up I blacked out and fell back onto the bed. I tried again, stumbled toward the door and flicked on the harsh overhead light. Looking down at my naked body I remembered what had happened. Horrific images invaded my brain and jolted me into action. I had to get out of there. Spinning in circles, not knowing where to look or what to do, I slipped on a puddle of spilled beer, and fell to the cold, dirty, linoleum floor. Standing up, I felt a gush between my legs and looked down to see thick, pinkish, yellow ooze leaking from my vagina down both legs. My blood mixed with their semen. I gagged and scrambled over to where my flowery peasant dress lay in a corner like a deflated being. My amber beaded choker was broken and there were beads scattered across the bed I was raped on. I loved those beads and that beautiful memory of buying them at a market on a Greek Isle but I couldn't make myself gather them off that bed. My underpants were nowhere to be seen, maybe tangled in the bed sheets, or taken as a trophy. I pulled my dress over my shaking, stinking, bruised body and limped upstairs — the pain in my pelvis made it hard to walk.

There was nobody around. The place was a shambles. There was no sign of Vince. I found my purse in the kitchen where I'd left it, got into my car and drove.

My parents had just moved out of our house, the one I'd grown up in, in Portman, a few miles away, and it hadn't been listed yet. It was a dilapidated wreck. In those days it took weeks for the phone and electricity people to come and disconnect services, so there was still power and phone. There were a few pieces of furniture they hadn't taken with them, a bed and a couple of chairs. I broke in through a window and ran to the washroom to vomit. All I could think of was my need to get clean. I turned the hot water faucet to full throttle in the old claw foot tub. And then I realized I'd be destroying the evidence. I had to report this crime. I'd been taught to believe if you were in trouble, call the police. I stumbled to the phone and dialed the police.

I've replayed that phone call in my mind countless times.

Hello, Bonjour, Portman RCMP.

Hello, something terrible happened to me last night.

Can you give me your name and the number you're calling from, miss?

Liv Andersen. This isn't my phone but it's Yellowstone 5 7170.

All right, Liv. Can you tell me what happened?

I was...raped.

Are you in a safe place now?

Yes.

Have you been injured, Miss?

Yes... no. It's mostly bruising.

Have you been examined by a doctor?

No.

It's important that you don't have a bath until you get checked over.

Okay.

Now can you tell me what happened to you?

I was at my birthday party and this guy gave me a drink and I think it was spiked...

Did you know the guy?

It was nine or ten guys — a hockey team.

Do you know the men that did this to you?

No. Sort of. Some of them.

Can I send an officer to your house, ma'am? What's your address?

No, I don't want to see anyone.

How old are you?

Twenty today.

So, you're not a minor. And where did this incident occur?

At a house where some of my friends live. They took me to the basement.

Were you drinking at this party?

I had one peach cider and then whatever they gave me. I think it was a vodka and orange juice.

Who allegedly drugged you?

One of the hockey players. Maybe two, I don't know.

Did you take any other drugs?

Well, yes, I shared a joint earlier with a friend.

How would you know if you had been drugged if you were already high?

I wasn't really high, I don't know. I feel sick.

Has this happened to you before?

No.

Were you a virgin?

No.

How many partners have you had?

I don't know how to answer that. Do I count the guys that raped me?

What were you wearing at the party?

A dress, a long dress. Why are you asking me that?

How many guys were there again?

Nine or ten. I passed out and I don't really know.

Did you say "No" when you could see what these guys wanted?

Excuse me, I need to throw up.

I ran to the bathroom, not knowing if I was going to cry, scream or throw up, leaving the phone dangling at the end of the black spiral cord. The tub water was about to spill over the sides. I turned it off and teetered on the edge of the tub, pondering that phone call. Then I threw up into the toilet again. There was nothing left in my stomach to throw up, so it was only yellow bile. Then I cried, for a long time.

I couldn't answer the cop's questions — I couldn't even remember whether I said "No." Just the way he dealt with it implied it was my fault — I was asking for it.

I remembered that the father of one of the guys was in the RCMP — he could've even been the one I was talking to. No one was going to believe that I was raped.

I held my mouth to the cold water tap and drank what seemed like a gallon of water, then peed and gingerly dragged my body into the hot water. I stayed in there for hours and hours, draining and refilling the tub as soon as it began to cool.

I remember living in and out the bathtub for several days. The phone rang and rang, but I didn't answer it.

To say it was the darkest and loneliest time in my life would be a gross understatement. I suppose I was in shock. Ten years later it's hard to remember the way I felt other than numb. I know I cried until I could no longer cry because my throat was swollen and raw. Then I sobbed silently until even my tears dried up. With the tears used up, I had nothing left to express myself — no words, no coherent thoughts and no one to hear my thoughts, share my pain or comfort me in any way. Just me alone for days.

I could have called my brothers, they would have come, but I didn't even think of it. They wouldn't have known what to do. I could've called my mom — she would've been there in a heartbeat. She would have made me go to the RCMP and report. She probably would've taken me to the hospital to get checked. She would've brought me to her new house, cried with me, been angry, made me drink tea and homemade soup. But my dad would've been there and he was the last person on earth I wanted to know about this. I had old high school friends whom I'm certain now would've been supportive, helpful, understanding — maybe they had similar experiences themselves, maybe even with the same guys. But it didn't even occur to me to call any of them.

It must have been the shame that kept me from reaching out. I felt like a sick animal crawling into a dark place to be alone, to either heal or die. I had no wish to share that darkness with anyone. I remember wishing the house would burn down with me in it.

The old house had a free-standing hot water tank in the kitchen. It was metal, painted brown, and I remember holding onto it for warmth and support just as I had as a little girl — it felt safer being in-between rooms. The emptiness and quietness of that old house was distressing to me. During my childhood, I don't believe I was ever there by myself. Seven of us lived there and our mom rarely went out. As a teen, I had longed to be alone there, but now that I was, it was frightening. It rained most of the days — a driving, hard rain pummeling the patched metal roof. I tried to find rhythms and patterns in the rain but would lose track. Mostly, I longed to look out the window and see the clouds clear, the blue return and the sun come up over Mount Baker. Maybe I could get my bearings back if I could see the mountain of my childhood.

Sometimes I'd glance in the cracked bathroom mirror and note the changing colours of the bruises on my neck, from red to black and blue and the broken skin on my lip, the blood blisters and bites on my breasts, then I'd look down at my discoloured arms and thighs. But for the most part I tried not to look at myself at all.

I slept during the day and stayed awake all night. I'd scramble out into the rain and sit in my Volvo, listening to sad, soothing songs by Janis Ian, Leonard Cohen and Joni Mitchell. When I felt able to handle the phone, I called the college in Twin Rivers and dropped out of all my classes. It was too late to get my tuition back, but I didn't care.

Hunger began to win out over nausea and I discovered my mother had left a few packages of saltine crackers and there were still some MacIntosh apples on the tree outside the kitchen window. I ate those and drank water from the tap. The bruises spread far and wide like maps of an unknown country, then changed again, from black and blue to greenish orange.

On the morning I was finally able to leave the property, I looked closely at my face in the mirror. My reflection had changed. Not just because of the remaining bruises — it had been a couple of weeks, so they were mostly faded to yellow. My face was no longer the open, shiny face of a joyful, free-spirited young woman. My eyes revealed a shadow beneath the blue.

I got in my Volvo and headed back up to Twin Rivers, not sure of where I'd live or what I'd do, but I knew I'd never live in Portman again and I knew I'd never be the same.

It was several weeks before I went to a doctor. I was very ill and quite sure I had a life-ending disease. The world had recently become aware of AIDS and I was fairly certain that's what I had. Turned out, the lingering pain I felt was a massive bladder infection, much like the ones I got as a child. Uninvited intruders my body was unable to fight off. I responded to the antibiotics the doctor prescribed and when the results finally came in for the STD tests I had asked for, I was clear. A bit of a new lease on life was afforded me and I decided that yes, perhaps I did want to live, or at least not actively die.

I have told no one other than that one police officer on the telephone about the rape, until now.

Throughout Liv's story, Celeste has been conveying her support with small empathetic noises, reaching now and then to touch her arm. Now she waits patiently to be sure Liv is finished. After a minute or so of silence, she turns off the tape recorder and moves over to sit beside her friend.

"Oh, my poor Liv. I'm so sorry that happened to you. Those bastards. They got away with it. They should've been sent to jail for what they did to you. You didn't deserve any of it," she adds, tears welling in her eyes.

Liv speaks slowly. Her racing heart has slowed, her face is pale, her eyes dull. "And what they did to me I'm sure they did to others.

I've always felt guilty for not reporting it. Imagine, I've felt guilty and ashamed for ten years, and they have probably not had a twang of regret or guilt."

"You tried to tell the police. That cop made you doubt yourself. He's as guilty as the rapists. You can still report it, you know."

"I don't know. One part of me wants to punish them, to make sure people know what monsters they are. But I also recognize that the time for making a strong case is long past. It just makes me so angry that these guys felt entitled to violate me. It seems worse that they are privileged, middle class guys with every opportunity in the world. It's easier for guys like that to get away with crime."

"You know, things haven't changed much since the time of Moragh. If you'd had a knife, like Moragh did, they probably would have overpowered you and used it against you because you were drugged. They committed more than one crime that day and I hope their karma catches up with them. You're the strongest person I know! To survive that and to do this incredibly hard work of healing."

"After all these years, when I hear a hockey game on TV I can't look at it, and the sound of the sporty fanfare and dimwitted commentary gives me flashbacks to that night. People think I'm being un-Canadian! One day, I'd like to speak out about this, to help other women and girls, and to bring it out in the open that being on a sports team can make guys feel like they have the right to harm people. Parents need to know that, so they can teach their boys it's not okay."

"I will absolutely be there to help with that. You're right, though — the first step is to heal yourself."

They sit in exhausted silence for a few moments. Liv leans back on the sofa and shuts her eyes. Then they open again.

"That was ten years ago and it's been hanging over me since then, locked away in the same place as the childhood abuse," she says, her voice rising with the sudden realization.

"You know, Liv, because your father violated you, you weren't able to experience emotions in the same way as a person who's been able to develop healthy boundaries. Anger about what happened and the ability and drive to reach out for support were foreign concepts to you. It's no wonder at all. It's good to hear some anger in your voice now when you talk about how you feel about the rape. And it's really awesome you've been able to finally reach out for support. Some people are never able to.

"Yes, I am angry. I'm sure it affected every decision I've made since. It took me a couple of months to recover enough to do anything, and then it seems like I put whatever lifeforce I had left into burying the past like a dead thing. But it was alive and bleeding.

"After Christmas I went back to college. I took a sociology class with Ross and we got together shortly after that. I think I saw him as a chance to start a brand new, happy life, away from my home town, safe from the shame and fear that would haunt me if I returned. What I didn't know was that geography changes nothing when it comes to matters of the wounded spirit."

"Marriage to Ross was your barrel," Celeste offers. "If you hadn't been assaulted, your life would have unfolded differently."

"You're right. I might have had a thing with Ross, but I wouldn't have been so eager to settle down. It was because of the rape. It wasn't enough to stuff my pain deep inside, I suppose I felt I needed to put myself in a container of some kind — marriage felt safe.

"I was physically healed by the time Ross and I got together, but I couldn't make myself tell him about the rape. Fortunately for our relationship, Ross' passion was far more intellectual than sexual. Despite my attraction to him, I wasn't able to enjoy sex or even have an orgasm for many years, but he was always gentle and undemanding in the bedroom — kind of old-fashioned. I'm sure he would've understood and been supportive had I told him.

"We conceived about the third time we had sex and began planning our life together. I think I convinced myself I was madly in love with Ross and with the idea of being a mom. I'm not offering this up as a recommendation for other women who have been sexually assaulted, but somehow in my case, that little bean growing inside of me was a lifeline. Carrying a child inside of me gave me a fresh and all-consuming focus and made me feel clean again — joyful, really. Being pregnant and knowing I was going to be a mother actually seemed to transform my negative karma into something beautiful. My spirit became shiny again and I became strong. Strong for my child, if not for myself."

19

~ Shadow Monster ~

Racing around the house trying to make herself look presentable for the first time in ages, Liv locates her cleanest blue jeans, sets up the long-ignored ironing board to give her lacy white blouse a once-over. She rips through her pottery bowl of jewellery to locate her turquoise and coral beads from India to add a splash of colour around her neck. Even though it's November, she's sweating, partly from racing and partly because she's nervous about tonight. She knows it'll be a lot of laughs and she loves being with her girlfriends, but she's pretty sure she'll drink too much and act like a lunatic. She's feeling vulnerable, as it has only been a few days since she shared her story of being raped with Celeste. *I don't think I'm ready to share this with all my friends yet, but I do feel like I could share it now given the right circumstances.*

Liv's telling of the rape has turned it into just that — a story rather than a nightmare she's repressed. Her marriage and her move to rural Little Mountain seem like a reasonable, intuitive choice — a soft landing, rather than a mistake.

Tonight is "Ladies Night" at the local bar, featuring an Australian comedy troupe that's passing through town. Her friends thought it'd be a perfect thirtieth birthday celebration. Ross is overnighting somewhere and she's needing the kids to be good, eat dinner and co-operate, so, sensing this, they are being jerks and not co-operating at all. Leah is feeding her chicken burger to Ruby, who is waiting under the table. Micah won't come upstairs at all as he's so focused on dismantling an old lawn mower in the basement with his dad's tools, which he isn't allowed to use. Molly is arguing with Liv because she can't get their usual, wonderful babysitter and has to settle for someone they don't like nearly as much.

"Why don't you just not go?" Molly pleads.

"Because I haven't been out in months and it's my very belated birthday party," Liv answers and then thinks to herself: *Why am I justifying myself to my seven-year-old?*

"You'll be fine with Melanie. I need you to help with Micah, okay?" Last time Liv had left them with this sitter, he'd hammered a screw driver into the log wall of their living room.

Hearing the beep of Kat's horn, she calls the kids together and gives them a hug and a goodnight kiss, tells them to be good for Melanie, who walks in the door looking like a sad sack. Liv thinks to herself, *For crying out loud, can't she at least pretend to be enthusiastic?* (Years later, Liv learned that Melanie had been beaten and abused by her stepmother. She felt bad for not being more interested in the girl's life and the source of her sullenness.)

This rare night of being out with her female friends is transcendent for Liv — to have the unfettered freedom to drink wine and swap stories without interruption makes her feel free. She is a valued member of a beautiful, vibrant pack of women capable of anything.

The comedians are outrageous. At one point, Liv's eyes well with tears of mirth — she looks around the table and sees her closest friends, all senseless with humour, and she feels so embraced by community that she is overwhelmed. She catches Celeste's eye and they beam at each other across the table.

The male comedians join the group of six Little Mountain gals at their table and the conversation is lighthearted and flirtatious. The women all agree they need to explore Australia one day, if all the men are so funny and sweet. One young man pays a great deal of attention to Liv, saying "I can't believe you're thirty years old with three kids and a farm — you're a beaut."

It's what she needed to hear — that *that* part of her is still alive and attractive. It's what she needs to tell herself. It doesn't matter what happened ten years ago or that her marriage is failing and her husband no longer desires her.

Ross will not ruin my life, she realizes with a start. *My father didn't ruin my life. That hockey team did not ruin my life. I've nothing to feel guilty or ashamed about. I have, I can and I will start over again, and again if I have to. I won't have the weight of painful secrets dragging me down.*

Their next hypno-therapy session is a few days after the comedy night and Liv tells Celeste she feels ready to explore the past life she's been avoiding. There have been recurring nightmares starring Liv as a Nazi soldier. Celeste agrees to help her go there and believes Liv will be able to look at this possible past life without taking on the guilt or trauma of it, so they proceed.

Session No. 10 transcript, Nov. 12, 1987
Detlef, 1943

He's riding a bicycle across an arched stone bridge that spans a canal — it's rural, probably in Europe. He's in his late teens, maybe eighteen or so, and he's wearing a uniform — khaki-coloured with a red swastika armband. Oh my God, this is the past life I've had nightmares about since I was a little girl.

I'm feeling reluctant, but at the same time know I need to force myself to look at this experience of my soul. I'm not sure why.

The countryside is lovely and pastoral — stone fences and pastures dotted with sheep and black-and-white dairy cows. It's late afternoon — the sun is low in the sky, beaming through a bank of clouds. The shadows are long and deep. Two golden palomino horses run up a hill in the distance and are silhouetted against the azure sky.

He passes old farm houses painted white, neatly decorated with brightly coloured wooden windmills and weather cocks, as if lifted from the pages of an idyllic, quaint children's story book. But, just like a Grimm's fairytale, I have a feeling this charming setting will belie an ugly plot!

His name is Detlef. I hesitate to allow my spirit to merge with a young man who's clearly enlisted with the notorious Nazis. There it is, though, the luminescent thread that ties my soul to his. I see that it is not a pure blue — it has a faded, muddy grey hue.

Damn! I knew something like this was going to rear its head. I swear he's smirking at me as my soul observes him.

Detlef is whistling a song. I recognize it.

I love to go a-wandering, my knapsack on my back.

And when I go, I love to sing, my knapsack on my back, fallerie, fallera...

He stops in the shade of a roadside oak and leans his bike against its rough bark. He lights a cigarette, then reaches into his pocket and pulls out a small round mirror. He looks at himself with a direct, appraising eye. Then he pulls his mouth into a smile — he's pleased with the way he looks, proud of his uniform and the idea of belonging, of being powerful.

Before he returns the mirror to his pocket, he turns it in his hand and runs his thumb over the smooth ridges that form a pattern of Cloisonné flowers. It's a strange thing for a young man to carry, but I sense it's a memento — or perhaps a trophy? The mirror inspires a flash of pride in Detlef.

He resumes his ride and, as if in response to my curiosity, he calls up a memory — a jostling crowd of children lined up to enter their school. A young Detlef, maybe eight or nine years old, stands slightly apart. His clothing is threadbare, his trousers too short. He feels panicked and trapped. He's a poor student and dreads feeling stupid in front of the other children. A girl around the same age comes up beside him, smiles and says hello. Shoshanna. He lingers over the sight of her, standing there clutching her books, gazing at him with her deep brown eyes. Shoshanna's face is round, her complexion fair, her skin almost translucent. Her smooth dark hair is pulled back into a low ponytail held by a scrap of yellow silk ribbon.

Her simple, friendly act puts Detlef more at ease — he gets carried away with the idea that perhaps she likes him in a particular way, but he can't bring himself to ask.

Now a little older, Detlef has filled out and is looking muscular and strong — handsome in that Eastern European way, fair hair, cool blue menacing eyes. Just like my dad's. His round face reddens as he exerts himself and I focus in and see him beating up another boy in the school yard. With each blow, each kick, Detlef vents his rage — the boy is "an idiot, a gimp, a dirty gypsy, a lying thief." Detlef's pen has gone missing and he's certain this boy had taken it. The smaller boy flails back at Detlef, but soon he's knocked to the ground. He gives up and curls into a ball with his arms wrapped around his head. Detlef lands a kick to his ribs — and then Shoshanna pushes between them, shouting at him to stop. She bends to attend to the gypsy boy, then helps him to his feet and back into the school. She casts a glance at Detlef — he reads disgust.

How dare she judge me? Detlef's temper surges at the insult. That look from Shoshanna reminds him of the dismayed expression on his father's face when Detlef is rude to his mother. Stupid, cowardly man. Detlef will have to find another girl to fantasize about — one that is blonder, with a more ample bosom. More of a true German.

Back to the present. Detlef's legs ply the pedals of his bike rhythmically along the country road. He's been unable to find a job, so he works on the family farm. He hates it — considers it drudge labour, far beneath him. He has no respect for his parents, who have spent their lives in the dirt and the muck and are still no better than peasants.

The only farming chore Detlef enjoys is the slaughter. Even as a young boy, he took pride in his own ability to exercise power over the farmyard creatures, sometimes kicking a cow unnecessarily as he walks past, or withholding food just to see them bawl and beg. Today he killed one of the boars, cut its fatty throat and watched its red blood gush. He looks forward to ham and bacon. They do eat well on the farm — although his mother had cooked the offal from the pig today, which he didn't like. Typical peasant farmers, making do with guts while conniving Jews live in big houses and amass fortunes. He's learning a lot at about the problems in his country from his Hitler Youth meetings. He's found others who share his ideas and it's an outlet for his anger.

Maybe Shoshanna would prefer a weakling like his father, who kowtows to his wife's every command. Men like him will always be the peasants of the world. Detlef will never be like him — he's strong, he'll take what he wants. If that means girls like Shoshanna won't like him, then so be it. He smiles to himself. There will be no shortage of girls for him when he's a decorated soldier in Herr Hitler's army.

She's is just a lowly Jew, a Kike, who has to wear a star on an armband. Even if she were to beg him, he thinks, he would reject her — still his penis hardens at the thought of taking her against her will.

Oh my god, I hate this guy so much! There's no way I can relate to him in any way! I don't know if I can stay here and watch this Nazi pig.

"Liv, would you like to come back from this past life now?"

No, I'll stick with it. I remember in one of the books you lent me, Buddha said that in our past lives we have all been the murdered and the murderer, the victim and the perpetrator. There must be a message here somewhere.

With each pump on the bike pedal, the mirror in Detlef's pocket taps solidly against his leg, reminding him. He knows he shouldn't carry such an item around, but he couldn't resist today — he wants it close to him. Tomorrow he'll leave it hidden at home.

He acquired Shoshanna's mirror the night before. His memory plays the scene in his head — he's marching with five of his Hitler

Youth cohort in formation down the dark city streets, accompanying the SS on a special mission. Detlef's pride soars as he marches with his peers, well-dressed and more powerful and purposeful than he ever felt as a farm boy. Their route takes them into the Jewish section. In his training, Detlef has learned from his superiors that the Jews are destroying Germany and must be forced to leave, beginning with the rich Jewish families who have a great deal of influence in their community. He believes this is an absolute truth.

They stop at Shoshanna's house — her father is a successful jeweller in Munich, but they live in this smaller village in a large, stately home. The officers bang loudly on the door and Shoshanna's father opens it. Detlef watches as he's dragged onto the street. Soldiers burst inside and soon emerge with her mother, who is weeping and calling to her husband. The commandant shouts at them, demanding to know where their children are.

The father, flanked by two officers, stands upright, with quiet dignity. He swears that they have sent their children away; their daughter is in university and their son in boarding school, both in Switzerland.

"You are lying," the officer spits at him. He strikes Shoshanna's father on the head with the butt end of his rifle and he falls on the ground. Detlef hears this and sees it as his chance to garner favour with his superiors.

"Heil Hitler," he salutes and moves forward, addressing his superior. "You are right, sir. These Jews are lying. I saw their daughter walking on this very street the other day — she was carrying jugs of milk. She's not in university in Switzerland."

Detlef is glad to be among the group of soldiers that flood into the house, which fills with the sound of smashing china and stomping boots. They move through hallways and rooms ransacking and destroying, searching for valuables, which they pile up and drag down the stairs wrapped in the rich carpets from the floors.

Detlef is excited, almost euphoric. He enjoys looting — moving in with his pack and laying waste to a house, ripping paintings from the walls, slashing furniture, searching for a cupboard full of silver or a jewellery box. He relishes the idea of Shoshanna seeing him in this new, powerful position.

Detlef makes his way into what is certainly her bedroom — a charming, feminine room with a gabled ceiling, painted white with touches of pink. The others have already been in here — the linen has been torn from the bed and lies in a pile of white eyelet. The mattress is awry, the floor is littered with garments and belongings. He picks up a small cotton brassiere and feels something resembling regret. Not for what he's about to do but for what he will never be able to do. He imagines what the soldiers might have done with Shoshanna if they had found her. It excites him. He looks under the bed, then walks around, inspecting, intrigued by her collections of miniature castles and cottages. He spots the miniature mirror, half-hidden in the corner and puts it in his pocket.

He's about to leave when he hears a muffled bump — there's someone hiding in the wall behind the dresser. He instantly knows it's probably Shoshanna and her brother. He stands quiet, his mind churning with possibilities. He could walk out — he's the last to search, so the fault will not only be his. But perhaps this is a test of his loyalty, the strength of his commitment. They are Jews. They are ruining his country. It's his duty to expose them.

"Sir! They're up here, hidden in the wall!" His voice rings loudly in the stairwell.

His chest puffs with pride at their congratulations. He helps tear down the hidden wall, exposing the terrified Shoshanna and her younger brother. "Mother! Father!" they cry. Shoshanna tries to shield her brother and fights the soldiers, battering them ineffectually with her fists. "Leave my brother alone, he's just a small boy, you filthy pigs." They are both dragged out of their hiding place, down the stairs and into the dark street.

As the family is roughly loaded into a transport truck, Detlef catches Shoshanna's eye, expecting to see recognition, some sign of regret for her treatment of him. But all he sees is blind fear and loathing.

Later that night, lurching with drink, leaning against his friends in front of Shoshanna's empty home, Detlef grins. It has been a good night for Hitler's army and a good night for him. There has been much laughter and back-slapping as they celebrated, guzzling back fine liquor confiscated from Jewish homes. "Blood and Honour," they chant in unison. There's talk of a raid on a gypsy encampment the following evening — not as profitable for looting, but the gypsies put up a great fight. There's sure to be blood. Perhaps now that he's proven himself, the officers will initiate him into some of the fun that is to be had with those wild dark-skinned girls.

Detlef's bike bumps off the dirt road onto a narrow cobblestone street. He rides to a streetlight and stops and props his bike against it. He lights another cigarette and smokes it quickly, almost impatiently, looking around. He grinds it out and pulls a rag from his pocket and buffs the dust from his black boots, then inspects his trousers, brushing them off with his hands. It's imperative he look his best — he'll be reprimanded if his uniform is not impeccable. His face flushes as he recalls the humiliation of being upbraided in front of the others for having a smudge of dust on his pant cuff. That will not happen again.

As he stands upright and reaches for his bicycle, a shot is fired — Detlef's head snaps back and he is thrust against the brick wall and slumps to the ground. Oh, the sickening rush of blood.

I felt that enter my chest just as certainly as I felt the bullet that killed Veda in India — but this time, I have a chilling sensation as his soul flees his body like a whoosh of dark vapour. I'm instantly set free to hang weightlessly over the scene.

Detlef's body is propped against the wall, his head hanging to the side and his legs splayed before him. In the shadows on the other side of the street, there's movement — I see the startled face of a young man, his jaw open, staring. He is dark-haired with an angular face, dressed in rags. It's the gypsy boy Detlef beat up when he was nine years old. He has a rifle in his hands. He spins and runs away, his footsteps sharp on the cobblestones. He swerves out of sight down a side street.

I look back at Detlef and notice a symbol scrawled on the wall above him — a white rose drawn in chalk on the red brick.

Liv's return is instantaneous — she sits bolt upright and clutches Celeste's arm.

"Oh my god, I feel so horrible about this lifetime as a Nazi! Could my spirit really have been in somebody as vile and hateful as him?"

"We're each capable of both good and evil, given the circumstances. Buddhism suggests that we have all been both the tortured and the torturer and we need to have compassion for both. Sometimes in that big library in the sky, maybe souls contract to be reborn into an existence where their main purpose is to provide a lesson for someone else."

"But this is just too weird, Celeste. When I was eleven, I read The Diary of Anne Frank and began having this recurring nightmare. I still have it occasionally.

"In the dream, sometimes I'm a soldier, sometimes I'm just myself. People are seeking my directions — I have to decide which way to send them. I always tell them the wrong way. I've been told to follow orders and I do. It always ends the same, with me realizing, too late, that I'm sending people to their deaths. Now I have my own children, they're in my dream too, and I give them the wrong directions and I send them to their deaths before I realize it's them! I wake up terrified and feeling sick to my stomach."

"Liv, what a horrible thing for you to have to experience over and over."

"Do you think it's connected to Detlef? Could his miserable spirit have carried over into this lifetime? I'm so relieved Detlef died young, before he could do more harm!"

"I would certainly say the dream is an echo of your soul's experience as Detlef. If you carried anything into this lifetime, it would be the fear you might be capable of evil. Knowing about your childhood and how you lived in fear of your abusive father, it could also have been your subconscious mind trying to find a way to make sense of it all, by making you feel responsible for everyone in the world. That's what can happen with children of trauma, Liv. They either take on the addiction, or they take on the world."

"Well, that's a heck of a choice. What I want to know is, how is my soul going to make up the karma points for being a vicious Nazi?"

"I don't think you have to worry about that. Maybe you already have! Think of it — Detlef was one of millions of soldiers, on all sides in all wars! That's universal karma — it aims to raise the awareness

208

of all humanity. A Buddhist monk once explained to me that karma doesn't work as we might think it would. It's not a steady progression of lessons learned and insights gained. It doesn't always progress logically toward enlightenment.

"Sometimes, after many lifetimes of good deeds and happiness, we're born into a very negative, challenging life, where we die of a terrible illness or where we inflict pain on others, like Detlef and your father."

"That really does help, Celeste. Now I feel so much better about being a horrible, racist, murderous Nazi! Just kidding, I actually do! It also helps me to understand that Ross isn't evil. He's not the bad guy any more than I am. He's misguided and doing harm to himself and others and he needs to be stopped — just like every brainwashed, delusional soldier who ever fought in war created by evil. Mental illness is like a war in a person's mind."

"I've really found Buddhism has been a blessing in my life. It helps me make sense of the world and my place in it. The other cool thing is that it doesn't mutually exclude all of my other spiritual beliefs. One day I might get more in touch with my birth mother's Ojibway or my father's French roots. All this 'accepting' doesn't mean we should sit back and do nothing about the bad in people or in the world — social action in Buddhism and also in First Nations societies are long-standing traditions."

"Well, when my life feels more in order, I'm going to take a long, solo holiday by the sea, take along a couple of dozen of those books you keep lending me that I never find the time to read, and figure out what, if anything, I truly want to be — a Buddhist, a Wiccan, a Quaker, or some crazy combination of all of them."

"There'll be time. If not this life, then the next."

Liv ponders their conversation. *The injustice and the horror of that war plays havoc in my mind, juxtaposed with what my unconscious mind plays out in my Nazi nightmares. Is every human capable of great good and great evil and everything in between? Will I be able to find a way to move forward in my life with this knowledge, with more compassion or with more forgiveness?*

Liv suddenly feels grateful for this knowledge and experience. Guilt and horror have been replaced by insight. She could be someone who helps people because she understands both sides of human nature. Instead of pointing people in the wrong direction, out of malice or ignorance, like in her nightmare, she could learn how to help people find their right trajectory and do no harm. Her mind dances at the thought of signing up for college classes as soon as she can. Let the learning begin.

20

~ Crisis and Catharsis ~

The call comes in shortly after noon. Celeste has just finished adding fresh thyme to a large pot of tomato soup. She intends for it to last her a week until Jacques gets home. He's still away working in the bush but will return in a few days for the Christmas break.

Liv's voice is breathless and harried. "Ross has barricaded himself in his office at the college and the police have been called. They want me to come and try to talk him out, but I need someone to be here when the kids get home. Could you possibly do that, Celeste?"

Celeste has been expecting something like this would happen. Ross' bizarre behaviour has been escalating steadily for months, so it was only a matter of time.

"Of course. I'll be at your house at four when the bus arrives. Don't worry about the kids. Actually, I'm coming over right now and we'll spend a minute doing some breathing and talking about how you can get through this. You shouldn't drive when you're so distraught. And you can take my car instead of your farm truck. It's not safe to go to town in that thing."

As Liv pulls up to the faculty building, the rock-hard knot in her stomach tightens and blood rushes to her face. She sees two police cars and an ambulance with flashing red lights. *Oh my god, has he hurt himself...or someone else?*

In a panic, she hurriedly parks the car in a No Parking zone and runs toward the building. Just inside the door, in the hallway outside Ross' office, are several RCMP officers, emergency workers and — thank goodness — Ross' good friend and coworker, Drew, who is talking to Ross through the door.

"Ross, are you okay? Are you drinking? Maybe you just need to come out of there and I'll take you home?"

"No, Drew, you don't get it." Ross' voice sounds slurred. "They want to get rid of all of us — mark my words, these people are KKK. They've taken all the money now they want all the power. I can stop them. God wants me to stop them."

"You don't even believe in God," Drew interrupts. "Come on out of there. The police are going to break the door down if you don't come out now. We can talk. Liv just got here. The three of us can go out for coffee."

"The shit is going to hit the fan, we can either be the ones getting hit or the ones doing the hitting." Then in a quieter voice. "Why is Liv here?"

"Sir, do you have a weapon?" an RCMP officer interjects.

"Who the fuck are you?" Ross yells. "No, my only weapon is my mind and they're trying to destroy that too!"

As Liv walks toward into the scene, she's nervous, absolutely unsure about what she can do that could possibly help the situation. An RCMP officer approaches her and takes her aside, now she's been identified as "the wife."

He asks her a few questions about Ross' drinking and whether he's done things like this before. Even though Liv tells him her concerns about Ross' mental health and his behaviour in recent months, the officer seems determined it's an alcoholic episode and all he needs is to dry out. He does want to determine if there's a weapon, though, so Liv assures him Ross only has a shotgun for farm use and it's at home to the best of her knowledge.

The system is not going to help, Liv realizes. He hasn't hurt himself or anyone else at this time and it's not illegal to rant about nonsensical things. The police want to take him to lock-up for the night so he can sober up, but Liv knows that won't help at all and will just make him more paranoid. The officer lends her his car phone to call the emergency ward at the hospital to see if he can be admitted, but they tell her he's not 'commitable' and she knows he won't go willingly.

Recalling her sessions with Celeste and calling on the strength of her past life characters, her fear and anxiety evaporate and she says, with confidence, to the officer, "I'll be able to talk him out of there and take him home."

She walks up to his office door. Inside, she can hear Ross weeping. She can't recall ever seeing Ross cry during their ten years of marriage. She's frustrated the police can't help, angry the college is so unsupportive — they just seem to want Ross gone. The lump rising up in her throat is extreme sadness, for Ross and for herself. The man she married seems to be gone.

"Ross, it's Liv," she says. "I've come to take you home. Everything will be okay. You need some sleep."

He opens the door and falls into her arms. Liv feels a sense of control and calm in herself. She suddenly knows his behaviour isn't about her, not at all. *He's not a bad man, he's just a victim of circumstances. I can't feel anything but empathy for him right now.*

Celeste has the kids settled in bed by the time Liv arrives home with a silent Ross. He doesn't even look at Celeste, just shuffles into the den and shuts the door.

"My head feels like it's going to explode," she whispers to Celeste, "I don't even know the man I drove home." She takes a deep breath, "Did the kids do all right?"

"They were thrilled to see Auntie Celeste waiting for them — a bit worried that you weren't here, but I told them you had an appointment in town. We made it into a party. The soup is still warm if you're hungry."

"You're fantastic."

Liv moves to serve herself, but Celeste frowns and guides her to a chair at the table and dishes her up a steaming bowl. It's tangy and fresh tasting and it warms her insides.

"Okay, tell me what happened," she says, once Liv's had a few bites.

"Oh my god — such a nightmare." She talks softly, aware of Ross in the next room.

"I could have let them take him to jail. The police thought a night in the slammer would scare him straight and sober, but I knew it would just make it worse. I tried to tell them how unwell he's been but they said unless he has a mental health history or diagnosis, he can't be committed against his will. He didn't say a word the whole way home. He just passed out."

To Liv it felt like she was living in a movie about someone else's life, only she didn't know the script. She hesitates for a moment and takes Celeste's hand in her own. "Thank you so much for stepping in with the kids, I'm so glad they didn't have to see their dad like that."

"You aren't alone Liv. You are going to get through this, I know it."

"Yeah, I know. I do feel I will. I'm worried that Ross won't, but I'm even beginning to let go of that worry. Drew said he thinks, like us, that losing the election played a big part in knocking Ross off the rails. And the insane amounts of drugs and alcohol he's been consuming for months. Drew and their other co-workers at the college know he dances on the edge of weird, but other than his left-wing shenanigans, Ross has been pretty good at keeping up the façade of normalcy at work — until the China incident, and now this."

How much worse can he get before he's forced to get help? Liv wonders. *Does somebody have to get really hurt? Maybe I should have let them take him to jail. No, I think I did the right thing but now I need to firmly hold my line and if Ross refuses to get help, the kids and I will have to leave.*

Celeste calls the next day to check in. Liv tells her that Ross has installed himself in the den, getting up only to use the bathroom and get more medication for his never-ending headache.

"He's taken to chewing his pills like Jack Nicholson in *The Shining*. Now I officially feel like I'm living in a horror movie. Worse yet, I'm playing the dutiful wife, even though everything in me wants to grab the kids and run screaming out of the house." Celeste laughs softly and encourages her, "Do it," she teases, although she knows Liv is just venting.

Liv demurs like the housewife she no longer is, "He won't eat anything, but does drink the fresh-pressed apple juice I make."

"Spiked with scotch, I'm guessing?" suggests Celeste.

"Oh yeah, for sure, he's got a bottle stashed under the couch in the den. I don't even go in there. Last night he summoned the kids to his bedside and apologized for being so sleepy and thanked them for being so good. He snuggled them for a few minutes and read them his favourite story, *Jumping Mouse.* They were absolutely beaming, they're so starved for his attention. Leah scurried off to bring him more juice and three of his favourite oatmeal raisin cookies. At one point I would have considered it heart-warming, but this just enraged me — nothing that he does seems authentic anymore."

Liv has moved into the kid's bedroom downstairs — a huge room with three single beds in three separate nooks. Even though she has successfully kicked Ross out of the marriage bed, she doesn't want it either. That room seems to give her insomnia. The kids argue over whose turn it is to have Mommy in their bed. In the mornings, they all tiptoe upstairs, being as "quiet as mice" so as not to disturb Daddy. Liv finds herself seeking any excuse to be away from the house — shopping, visiting friends, getting out to do some of the farm work. She winterizes the rose and lavender garden and harvests the last of the onions, garlic, potatoes and carrots. It gives her focus and a feeling of satisfaction — she had resigned herself to letting them rot in the field.

She's been able to negotiate a medical leave from the college for Ross, as long as she can get a doctor to sign some papers, so that is a relief — there will be at least be a paycheque and they won't lose the farm to foreclosure.

"He's postponed his appointment with the psychiatrist, even though he knows it's now both a legal and employment requirement," she tells Celeste over tea one day.

"And you've told him more than once it's a marriage requirement as well," Celeste reminds her.

"Yes, I've given him two weeks to show me he's making changes and getting medical help. He's agreed to it, but he says the problems are with the world, not with him, and he really believes that. He knows our marriage is hanging in the balance, but he seems unable to step up. The headaches are relentless and he seems so depressed he hardly speaks. He told me last night he'd see the doctor to get some new painkillers this week and he grudgingly agreed to re-schedule his psychiatrist appointment."

Celeste has tracked down a library book about mental health disorders. She cracks it open and finds a section she wanted to share with Liv. There's a checklist of symptoms of bipolar disorder. She reads out loud from the first paragraph.

"The first and foremost symptom of many mental illnesses, particularly bi-polar disorder, is the patient does not believe there is anything transgressive about their behaviour." Liv smiles, "Bingo!" Let's do this test on Ross' behalf, then, shall we?"

Out of twenty questions, Liv answers yes to all of them, except one: "Have you lost your relationship with your significant other or important friends because of your behaviour?"

"Not quite yet," she says, "Put that one down as a maybe, I guess."

"I know you don't want to abandon him when he's so ill. You're doing the right thing, gathering your strength and resources, setting boundaries and making plans for you and the kids. You have to stop trying to figure out what's going on in his head. It's never a good idea to get inside the head of a mentally sick person. Remember how you felt when you looked at Detlef's life? It's the same here — you can't possibly figure out how to fix it because you have no control over him and he has no control over his illness."

Liv boldly brings the book home to give the test to Ross, hoping it will help him shed some light on the seriousness of his condition. He grudgingly answers some of the questions but only answers affirmatively to three of them: Do you have difficulty sleeping at times? Do you find that your thoughts race? Do you believe you are destined for a great purpose? Ross becomes agitated and snaps, "It's all because of these God-dammed fucking headaches — you have NO IDEA. Now get the hell out of my room!"

"Oh, I'm getting out of YOUR room all right. And you might have to re-think the answer to question 14: "Has your behaviour ever caused you to lose a relationship?" It feels good to speak her mind. It's a new habit she might want to keep.

Through the door she hears him shaking out a bunch of pills and pouring a rye from his hidden stash. He usually only drinks it with ice but apparently cannot be bothered to get up to go to the fridge.

Liv has a noon appointment at the school and she's worried about leaving Ross alone because he seems to be amping up.

As she leaves, he's holed up in the den, frantically making phone calls and ranting about the college. It sounds like he's caught up in one of his conspiracy theories. She hopes he's not getting himself fired but she knows she can't stop him. The part of her heart that was just for him is feeling emptier and emptier. *I don't think I can keep doing this till he sees the psychiatrist in January. The kids and I might have to leave sooner.*

She's been summoned to the school. Her children's teachers have unanimously expressed concern about their academic performance and behaviour. Molly, normally a social little girl, is isolating herself during class activities. At lunchtime, when she would usually be playing and having fun with her friends, she sits by herself, twirling a lock of her copper hair around her finger. Micah has been caught on three occasions launching spitballs at his classmates and his teacher. Leah's teacher reports that she seems distracted and tired. She's always been her star student, but now she hides Babysitter's Club books inside her textbooks and reads when she thinks it won't be noticed. She's not completing assignments.

Liv's heart sinks with that kind of guilt that all mothers are familiar with. *How could I not have seen that my kids have been struggling? They need me to fix this mess our family is in.*

She doesn't have any solutions, and nor do the teachers. But at least she's able to inform them (without going into great detail) about the current situation in her home and assure them she's doing her best to resolve it one way or another. She hopes the small amount of information she shared will help the teachers feel a bit more understanding towards her children. Liv arranges for Micah to see the school counsellor for some play therapy, as the teachers and Liv herself don't want to see his aggressive behaviour escalate. She knows he has some problems with attention and behaviour, but is opposed to putting him on medication at this point in time. She'll be able to talk to Molly and Leah — she realizes she hasn't really been honest with them about what's happening in their family, and it must be as crazy-making for them as it is for her. Liv has only recently realized her own family dysfunction was not her fault, and she doesn't want her kids to have to wait until they're adults too.

After the meeting, she picks up a few groceries and goes to the hardware store to get plastic tubs with lids, in case she needs to pack in a hurry, and heads home.

Celeste's car is in Liv's driveway. She waves when Liv drives in. She's sweeping the first snowfall from the steps.

"Hey, what's up?" Celeste's welcoming grin quickly melts into a serious expression. Something has happened.

"Hey, Liv," she gives her a quick, tight hug. "Sit down and I'll tell you what's going on."

Liv sits in one wicker chair on the porch and Celeste takes the other. She can hear Ruby whining at the door from the inside so she hops up to open it, but the handle won't turn. The door is locked.

"The police locked it when they left."

"What?"

"The police were here because they got a 911 call from a terrified semi-truck driver. He said there was a man firing a gun at passing vehicles. A bullet hit the side door of the guy's truck and nearly gave him a heart attack."

"Oh my god, Celeste. Ross did that? How did you find out?"

"Liv, this is Little Mountain — everyone in town will know by dinnertime. The truck driver stopped at the gas station to phone the police and Jacques was there. The trucker said the guy looked like Moses, wearing a striped bathrobe, firing off his porch. Jacques knew right away by the description that it had to be Ross. Jacques rushed home and told me and I came over right away. The RCMP were still here when I arrived. Ross was cuffed in the car and they told me there was no one in the house, so I knew you were okay."

"He could have killed someone. Was it awful? They took Ross away?"

"He was very drunk and delusional, raving about being in a war zone and needing to protect his family from the invaders on Highway 5. He apparently didn't resist so he wasn't hurt."

"I can't believe this," Liv says, holding her hands over her face. After a moment's thought, she adds, "But then, I guess I can. He's been building to this."

"Yeah, he has. I know this sounds weird Liv, but I'm glad this happened — particularly since nobody got hurt. Now Ross will be forced to get treatment. It's no longer up to him."

"So, he's in jail?"

"No. I had a talk with the corporal — I explained to him that I'm your counsellor, so he told me Ross would be involuntarily committed to the psych ward. He said you shouldn't go into town, but he wants you to call him — he gave me his card," she says reaching into her pocket. Liv's heart is racing. The north wind howls through the valley and into the alcove on her porch. It blows her long hair into her face and she impatiently sweeps it off with her left hand while her right hand shakes and fumbles with the key in the lock.

Ruby tumbles out, wagging her whole body, snuffing and nudging.

Corporal Brad Minnick answers the phone with brisk formality but shifts into a more considerate tone when she introduces herself. He says the psychiatrist has signed a committal form on the basis of Ross' previous offences, but that her input and agreement would be appreciated.

"What exactly were these other offences?" Liv asks, aware that her voice is tentative and up an octave or two. She's been wondering about this for weeks.

Confidentiality apparently void once a person starts acting really crazy, the corporal reels off a list of previous infractions. As well as having attempted to bring a handgun on a flight to China, Ross' violations include driving while impaired, a bar fight in Hope, soliciting the services of a prostitute and an eat-and-run on a $300 dinner for two at a posh Vancouver restaurant. At last Liv gets some details about the China affair — he had been detained at the Vancouver airport, his weapon was seized and he had agreed to undergo psychiatric testing in lieu of legal charges.

So there was someone coming after him with guns when he was on the phone with me that time. It was the police.

The corporal explains that there is a criminal file still open on him in another city, and the police have been waiting for confirmation of the psych testing so they could close the case.

He goes on to say that today's incident does carry a legal charge of discharging a firearm illegally with intent to do harm. Ross' hospitalization is mandatory. If he leaves the hospital there will be a warrant for his arrest. A court date will be scheduled within a few months. Liv is sweating from the stress of this news but at the same time she's relieved that now she knows and now she isn't alone in this mess.

He gives her the psychiatrist's phone number and advises Liv to call him to get more information about her husband's condition and the plan moving forward. She thanks him and rings off, then tries the psychiatrist's number. The officious receptionist tells her the doctor cannot possibly talk to her at this time, but reluctantly agrees to take a message.

Liv sighs as she hangs up the phone. Celeste, who has been tending the dog and tidying the kitchen this whole time, assures her friend that everything will be all right.

"I know. I just feel so exhausted. This is really happening. What am I going to tell the kids? They'll be home in a few minutes."

"You're going to have to tell them the truth. But not tonight. It will be better to tell them when you know more about what's going to happen next. Tonight, you're going to tell them we're making Christmas decorations. Where's your glue and glitter?"

21

~ *Inspiration* ~

Liv approaches the following day with a strange sense of optimism. The outside temperature has dipped way below freezing, so there's lacy hoarfrost on the ferns and lavender in front of her house and the few remaining crabapples have freeze-dried blood red against the brilliant blue sky. A few straggling Canada Geese form a honking V just above the tree-line. She suspects these are the ones that don't have to go too far, maybe just to Vancouver. Ross is in good hands, safely ensconced in the hospital. The burden is no longer hers alone. Finally, they're moving forward. Even the kids seem relieved and now they're openly talking about Daddy being in the hospital because he has an illness that made it hard for him to manage his feelings and behaviours. He needs some medicine and some help.

She bundles up for the walk to Celeste's — still, a biting wind off the river stings her cheeks and the ground is hard frozen with a skiff of snow, making the footing icy.

"I had the strangest dream last night," she tells Celeste in the warmth of her kitchen. "It was like a hypno-session, but also kind of a whirlwind recap of my Geography 101 class. It began with that rotten

Detlef a moment before he was killed, just his face, and then the shot rang out and I watched as his shaky, cruel spirit was transformed into grey smoke. I followed it up into the atmosphere, where it was carried over the North Sea to Greenland, then over Baffin Island — I was sailing with him, looking down over the ocean, the land and the ice — over the Arctic archipelago, the Victoria Islands, over the forbidding Arctic tundra. We went over Great Bear Lake, over kilometres of forest and mountains to the coast. I could see Haida Gwaii off in the distance as we followed the coastline and then down a wide ocean inlet. As we went I could feel his damaged spirit becoming cleansed — not completely…he had a lot of karmic debt to account for. At a certain place, his smoky soul swirled and dove into the woods and I followed.

"A beautiful brown-skinned woman squatted between two strong trees near an outdoor fire. She was alone and labouring hard, but she wasn't afraid. Her large brown eyes were wide with concentration. She took a huge breath and bore down, delivering to the mossy bed beneath her a perfect, black-haired, round-faced baby boy. She lifted him to her face and breathed in his sweet smell just as Detlef's soul — my soul — bonded with the infant's squirming body."

"Ah, the next incarnation," Celeste says with a smile.

"Yes. His mother looked to the sky and said a prayer, then lovingly folded her child inside her shawl, close to her breast. They quickly warmed one another.

"The dream was so real, Celeste. I could smell the ocean, fresh and briny, and then a gust of strong wind buffeted the woman and suddenly I was in my own bed. I could hear my kids chattering away in the kitchen, and the snap, crackle, pop, as they poured milk on their Rice Krispies."

"That's amazing, Liv! This incredibly lucid dream tells me you're very much in touch with your unconscious mind right now, which is a good thing." She teases, "But maybe you just needed to get rid of Detlef?"

"Yes, good riddance to him, for sure, but I really do want to go to the Northwest Coast. That has to be the life that came just before mine."

"We can do that. I can see how you'd want to experience your most recent past life. You've endured so much and now you're navigating your way through. You have some tough decisions ahead of you."

"You're right. I feel like I'm sifting and sorting and soon I need to put it all together. As upsetting as these past life stories are, they're entrancing and bolstering me. Even though I feel pretty messed up over the situation with Ross, I'm stronger than I've ever been."

"Ambe — I just learned that. It means 'let's go' in Ojibway," Celeste says.

Liv cups the soapstone in her right hand, running her thumb over its smooth surface. Celeste's calm, clear voice draws her down the path, counting the trees down to the sands of time. A raven caws high in the trees up ahead, leading her into the forest.

Session No. 11 transcript, Nov. 24, 1987
Joey, 1953

My spirit line is azure, sailing along a steep, forested valley. Now it's dropping, travelling in a descending arc, like one of those parachute toy soldiers Micah loves to drop off our deck. I follow it, dropping dizzily from the tops of towering cedar trees and into the chilly shadows at their feet. Two boys, maybe six or seven years old, run laughing along a path spongy with red, decayed cedar. They're running hard, nimbly leaping over roots and clamouring over and under enormous deadfalls — they know this trail well. My glowing cord trails from the smaller of the two, who is valiantly trying to keep up with this friend.

I meld easily with him and instantly feel Joey's vigorous energy, which is exclusively focused on this race with his cousin Peter. Joey admires Peter utterly — he aspires to be just like him. He is his teacher and protector.

The trail suddenly widens and they stop abruptly, colliding boisterously, on the edge of a high riverbank. Peter won the race, of course. The river below churns and boils around boulders, lashing the shore on its journey to the sea. The boys slow their pace and descend down a steep path to a small beach created by a back-eddy. They start throwing stones. It becomes a competition to see who can hit a distant log. Joey cheers when he hits it first. Then Peter changes the rules — the winner is now the one who can hit the log ten times in a row. They comment loudly on every throw, taunting and teasing.

Peter finally reaches the goal and declares himself the winner. They wrestle briefly on the beach, laughing. As they try to catch their breath, Peter throws his arm over Joey's shoulder.

"Even though I won, you have good aim. You're gonna be a great hunter."

Joey's heart soars at the praise. I get a strong impression of this little guy's self-image — he sees himself as lesser than Peter, but well within range of bettering him. He's driven by this competition, eager to learn and develop skills. He's thin, but there's a solidness to him. In addition to being taller, Peter is also heavier. His face is rounder; he's stocky and powerful.

I realize that the boys are calling each other by different names, in their own language. Joey is called what translates as Cedar Standing

Tall. Peter is Eagle Feather. They reserve these names for times when they are all by themselves. It's dangerous these days to use names that sound too "Indian."

Now they've decided to try to catch a fish — they're searching the beach and surrounding forest for materials to make spears. Joey has the idea of making a fence in the water so they can herd the fish into the shallows and spear them more easily. It must be autumn, as the salmon are spawning. The boys wade out into the frigid water, struggling against the current, and try to plant the sticks, but they won't stay in place wedged between the rocks. They cheerfully abandon that idea and head back up the trail — hunger is leading them home.

These two keep up a constant stream of chatter as they saunter along, which provides me with more information.

Peter's father, Billy, who is Joey's uncle, teaches both of them the skills of hunting and fishing. Joey never met his father, the son of a Norwegian settler who went to fight the Germans and never came back. Joey and his mother are also reliant on Uncle Billy for meat and fish — as her brother, it's his duty to see that they eat.

My spirit thread is dancing forward through time. As if in a movie, I see Joey's life unfold, watch him grow, and observe how he lives. Their home is a one-room cabin, heated by a small cast iron stove. They have only candles for light, so they seem to rise with the sun and sleep with the moon. Their food comes from the forest, the river and the ocean — except for the fry bread Joey's mother makes when they have flour. She serves warm chunks of it from the cast iron frying pan and they dip it in oolichan oil, which smells as fishy as you might expect. Joey loves it.

You can see where Joey gets his delicate features — his mother's face is heart-shaped, with defined cheekbones, framed by her glossy black hair. There's a particular alertness to her eyes — they shine, especially when she's looking at her son. Her name is Ista, in honour of the first woman in Nuxalk culture. She has been widowed for seven years, since before Joey was born, and she hasn't taken another man. She tells Joey about his father, who was kind and brave, with laughing eyes. I wonder within this hypnotic dreaming if this Norwegian connection is where Joey and my blood and spirit lines met up.

She works ceaselessly, sometimes with other women from the village and sometimes on her own, foraging in the forest for all manners of berries, shoots and seeds. These she dries or smokes and stores for the future. She strips bark, collects roots and weaves baskets to trade for the things she can't get otherwise. She's trying to carry her weight, so as not to be a burden to her brother-in-law and his family.

Joey and Peter spend their days in the forest, playing games, competing and inadvertently picking up the skills they'll need when they are older. They're inseparable, except at night when they go to their own homes, which are not far apart in the cluster of dwellings known as Nuxalk, which is now called Bella Coola.

I cast my thread forward.

~ ~ ~

There's Joey. I try to join with him, but I meet with resistance. He's blocking me — I don't think he's aware of me — he's just closed. I'll hover in his company instead, as I did with Veda when she was an infant.

I now realize that Joey isn't at home. This is a large, drafty room with a high ceiling. The only light comes through the partly open door.

I can make out two rows of beds down each side of the room. Each bed holds a child, covered with a grey wool blanket. A residential school.

Even though I can't merge with Joey, I can sense that he is awake, lying rigid — alert, listening.

This is chillingly familiar to my own childhood — lying awake, dreading the sound of my father's approach. But this isn't Joey's father, a man who would never have harmed him. This is a man in a black robe.

On one hand, I feel compelled to stay, to be here for Joey through whatever happens, but it's excruciating — even though I have no corporeal shape, a traitor to my own past spirit, I'm jittery and agitated. I have to go — I'm casting forward.

~ ~ ~

This time Joey is less guarded and he allows me to bond with him. He's with a group of boys in the hallway of the school. Peter is there too. They're joking and laughing — tentatively enjoying a rare moment of unsupervised play. I hear one of the boys speaking in an unfamiliar language.

"Number 527," a voice calls out — loudly, imperiously. The boys freeze. A priest looms at the end of the hall and strides toward them.

"What are you doing?" he asks, his voice harsh. Joey gathers his courage and steps forward. At the school, he's not Joey, not Cedar Standing Tall. He is 527.

"I'm sorry, Father." Perhaps he hopes his submissiveness will be enough. But the imposing black-robed figure sweeps forward, takes his arm roughly and begins dragging him down the hallway.

Joey feels the blows stinging his bare backside, but he doesn't react. He's absent. I sense him closing his mind, taking himself elsewhere — he conjures images of tall cedars, a tumbling, rushing river.

I see a ship slowly plying its way through choppy waves down a long channel. The shoreline is a wall of enormous trees broken by the occasional rocky point or towering cliff. I am drawn inside to a passenger area, where Joey and Peter sit on a hard bench. A dour priest sits behind them, his head bent over a black-bound Bible. There are a few other passengers, but they're on the other side of the ship.

A feeling of dread overcomes me and I'm suddenly nauseated. It is different than what I felt when I met up with Detlef — with him, I despised his tarnished soul. Now, it's the circumstances that scare me. I'm horrified at the damage being inflicted on these two boys. The blue thread shimmers between us, but again Joey is closed to me. I can only watch.

Peter is leaning against Joey weakly. His hands are pressed against his chest, his breathing shallow. Both boys rock with the movement of the ship, but Peter lolls as if he might slip off the bench. He begins to cough and lurches upright, his body clenching with the effort. Joey steadies him.

The school is sending them home to see their families, not out of kindness, but because Peter is dying. They probably hope he'll die at home to save them adding another death to their statistics.

Joey walks slowly up to his uncle's house to find Peter propped on the step with a blanket over his shoulders, enjoying the sun, the cool breeze and most of all the freedom from the torture and abuse of the residential school.

"Hi," he says when Joey sits beside him. "I like to be out here. Inside, I cough so much, my mother is afraid I'll give the sickness to my sister."

Joey gives a little grunt of understanding. His once strong cousin is now a featherweight and he's disappearing.

"I know I am dying, Joey. We've both seen other kids at the school sick like this. I'm ready to die."

Joey nods. "Remember right before they took us? That was the last time I felt good."

Peter shifts against Joey, groaning quietly that he's tired. His illness has made him weak, but it won't let him sleep for long because of the coughing.

"I will not go back to that school," Joey says firmly. "They took us from our families, starved us and beat us. They do those horrible things to our bodies. Sex things. I'm not doing that any more. I know what we can do."

Peter glances quickly at him, a question in his eyes. "The father says that if we stray, the devil will throw us into the fiery pits of hell."

"The father is wrong. He's not our father anyway."

Joey opens the door and talks to Peter's mother, telling her they're going for a walk. She comes out, touches Peter's forehead and looks into his eyes.

"Do you feel well enough, Peter? Are you sure?"

He smiles and assures her that he feels stronger from sitting in the sun. She tells Joey not to take him too far.

They follow the trail to the river — the same one where I first encountered them. Bound by the blue cord, I follow, filled with apprehension. Peter has to stop frequently to cough — great wracking coughs that leave him shaken and gasping. Joey attends to him, wipes his mouth — and finds blood.

When they reach the top of the canyon and stand overlooking the great river, they stop and turn to face each other. I hear them softly address one another, using their Nuxalk names.

"Eagle Feather."

"Cedar Standing Tall."

They know there's only one way to escape fire, and that's with water. Oh no… They're going to jump!

Adrenaline rushes through Joey's body. He feels more alive than he's felt for a very long time. He hears the high-pitched call of an eagle and he takes it as a sign — it gives him strength. He tightens his grip on his cousin's hand.

"Now," says Joey.

I stay with them. My spirit stays with Joey. I can't let them do this alone. My stomach lurches as he drops through the air. Peter's hand lets go and it seems to Joey as if Peter is falling upwards — no, he's flying! He imagines wings growing long and strong for his cousin. The energies of all their ancestors and relations are in the sky with them. Peter becomes an eagle.

And still Joey is falling, almost like he's sliding down a glowing band of blue toward the water, which now teems with the movement of thousands of large fish, their silver scales flashing. They've gathered to meet him. As he finally crashes into the turmoil of water, he has no fear and feels as whole as when he was made by Creator. He's suspended, swept downstream by the endlessly moving water, limp.

My soul swims free — I am the salmon.

Celeste is sitting in front of her on the footstool wiping tears from her eyes.

"Such courage. My heart is breaking. They were so proud, refusing to allow themselves to be taken again. It's a fucking travesty what was done to them. To all of them, all of us."

Liv is beyond words. An ache in her chest threatens her breathing. Tears trail down her cheeks. Celeste hands her a tissue. She can see the deep pain in her eyes.

"That must have been hard for you too," she croaks, "With your family history."

"So many sad stories — and they get sadder with each generation that suffers new hells based on the one before."

Liv knows her friend's story — at least the part Celeste herself knows. She was adopted to a white family as a child. It wasn't until she was an adult that she found out that she'd been forcibly removed from her Métis parents. Her French/Cree father committed suicide. Her Ojibway mother died on the street. Both had spent their childhoods in the red brick fortress of the residential school system.

Celeste went to university out east and studied psychology and anthropology. While there, she had the chance to explore her own roots, history and culture, and with the help of an amazing Indigenous counsellor, find a way to not only heal herself, but find her own calling.

They sit quietly for a long time. Then Celeste rises and puts the kettle on.

As she walks home Liv ponders the devastating stories of Joey and Celeste. The only other First Nations person she had known well, a girl named Suzy, had a similarly tragic story.

Suzy showed up in September of grade four and Liv knew right away she wanted to be her friend. She'd always felt, and been treated, like an outsider, with her hand-me-down clothes and rough family life. There was a sadness to Suzy that told her they had that in common.

They gravitated to each other and were soon inseparable. Together they learned how to be the best rope-skippers, hop-scotchers and monkey bar athletes. They shared the ability to shut out the rest of the world and create their own safe one.

She never liked to bring friends home after school, not knowing what kind of mood her dad would be in, so they went to Suzy's squalid rented house at the bottom the street. The mess didn't seem to embarrass her. The first thing they'd do is forage in the kitchen for something to eat — a box of cereal or crackers or cookies. Liv would never do that at home — she and her brothers were never free to self-serve, probably because money was scarce and her mom had to make the groceries last.

It soon became apparent that both of Suzy's parents had drinking problems, although her dad was in AA. Suzy's mom was always there, but she rarely got out of bed. She'd call out and Suzy would stand in the doorway and talk to her. She seemed to only care about herself and often got Suzy to bring her a bottle of beer.

Her dad was always friendly when he got home from work. He was Blackfoot, from southern Alberta, and he had some great stories about his childhood, working the trapline, picking berries and fishing. Liv got the feeling he knew her dad, perhaps from his drinking days. It was a small town. He once called Liv a blonde Indian. He said she wore her sad face on the inside. She was ten by this time, so she kind of knew what he meant. Most of the world saw her as a happy, sweet kid, but those who knew pain could see it inside of her as well.

One day they arrived at Suzy's after school and found her dad really drunk. He'd fallen off the wagon hard and he was ranting. Liv just went on high alert — she immediately made an excuse to leave, because she just wanted to get out of there.

Suzy came after her and they hid behind a bush in the park and Liv told her about her dad — not about the sexual abuse, but about his drinking and how he physically abused her family. That was the only other time Liv came close to telling someone, but she didn't.

The following Saturday, Liv went to Suzy's house bursting with ideas for things for them to do. The house was empty, littered with trash and abandoned belongings. She never saw her again.

All this misery and suffering in the world — so many lives fraught with unhappiness and injustice. What purpose does all this turmoil serve? It seems like nobody has any control over what happens to them.

Then she feels a surge of inspiration. *That's the Wyrd — the rigid fabric of life, woven with everyone's stories. It's not just about one person's story — it's how they're all woven together.*

She begins walking faster, excited by this revelation.

I can alter my life with my own choices. I can change the colour and pattern, just as Ingaborg said. I'm lucky to have been born with choices. I'm a grown woman, and I have changed — I'm no longer the little girl in an unsafe situation. I can use my brain and the cultural privilege life afforded me in far less selfish ways than I have been. Guilt and pity help no one. What of Joey, Veda and Suzy — or any number of other souls who, through no fault of their own, are unable to determine the course of their lives, much less live them?

22

~ *Committed* ~

Ross is still in the lockup section of the psychiatric ward and not allowed any visitors for another week. Liv is used to being on her own when it comes to the kids and the farm. It's now snowing almost every day, which means all her chores are preceded by shovelling paths and sweeping steps. Neighbours have dropped off plenty of firewood, but she still has to chop it and bring it in the house to feed the hungry woodstove at frequent intervals. Without being asked, their neighbour Rob ploughs her driveway on snowy days, so they wake to the rattling engine of his tractor backing and forthing in the yard. The farm is blanketed in a purifying coat of white. Liv smiles to herself at the thought of these lovely neighbours and country folks, who know Ross has been locked up in a psychiatric ward and wouldn't in a million years want to talk about it — at least not with her — but still know exactly what needs to be done to help this little family survive. They pitch in without fanfare, to make sure there is wood for warmth, food and a cleared path to the highway.

The psychiatrist, Dr. Vindloo, has called her several times. He has an earnest tone, with a cultured British accent. He speaks precisely and formally, referring to her often as Mrs. Edwards. He reports that he's trying to find the optimum medication to manage Ross' illness, which he has now diagnosed as bipolar disorder with psychotic and delusional features, further complicated by alcoholism and drug addiction. Hearing this, Liv feels a jolt of panic, but she remains attentive and assures him that she's willing to be a part of Ross' treatment plan.

He tells her Ross is not adapting well to being in the hospital.

"He has been resistant to therapy, Mrs. Edwards. It's unlikely he would have come in for treatment without being committed against his will." Liv recognizes this as a huge understatement. She knows Ross is likely acting like a caged animal, pacing and cursing his captors.

After two weeks, Liv is encouraged to visit. The psych ward looks like any other — a long hallway lined with rooms, grey walls, a bustling nursing station. The pervasive scent of disinfectant has an underlying tinge of body odour and feces. There's a lounge with a pool table and some couches. Liv wanders up the hallway, feeling uneasy. She follows a red linoleum line to the nursing station and stands tentatively, waiting for one of the staff to notice her. A young woman with dreadlocks and missing front teeth, wearing mint green cotton hospital pajamas, shambles up and takes her arm.

"You don't want to be here, lady. They won't let you go."

"Oh, I'm just visiting," Liv says, flustered.

"Ya got a cigarette?"

"No. Sorry," she smiles apologetically, guiltily, as she's aware that she actually does have some she brought for Ross.

Thankfully, a nurse finally notices her and comes to the counter. "Marnie, go on now," she says to the patient, who sneers and slides off down the hallway.

"Can I help you?"

"Yes, I'm here to see Ross Edwards?"

The nurse runs her pen down a list on the clipboard attached to the desk.

"He's on the secure ward. If you wait in the lounge I'll get someone to bring him out."

She doesn't recognize him at first. He's following a male nurse down the hall toward her, moving reluctantly, his head down and face turned to the side as if he doesn't want to see where he's going. His arms are slack at his side. The baggy green hospital robe hangs loosely from his narrow shoulders. He's emaciated — only his face looks fuller, kind of puffy and pasty.

She rises and goes to him, unsure whether to hug him or not. He hasn't seen her yet, she doesn't think. The nurse sees her coming. "Mrs. Edwards?"

"Yes," she says.

Fortunately, the nurse seems to know this is an awkward moment. He reaches for Ross' arm.

"Hey Mr. Edwards, it's your lucky day. Your wife is here to see you."

Ross gives her a brief, surprised glance. Then he makes a huffing sound — air escaping quickly through his lips.

"How about we go to the visiting room," the nurse suggests. Liv nods gratefully, and he guides them to a small room down the hall with two hard chairs in it and an oil painting of a sailing ship on a stormy sea hanging crooked on the far wall. The nurse withdraws to stand just outside the open door.

"Welcome to my nightmare," Ross says, still not making eye contact. "I didn't know if you would come."

"Of course I came," she says lamely. She'd considered not coming — who would blame her, considering all the things he had done? *But the illness is the demon here.* She has to keep remembering that and give him a chance.

"I brought you some cigarettes and some black licorice."

"Thanks."

"Is there anything else you'd like me to bring?"

"Well, you could ask Nurse Ratchit if she could spare some Fiorinal for this goddamn headache."

"You're still suffering with them? I was hoping..."

With an ice-blue glare, Ross interrupts, "That they'd make me better? Not likely. This is really just a holding pen. They dope you up so their job is easier."

"Oh, Ross. You know they're trying to help you." She has been hoping he'd be contrite and apologetic, willing to go through this step so he can return to his life, and to hers.

He seems to consider her words and is about to argue. Then he gives her a sheepish sideways look and one of his closed little smiles and, for the first time in months, she sees a trace of the Ross she remembers, just for a flash — the clever, erudite professor with the knowing smile and mischief in his eyes.

And in that deep, rich, radio DJ voice that used to be able to convince her of anything, he says, "Oh Liv, my beautiful and brilliant wife, I'm not trying to be a hardass. I'm sorry about all of this. Can't seem to help myself. I know they want to help me. I'm just not sure they can."

This is true, she can tell.

Liv realizes she's used to talking to Ross when he has a drink in his hand and a smoke to his lips — it seems weird for him to have neither. She asks him if he wants to go for a smoke, and he says yes. Of course, it's a big production — it's minus ten degrees and windy outside, so the nurse has to get Ross a jacket and then accompany them to a breezy outdoor corridor. They sit on a frigid cement bench and Ross smokes three cigarettes in succession while they attempt to talk.

"Everything okay with the kids?"

"Yeah. They're loving the snow, of course. And looking forward to Christmas break." Liv takes off her mitts and fumbles in her handbag, "Leah sent you this card she made. Don't you love her rendition of us as snow people? She even put a cigarette in your mouth."

He asks about Ruby. Liv describes her burrowing in the snow and coming up with a snowball on her nose. He laughs fondly.

When she leaves, they hug awkwardly. She doesn't turn back to see if he's watching her.

She makes the drive every second day, an hour each way, often arriving in a state of nerves because of the snowy, icy conditions. During these drives she thinks largely about her marriage and how to minimize the damage to her children, but also about her therapy with Celeste.

After one particularly bad visit, when she tried to start conversations but Ross sat and stared at her for twenty minutes without saying a word, she spent the drive home reviewing the gifts in her recent past life explorations. *I know I need to start over like Hannah had to do. In some ways it would've been so much easier if Ross had died, then I could just grieve the loss and eventually get over it.*

Even if by some miracle Ross and I stay together, I'm not the same person and our relationship will have to be completely different.

Moragh's courage and wisdom and Veda's belief in standing up for what's right are part of me now. Ross may or may not be accepting of the new me — that is, if he ever gets well enough to know or care about who I am or how I've changed. Or, maybe I won't like him as a sober, saner person?

She brings him treats to brighten his days — homemade oatmeal raisin cookies, shoestring potato chips and the obligatory cigarettes. She tells him anecdotes about the kids, the animals, their neighbours. Sometimes he's warm to her and speaks of the future, as if trying to keep her invested in him. He tells amusing stories about the other "crazies" on the ward — presenting himself as compassionate and caring and wanting to do what he can to help. At other times, he accuses Liv of colluding to lock him up, implying that it's somehow her fault he ended up in this "prison," as he calls it. He refers to the nurses and doctors as "wardens" and "guards" and then he winks and says, "Yes, I know. Just kidding," when they correct him.

He either seems exhausted and depressed and on the verge of tears, or angry and agitated. If Liv's guard is down or she stays too long, she feels at times like she's bipolar by proxy, with his moods tied directly to hers. One visit is taken up entirely by him trying to convince her to sneak him out.

There are other days when he's unable to speak at all and just curls into himself, actually dozing while she's there, not even interested when she suggests they go outside so he can smoke. On one such occasion, one of the nurses tells her Ross has been belligerent and has been given a sedative to calm him down. The front of his pajama bottoms is wet with urine. He has drool running from his mouth, down one side of his chin. In a snippy voice, the nurse tells her he kicked one of the guards who tried to restrain him.

Liv feels like throwing up when she sees Ross in this state. *He's not getting well at all...he's getting worse.* She desperately wants him and the medication to do the work and get him well, but she doesn't blame him for not buying into this kind of treatment. On the drive home that day, Liv turns on the radio and hears Stevie Nicks's smoky, sage voice singing Landslide. She can relate to the lyrics.

I took my love and I took it down

Climbed a mountain then I turned around

And I saw my reflection in the snow-covered hills

Well the landslide brought me down

I've been afraid of changin'

Cause I built my life around you

But time makes you bolder

Children get older

And I'm getting older too...

Finally, after a few days of relative calm, the psychiatrist suggests she bring the kids in for a visit. They're shy and weirded-out, especially Molly who can't meet her Dad's eyes and won't give him a hug. Ross takes them to the games room and shows them how to play pool, which they think is pretty cool. He gets them each a can of pop and a package of Smarties — things they're rarely allowed — out of the vending machine. Soon, outgoing Micah has made friends with a pool playing young schizophrenic guy named Josh. Leah is telling her dad all about Ruby's escapades and Molly is munching on shoestring potato chips, smiling in spite of herself.

They all hug Ross spontaneously when it's time to say goodbye. Liv finds it kind of heartbreaking to see how easily the children can be won over with treats and a bit of attention. Yet she suspects each of them is holding their real feelings inside, just as she is. They arm-punch each other and argue about ridiculous things most of the way home in the car.

Liv begins to participate in support classes for families of people with bipolar disorder. She finds it fascinating and also more than a bit embarrassing that it took her so long to figure out that Ross is mentally ill. Now she recognizes he's shown signs of bipolar disorder since the beginning of their relationship.

The counsellor tells her that people with the disorder have a good chance of recovery if they get on and stay on the medication, stay off alcohol, have family support and attend counselling. Without that support, the odds go down to pretty much zero for having a happy life, successful relationships or a career. She decides the least she can do is provide support, as it seems to be integral to success. She and the kids are his only family — Ross' parents died several years before.

Admittedly, she feels a bit of pressure from the other shiningly optimistic participants in the group, who, unlike her, have not been pondering a break with their mentally ill loved one. She feels guilty and isn't sure at all about trying to make the marriage work. In fact, she's pretty sure it's over. But if he's willing to do his part, the least she can do is stay in it long enough to help him get well. It seems like the right thing to do.

Meanwhile, though, Ross has become a bit of a problem on the ward. He's been cheeking his medications and avoiding therapy sessions, usually citing migraines as the reason. In his charismatic, college professor way, he's been able to round up audiences and hold court with the other patients and even some of the nurses, many of whom have been his students in past years. They seem to be especially intrigued by him. Liv can't help but wonder if he's had sex with any of them, more out of curiosity than jealousy.

Liv arrives at Celeste's one frigid but clear day, just before Christmas, after one of her journeys into the city.

"I don't have long — the kids will be getting home soon. I just had to talk."

"Come on in." Celeste motions her into the living room and Liv gratefully relaxes into the sofa that has been her vehicle for so many forays into her soul's past.

"Ross went on a wild escapade last night. According to the doctor, he incited some of his fellow patients to leave the hospital without permission during the evening shift change. They wound up at a strip bar downtown. Ross somehow produced a credit card and bought booze for everyone."

"That won't do much good for his recovery," Celeste says, shaking her head sadly. "Or your bank account."

"When the ward clerk discovered they were missing she called the police, who had no trouble locating them, of course, since they were wearing pyjamas and hospital ID bracelets. They'd had time to down lots of beer and possibly some cocaine. When the paddy wagon brought them back to the hospital, it was discovered they had one extra passenger — Ross thought it would be hilarious to bring his new friend Tiffany, an exotic dancer clad in a gold-sequined mermaid gown, along for the ride. She was apparently game to perform for 'the inmates', but instead the RCMP escorted her home."

They can't help but chuckle, imagining the scene. "Man, I live a sheltered life here in Little Mountain," Celeste laughed.

"Anyway, Dr. Vindloo was not impressed — it kind of seems like he's giving up on trying to help Ross. He's clearly not trying to help himself and he refuses to engage in any of the programs. He said he'll let him stay to finish the assessment time required by the law for the sake of community safety and for the kids and me — his loving, supportive wife — which I don't know if I am anymore.

"From the classes I've been taking, it sounds like I've been the worst enabler there ever was. The other spouses in the group can't believe I've never really held Ross accountable for anything. When I think of how I rushed around like a madwoman every day, making everything perfect so he'd be happy and relaxed when he got home. Never questioning his decisions, even when they affected me and the kids. Like a 1950s housewife. I'm not that person anymore!"

"You did what you knew how to do, Liv. You did what you learned to do as a child survivor of abuse and addicted parents. And besides, you've also learned you can't help someone who doesn't want to be helped."

Liv's next few hospital visits are even more difficult. Ross is agitated, pacing with frantic energy one day and weepy and paranoid the next. Sitting with him out in the smoking area one afternoon, she tries, somewhat awkwardly, to reach out to him.

"It must be so hard for you, being away from your work, your home and us. I was going to ask Dr. Vindaloo if you can have a Christmas pass — come home for a few days?"

"Is that the best you can do, Liv? Maybe you better take some more of those classes to see how to deal with mental patients!"

She stares at him in shock, her lips trembling.

"Well, don't think you need to feel sorry for this sicko. You put me in here and you want me in here. Fuck off."

Liv leaves quickly and phones Dr. Vindloo when she gets home. She asks him why Ross is so angry, and why the medications aren't working for him. Dr. Vindloo tells her it's time for a family conference and books one for the following day.

Ross enters the room looking both sheepish and agitated. His demeanor is that of a schoolboy being hauled into the principals' office — eyes downcast and shuffling feet — but his fists and mouth are clenched as if he's preparing to defend himself.

Ross remains in the doorway of the doctor's office, hands pushing against the frame in a display of strength and launches into an oration of sorts. He declares that he doesn't need treatment and will not take the medication any more. His behaviour immediately confirms Dr. Vindloo's suspicion that he's been hiding his medication.

Ross moves in front of Liv's chair, bends forward and dramatically takes her hands in his.

"Kahlil Gibran explains it better than I ever could." And then, drawing on his steel-trap memory, he recites an entire poem, dropping Liv's hands and pacing the room as he speaks.

Your joy is your sorrow unmasked.

And the selfsame well from which your laughter rises

was oftentimes filled with your tears.

And how else can it be?

The deeper that sorrow carves into your being,

the more joy you can contain.

Is not the cup that holds your wine

the very cup that was burned in the potter's oven?

And is not the lute that soothes your spirit

the very wood that was hollowed with knives?

When you are joyous, look deep into your heart

and you shall find it is only that which has given you sorrow

that is giving you joy.

When you are sorrowful look again in your heart,

and you shall see that in truth you are weeping

for that which has been your delight.

Some of you say, "Joy is greater than sorrow,"

and others say, "Nay, sorrow is the greater."

But I say unto you, they are inseparable.

Together they come, and when one sits alone with you at your board,

remember that the other is asleep upon your bed.

Verily you are suspended like scales between your sorrow and your joy.

Only when you are empty are you at standstill and balanced.

When the treasure-keeper lifts you to weigh his gold and his silver,

needs must your joy or your sorrow rise or fall.

As he finishes, he goes down on one knee before Liv and looks straight into her eyes, his own narrowing to slits.

In a low and raspy voice, he tells her, "Their pills make me bland. I have no joy and no sorrow — I am an empty, boring shell of a person."

Dr. Vindloo takes issue with this — the poet, Gibran, is from his country, so he knows the poem well. He feels Ross is missing the whole point.

"By choosing your illness over the treatment of it, you are relinquishing your chance to experience the real ups and downs of life, as well as what you yourself describe to all as your greatest joys — your wife and children.

"Your highs and lows, as an untreated bipolar person, are based on delusions and distorted thinking," the doctor explains. "They are not the real joys and sorrows that life can bring. It's my opinion that you're making a wrong decision, but I cannot keep you against your will — at least until the next time you break the law."

Dr. Vindloo takes Liv aside and genuinely apologizes for the outcome, saying he's "never met a more brilliant, or less insightful, person," in all his years of work. With that, he ushers her back into the examining room where Ross is waiting, looking pale, nervous, wired. His hair has come undone from his pony tail and it hangs in his face. He rushes to her.

"I want you to stay with me, Liv. You know I love you and the kids, but I cannot and will not take the medicine or stay in treatment. I'll try to lay off the alcohol and drugs, but that's the best I can do. I can't be less than who I am, and that's what the Lithium and anti-psychotics do to me. They make me feel numb and dull. They make me drool, Liv! My hands shake so much I can't even sign my name. I get piss on the toilet seat and the floor, because I can't even hold my pecker still!"

Ross stands facing Liv and gently places his two hands on her cheeks, cradling her face, "I love you so much, Liv. I do, and I don't blame you if you choose to leave me. You're the best thing that ever happened to me and I've hurt you badly, I know that. I'll try to control it, though, if you stay. I'll try so hard to fight it."

Both of them crying, they embrace. The psychiatrist discreetly leaves the room.

Wrapped in his arms, Liv can feel the taught, almost electrical disharmony in his body. And yet, against her will, she stirs to him, still drawn to his energy. For just a moment, she sees past his disheveled appearance and chaotic mind and is transported back in time to the attractive, charismatic man she fell in love with. She snaps to, consciously pushing away her indecision, her empathy, their history and then speaks in a quiet, cracking voice.

"I love you too, and I have loved our life together, Ross. If only that were enough. I can't be less than I am either. If you want to be with us, you have to do this for us, and for yourself. You have to take the medicine and the counselling."

His arms tighten around her and he turns his head to breathe in the scent of her hair. He gives her a soft kiss on the cheek, then loosens his hold gradually, and steps back, definitively.

"Well, this is it then," Ross says.

"This is it then," Liv says back. They step back from their embrace, wiping away their tears.

Walking away from him down the hospital hallway, Liv feels almost disembodied, as if she's watching herself leave, a wobbly reflection on the shiny hospital floor.

It's never occurred to Liv that her marriage would end by mutual agreement. She assumed that Ross would choose her and the kids over anything. She thought he would be so happy when he heard that she would stay in the marriage and try to make it work if he did his part.

She sits for a time in the parkade feeling numb and alone.

It's December 20th, around 8 p.m. Liv imagines the babysitter is probably tucking the kids into bed about this time — her sweet kids, blissfully unaware of the change that's coming to their lives.

On the outskirts of the city, she slows the car down and pulls over to blow her nose again. The night sky is alive with dancing stars and northern lights, flaring brilliant blues, purples and greens. It seems to her a sign that everything is unfolding the way it's meant to. The moving curtain of celestial light brightens her path and reminds her of the strength, love and wisdom that have been forever woven into her spirit.

Later, she finds out that Ross checked himself out of the hospital that same evening, against medical advice. He booked into the hotel with the strip bar and Liv didn't hear from him again until mid-January.

It wasn't the worst Christmas ever. Liv couldn't bear the thought of travelling to the coast to spend it with her parents, especially with her father dying. She hadn't even told them about the separation yet. But Liv's Little Mountain friends included her and Leah, Molly and Micah in all their family traditions and turkey dinners. The usual Little Mountain festivities, sleigh riding, consuming mass quantities of marshmallowy hot-chocolate beside blazing bonfires after ankle-destroying ice skating in ill-fitting skates on crystal frozen ponds, weren't quite as fun without Ross and he was missed. But it was still fun. It did her heart so much good to see she was able to make Christmas magical for the children, because that was what really mattered.

23

~ *Resilience* ~

Liv arrives at Celeste's, exhausted, putting one foot in front of the other, doing all the things she needs to do to get ready for the divorce, but today she needs a boost, a distraction.

"I need to know the final chapter in Hannah's life. All my other past lives I looked at ended with death, but Hannah's life was just beginning to unfold. I want to see what happened to her."

Celeste's living room glows golden with late-afternoon winter sun. Liv takes a drink of minted ice water and relishes the chill it produces as it flows down her sore throat. She's been fighting a cold the kids brought home from school.

"You know, of all the past lives I've visited, Hannah's still resonates with me the most. The characters are alive in my mind. It's like a feature-length movie where I haven't seen the ending. As I make my way through this divorce, I find myself thinking about them. Even her annoying, religious sisters are part of my soul's history and I love how Ingaborg infuriates them because she won't bow to the rules."

"She's certainly indomitable! She's like you, Liv — a free spirit, despite all the pressure to conform. She remains optimistic in spite of the punishment she endures," Celeste observes.

"Yes. Such a restrictive world, especially for girls. Strangely, despite the feminist revolution, I can relate to the pressure they're under. I've always been way too concerned about what people think I should be."

"We all fight that conditioning. Hopefully our daughters will escape it."

Liv takes another swig of water and smiles at her friend. She realizes she's always felt deprived being the only girl in her family and maybe that's why she's so interested in the Kleppen girls. She imagines what it would have been like for her to have a sister, someone with more in common, maybe someone who would protect her. As an adult, she's been able to surround herself with "chosen" sisters, friends who have been there for her and she for them.

"I'm so curious to see how Hannah and Ingaborg managed in their lives, considering the challenges they faced."

"Children have an amazing ability to find their way through troubled times," Celeste says.

"I sure hope my kids have that kind of resilience. They could sure use it right about now, with all the changes."

"Well, let's see how our girls fared, shall we? I hope it's a happy story, for everyone's sake," Celeste says, moving to her customary place on the footstool.

Session No. 12 transcript, Feb 1, 1989
Hannah 1858

Hannah is alone in the house. It's absolutely wonderful to be with her again. She's adding chopped cabbage to a pot of fish stew on the hearth when she hears something outside. She wipes the condensation off the window and sees Ingaborg approaching with two men. They're strangers, and even stranger is their attire — they wear black wide-brimmed hats and have the distinct facial hair of Hasidic Jews. It must be her uncles. The Kleppens have received a telegram about their impending arrival to claim her.

Her first impulse is to run. She clatters up the stairs to the room she and Ingaborg share and sits crouched on their mattress, her mind swimming with conflict. She has never met these men before and they have come for her from far, far away. While her life here is not particularly happy, she at least has Ingaborg — any thought of leaving her brings panic.

Ingaborg is calling her from below. Hannah resolves not to leave her friend — she'll send her uncles away, she decides.

Downstairs, she greets her uncles shyly, but begins to warm to them when she sees their joy at finding her and the kindness in their faces. They introduce themselves as her Uncle Benjamin and Uncle Samuel, her mother's brothers. It's clear they want to embrace her, but they just step forward and gently take her hands, looking into her eyes.

The Kleppens appear. They are shy at first, then it's bedlam, with everyone speaking at once in different languages. The uncles speak English, basic Dutch and no Norwegian. Hannah is surprised at how quickly she lapses into speaking Dutch. She can also recall a little bit of English, so she's the interpreter.

Her uncles extend their warm thanks to the Kleppens for saving Hannah and offer them generous compensation for caring for her for three years. Hannah observes the glint of greed in Mr. Kleppen's eyes at the mention of money, but he quickly declines, saying they cannot accept payment for doing God's work.

As Hannah talks and interprets, an idea begins to form in her mind. Perhaps there's a way she can leave this backward place and take her friend with her. She knows the Kleppens consider Ingaborg a misfit — her rebelliousness is an embarrassment to them and they're convinced she will never be a suitable wife or an active member of this strict community. If Hannah can find a way for them to save face, she hopes they can be induced to let Ingaborg go.

Speaking in Norwegian, she flatters the Kleppens, telling them she'll never forget their kindness to her. She says she fears she'll never adjust to a new life with these unusual looking men in their strange hats and long beards.

Hannah takes advantage of the linguistic limitations of the Kleppens and tells her uncles she won't go with them without Ingaborg.

"We cannot take this girl from her family," Uncle Samuel exclaims.

She tells her kind uncles that Ingaborg is beaten and abused by her father and she will suffer terribly if Hannah isn't there to protect her. She knows she's exaggerating in some ways, but she's desperate.

The uncles are horrified a father would treat a child this way. They tell her they will provide a home for Ingaborg if Hannah can arrange it.

That achieved, Hannah turns to the oblivious Kleppens and builds her case with them. Her uncles, she tells them, are aware that Hannah and Ingaborg have a strong bond. Negotiations continue and they offer

Ingaborg a position as Hannah's companion, with her salary to be paid to her parents until she's of age.

She knows this will not only appeal to Mr. Kleppen's greed but legitimize the decision in the eyes of the community. She clinches the deal by suggesting that Ingaborg will find great educational opportunities in England, which will make their family proud.

Hilde has grown pale with this talk. She and her husband confer quietly — it seems she's alarmed at the idea of losing Ingaborg. He speaks to her firmly, then turns to the uncles and agrees to the proposal with stiff formality. Hilde stands behind him, her face grim and her lips trembling slightly.

Hannah and Ingaborg join arms and dance in a circle singing, "Tusen Taks, Tusen Taks, a thousand thanks."

Hannah's uncles are mystified this couple would allow their child to go so far away but they're pleased a deal has been struck.

They must leave at first light the next morning so Hannah and Ingaborg run to Uncle Olaf's house right away to tell him the exciting news. Uncle Olaf is happy for his cherished niece and her special friend. They are surprised the next day when he makes the long trek to see them off and hands them each a small, carefully wrapped package. Thrilled, they unwrap them to discover two delicate and intricate pendants. He carved them out of black soapstone the girls had brought him from the beach. Both feature the three Norse Norn sisters dancing, one with a moon over the dancer's heads for Hannah and one with the sun for Ingaborg. He has hung them on fine silver chains he remade from a necklace he had bought his wife for their wedding.

They encircle him in a close hug. "Uncle Olaf, we love you and we promise to write to you about our adventures in Scotland!" Ingaborg has tears in her eyes realizing she'll likely never see him again.

~ ~ ~

It feels like I'm back in the barrel with Hannah but it's Hannah and Ingaborg, cuddled together on a narrow bed on a ship. Hannah is terrified — curled into herself, quivering under a heavy blanket. This voyage brings back the horrors of the fateful journey that took her family from her. Ingaborg is tucked in beside her murmuring words of comfort, although she's queasy from the motion of the rocking ship.

~ ~ ~

Now forward again. They're in a horse-drawn carriage, clippety-clopping up a long, straight lane overhung by arching tree branches toward a grand, imposing home. The uncles sit in front with a uniformed driver. In the back seat, Ingaborg is quiet, staring with wide eyes, while, beside her, Hannah is fidgety and agitated. I've never seen her so antsy. As the carriage approaches the manor, I see the entire household staff has been assembled to greet them. Housemaids, a butler, liveried footmen and kitchen staff line up one side, the family on the other. A footman comes forward and opens the carriage door. Hannah bursts out and runs toward a gangly boy who rushes to meet her.

"Finn!"

Unbelievably, there he is — Hannah and her brother fling their arms around one another. "Finn, Finn, Finn," echoes in Hannah's mind, but for the moment, she is speechless.

Hannah regains her voice and she and Finn talk breathlessly as the party is led into the palatial entry hall. She's introduced to a delicately beautiful dark-haired woman — her aunt Rachel, her Papa's sister, who in turn presents her husband, Uncle Haim. He's a tall, dignified-looking man who bends to greet them with sincere warmth. Ingaborg stands beside Hannah in silence, her eyes wide with amazement at the extravagance of this home.

Aunt Rachel fawns over Hannah and hugs her very tight, telling her she is lovely and very much like her mother. After three years of grief and uncertainty, she's overjoyed to know Hannah is safe. She smiles welcomingly at Ingaborg.

"God bless you for saving Hannah, my dear, and welcome to our family."

Aunt Rachel takes the three children to a grand salon with settees upholstered in rich gold velvet, where they settle beside the fire. A maid wheels in a trolley loaded with a pot of tea, cups and a platter of assorted sweets.

Aunt Rachel says she has always felt somewhat responsible for the loss of Hannah's family, as they had been travelling to Scotland to visit her when they met with tragedy. Everyone had assumed Finn was the lone survivor. He'd been spotted by some fishermen two days after the wreck. His lifeboat had been carried further out to sea by an easterly wind, and he'd been found clinging to a dead old woman, hypothermic but alive.

Hannah holds Finn's warm hand and glances at him often, drinking in his smile, as if she can't believe her own eyes that he's truly there.

Hannah and Ingaborg are taken up a stately staircase to a lovely room on the second floor with twin canopy beds heaped with pillows and luxurious comforters. A fire warms the room. There's a knock and a maid enters. She shows them where to wash and helps them change into matching velvet dresses in cornflower blue with white eyelet trim.

All the while, the girls chatter excitedly in Norwegian — they can't believe how their lives have so quickly changed. They stand side-by-side, clasping their carved, black pendants, looking at their reflections in an elaborately gilded mirror.

They're ushered into an intimidating formal dining room and seated with Finn between them. Along the wall, a row of servants stand in wait with platters of fragrant food. Aunt Rachel signals for service. The girls' eyes are wide with wonder at the generous meal before them. Before they begin to eat, Uncle Benjamin leads the table in a prayer of gratitude for the miraculous return of Hannah, for their new charge, Ingaborg, and for the blessed, hope-filled life they're about to begin.

~ ~ ~

I see glimpses — Hannah, Finn and Ingaborg running across an expanse of lawn, then in a forest glen, rolling with laughter on green grass. Then they're a bit older, exploring an ancient ruin, lingering on lichen-coated stones, entranced by the magic and lore of the Celts.

In a sunlit studio, perhaps at a music school, I see the three of them together, filling the room with music so affecting it takes my breath away.

Hannah sits erect at a grand piano, her mouth curved in song. She's taller now, maybe about twenty, and her voice has gained depth but lost none of its sweetness. It's perfectly suited to the rambling Scottish ballad she sings — strong and full of emotion.

Finn stands alongside, his face intent as he plies a violin with a bow. The change in him is remarkable. Gone is the awkward young boy. He's filled out and grown muscular. There's a trace of his father in his handsome features.

Ingaborg looks both womanly and angelic as she sways and plucks the strings of a graceful harp — her bright gold curls, tied back with a ribbon, cascade down her back.

Now they're playing on a stage framed by towering red velvet curtains before a large, rapt audience. As the last notes fade into silence, they rise to the applause, join hands and move to the front of the stage to take a bow. They beam at each other and bow again.

~ ~ ~

I see them now back in the salon in their Edinburgh home, sitting once again on the elegant sofas. Hannah is a mature woman now — her face is leaner, and her dark hair is arranged into a smooth, refined bun. She's reading a book, but as I watch she glances over, catching Finn's eye. They share a smile. He says something to the woman beside him that I don't catch, and she throws her head back and laughs. It's Ingaborg, and she has her feet in his lap! He gently places his hand on her belly, which is distinctly round.

Finn and Ingaborg are lovers and they're having a baby! How delightfully unconventional! Just like Ingaborg. This is astounding. I never could have imagined things working out so perfectly. I'm so happy for them, for myself. This seems like a good time to come home.

"Come back slowly to this time…" Celeste intones.

Liv takes a few moments to process, then slowly opens her eyes. Liv breathes in what she now knows is her own truth, "My spirit does contain Hannah's resilience and self-confidence and I will get through this time in my life."

She's certain that Hannah wasn't someone she dreamed up to keep her company as a child. Her story is far too complicated and touches hers on many levels.

"I absolutely recognize these stories and these characters from the past. Hannah and I shared a soul and Ingaborg and I share a bloodline! When I go home, I'm going to do a whole lot of research and make some phone calls now that I have time," Liv says, rising to go. "This is so exciting — in addition to being an awesome distraction from my divorce."

"You, my friend, are the perfect hypno-subject and what a story your soul has to tell. I'm so happy this work we've done has helped you find your way."

24

~ *Roots And Wings* ~

Celeste's kitchen windows are foggy with steam the next day when the phone rings. A giant pot of borscht bubbles on the stove and she tucks the receiver between her cheek and her shoulder — her hands are busy kneading bannock.

"Celeste you're not going to believe this! I know we don't have a session today, but are you busy? I need to tell you something amazing."

"Of course, come on over, my friend. Soup and bannock await you!"

Liv arrives half an hour later, pink-cheeked and breathless.

"I can't wait to hear what has got you so excited, but catch your breath while I turn the stove down."

Liv immediately begins relaying the stunning information she's learned from her morning's sleuthing.

"I couldn't stop thinking about Hannah's story. It was driving me a bit mad. So, I called around to see if I could discover whether and which of these people really existed. I got no information from my mom and dad. They were on their way to his oncology appointment, and they were pretty sure they wouldn't be receiving good news. I told them I'd call back later to find out how it went.

"I feel bad about it, but I can hardly process the health crisis my father is facing. I haven't even told my parents that my marriage is over. I don't want to burden them with it, plus there's absolutely nothing they can do to help. I'm doing okay with all that but have let myself become obsessed with finding out about the Norwegian connection. I dialed 411 and asked for information for Pickle Creek, Saskatchewan, the town where Dad grew up. I asked for the new number of my great Aunt Else Andersen. She's in a care home now.

"As I expected, coming from a defunct family where nobody shares stories or keeps in touch, Aunt Else wasn't very helpful, especially when I reminded her who my dad was. But she did give me the number for another of Dad's aunts, Greta, who turned out to be a gold mine.

"This sweet old lady was married to a Mormon fellow — she converted and has spent the past forty years contacting all the Norwegian relatives, trying to patch together a family tree. She was thrilled beyond words that I was calling to ask about the family. She wanted to know all about my family line as well, so she could add all of us to the Mormon Census. Apparently, they take great pride in having the most accurate census in the world.

"Anyway, Celeste, I for one am so grateful for the Mormons because it's all true. There *was* a Hannah, there *was* an Ingaborg and there *was* a Finn! There was a steamship wreck in 1855 and nine-year-old Hannah was found by the Kleppens and raised for three years, until her wealthy relatives came to claim her and take her and Ingaborg to Scotland! Oh my God, I nearly forgot — Aunt Greta swears that Hannah's family were the Rothchilds!"

"What? No freaking way — the famous Rothchild family?"

"Yes, that's what she says and I have no reason not to believe her."

"Holy Hallelujah, Liv. This is so fantastic and wonderful and crazy! You swear you didn't know of this story before now?"

"I had a weird inkling — all through our sessions with Hannah I've had the sensation that parts of her story were vaguely familiar from my childhood, as if I'd read them in a storybook or overheard some adult conversation I wasn't meant to hear. But Aunt Greta has documentation. She says my ancestors, the Kleppens, were offered a sizeable reward for saving Hannah's life and they apparently refused it for religious reasons. She says that Hannah, Ingaborg and Finn *were* musicians — she wasn't sure what instruments they played, but they performed all over Europe. Ingaborg and Finn were married and started a family line that leads to *me*. She's going to send me copies of everything she has.

"Oh, and Celeste, the most amazing thing — Aunt Greta says she inherited her great grandmother's old jewellery box, and found a pendant made of black stone with three little figures and a sun carved into it."

"Ingaborg's necklace? Is she sending that to you as well?" Celeste exclaims.

"Yes, and I absolutely cannot wait to wear it around my neck as a talisman, and to pass it, along with the story that goes with it, to my daughters when they're grown."

Throughout this animated debriefing, the two friends have been at the kitchen table, enjoying delicious dill and garlic infused borscht and aromatic, yeasty bannock smothered in honey.

They rise to tidy the kitchen together, both feeling satisfied and exhilarated.

"When we first encountered Hannah, I couldn't have imagined the relevance her story would have to your life," Celeste says, her voice conveying her wonder.

"The most startling realization that came to me is that, by saving Hannah, my ancestor Ingaborg essentially saved *my* soul."

"Wow." They sit in silence briefly, considering the implications of that statement.

Celeste says, "And then to learn that Ingaborg and Finn created a new generation by tying the two family-lines together, which led to your dad being born and then you... it's incredible. You have some good, strong roots after all."

Liv's face glows with pride, then she smiles at her friend, "Well, mixed in with the crazy, religious and completely dysfunctional ones!"

They both ponder for a moment then Liv continues, "Hannah was able to re-create herself and her life story after unimaginable trauma and loss. Ingaborg was able to escape the ties of her religious family. Just as Hannah's adversity forged her own strength, mine will too."

25

~ Balm of Gilead ~

It's rare for a marriage to end easily and Liv and Ross' was no exception. One night, in the depths of February, Liv is cleaning up after dinner when he shows up at the farm, laden with food and gifts. He says he's come for a visit with the kids, but as the evening progresses, it's pretty obvious he hopes to reinsert himself into his family. He's lucid and cheerful. He looks handsome and his eyes have a bit of their old spark. She notes that he's wearing a fitted denim shirt she bought him for his last birthday. She can feel herself warming to his intellect and charisma.

He plays with the children until bedtime, then tucks them in with a wildly funny story, complete with farting noises. They're giddy and delighted — she can imagine them building fantasies of their parents getting back together.

Before he leaves, they stand together in the kitchen.

"That wasn't so bad, was it?" he said, his eyes flashing with that familiar mocking amusement.

"No, it was great," she said. "The kids were so happy to spend time with you. But I would prefer you let me know when you're coming, that's all." She's aware that she softened her message with that last addition.

"I'm doing really well, Liv. I feel like I have some control again."

"I'm so glad to hear that, Ross, I really am."

She knows from her support classes at the hospital that people with bipolar disorder can enjoy periods of stability, but if they go untreated, they'll return to mania and depression.

Later, lying in the darkness, unable to sleep, she momentarily toys with the idea of trying to reconcile with him. The idea of starting a new life with her three kids is daunting. But she believes in the influence of the strong women from her past — Hannah with her courage and resilience, the intuitive, free-spirited Moragh and Veda, with her sureness and understanding. They compel her to take up the thread of her life and weave it herself. She resolves to no longer allow herself to fall sway to Ross' fine words. Another of her Grandma Olive's sayings pops into her head: "Don't believe what people say, believe what people do." She resolves to deal with him kindly, yet decisively.

The next time he visits, a few weeks later, he calls in advance. As he passes her in the doorway, he flashes her a brilliant smile and hands her a single red rose. She catches a whiff of alcohol on his breath. He tells her an amusing but far-fetched story about how he is helping his friend, a First Nations chief, deal with some land claims issues. His tone and speech are on the manic side and she has learned to be wary of the impassioned, grandiose demeanor he's portraying.

She stays in the kitchen while he has his time with the kids. She gathers her courage, calls inwardly to Moragh for support. She waits until he's about to leave and catches up with him outside.

"Ross. I want you to know that from now on, when you come, it will be to see the kids — not me. You need to be respectful to me. And you need to be sober. Our marriage is over — and not just because you refuse to take treatment. My love and trust for you has been irreparably damaged. I still really feel that ending our marriage is the absolute right thing to do, and the sooner the better, for all of us."

He crumbles in front of her in the driveway. All his brilliance, his arrogance, his confidence falls away to reveal a thin, emaciated, weeping wreck. Her heart clenches with compassion, but she can give it no attention — she can't give him hope on a path that will lead nowhere.

In March, they enter into divorce mediation through the provincial Family Justice Centre. Ross is angry and combative. He argues vehemently for joint custody of the children, but with his mental health and substance abuse issues, Liv presents a far stronger case for full custody, even with her minimal income. The most she will concede is joint guardianship and generous visitation. They agree to divide their assets and debts evenly. The farm will be sold.

Liv is stretched thin between caring for the kids and the farm and travelling into the city for mediation sessions, as well as group therapy at the sexual assault centre.

I knew divorce could be ugly and hard but I had no idea how much time and energy it takes to create a brand-new life for four humans, let alone a dozen animals.

Her energy springs from a deep well inside. With faith that well won't dry up, she puts one foot in front of the other, crossing things off the many lists she's made. Liv applies for the Bachelor of Social Work Program. She's always been drawn to the helping professions and believes this is the right path for her education and her career. She isn't sure which stream of social work — maybe child protection, advocating for women's rights, maybe mental health counselling or community development — all of these areas excite and inspire her and give her the fuel she needs to push forward. Gandhi's words echo her hopes and beliefs: "As human beings, our greatness lies not so much in being able to remake the world — as in being able to remake ourselves. In doing so, we can change the world." *I've been so lucky to have the support I needed to change myself, now I want to give that to others.*

She scours the newspapers, looking for a place to rent and jobs to apply for. She'll need to work to earn money to get through university, as she won't be able to count on Ross for any kind of support money. Prior to moving to Little Mountain, she'd worked with special needs children. Now, she freshens her resume and puts feelers out to some of her old contacts. She begins the daunting task of preparing for the move, sorting through the children's clothes and toys and taking bags of things to the local church thrift store.

Liv spends many long, dark winter evenings working on sewing projects — making pajamas for all the kids and creating a special gift for Celeste. She even fixes her favourite blue sweater — the one she snagged on the fence so many months ago. She holds it up to inspect her work. The repair isn't perfect, but it's pretty darn good. She slips it over her head and pushes her arms down through the sleeves. Finally, she can wear it again.

March and April come and go. Ross remains in Twin Rivers — he still has lots of friends who are willing to offer him a place to stay, even though it always ends badly. She hears stories of his escapades, and they make her mad at first, and then just sad. He's apparently dating lots of women, some even his own age, which Liv finds interesting. She's not jealous anymore, which confirms for her that she no longer loves him in that way.

Later in May, things start to fall in place. She's offered a job managing a respite home for special needs children beginning in July. She's found a place to live — the main floor of an old house on a tree-lined street, right near an elementary school. The four of them will have to share two bedrooms, and she'll be back to the laundromat lifestyle, but the home will be a home and it will be hers. She takes possession on June 1, but doesn't move right away — she wants the children to finish out the school year in Little Mountain. So, while the kids are away all day, she slowly continues to dismantle the dream home and the good life she and Ross had built. Celeste and some of her other friends pitch in to help and on those days there's laughter, but it's bittersweet.

The chickens are sent to live with Deanna, who promises to deliver fresh eggs to Liv and visit her in Twin Rivers whenever possible. Liv forces herself not to think about what will happen to her gentle cows once they become part of some rancher's herd. She worries about the pigs, as she's fond of them, but they were destined for the freezer anyway. She found an excellent home for Majic — an old friend who lives in Alberta now is thrilled to take him for her horse-crazed daughter. He will be prized and preened.

"Oh, my brilliant, understanding Majic," Liv weeps into his thick silver mane, taking in his scent one last time. "I've shared so much with you... and you've left an imprint on my heart forever." Majic places his velvety muzzle squarely on Liv's chest and lingers there for a few moments. He knows it's goodbye. He allows himself to be calmly led away by the very excited young woman who will have so much time and love to share with him.

One day in late June, Celeste arrives at Liv's to find the door wide open, letting in fresh, warm air. She calls out as she walks in.

Her footsteps land loudly on the wood floor of the living room. The moving truck has hauled away all the larger furniture and appliances, and all the art has been removed from the walls. The house has a cold, hollow feeling. She calls out again and hears a distant reply from the basement.

She finds Liv downstairs in the kids' bedroom, eyebrows knit in exasperation. She's sitting on the floor amidst a pile of children's artwork and papers.

"Hey Liv. The door was open. Are you okay?"

Liv sighs, "Come in."

Celeste sits across from her on the floor.

"I was trying to create a box of stuff for each kid, just the things that hold the best memories. But at this rate I'll need a boxcar for each of them."

"I know. It's hard to throw any of it away. I just recently got my girls to take care of the stuff they left behind. I've been studying the Buddhist practice of emptiness, letting go of attachments to things and feelings. Jacques is worried I'm going to get rid of everything in the house, including him," she laughs.

"I tried to get the kids to help. Micah put a giant firetruck in his, Leah piled hers with her stuffy puppies and books and Molly refused to even begin the task, loudly declaring that her babies are not going to be put in a box."

"Wow, this is a lot," Celeste says, surveying the pile of paper, toys and craft projects before them. "How about we go through the school and art stuff together? We can appreciate each one, sort of honour them, and then maybe it'll be easier to pick a sample for each of the kids."

"You know, that might really help — sort of like giving each of their creations that last bit of attention."

Celeste holds up a handmade Mother's Day card — orange construction paper adorned with a crooked figure with a mass of yellow curls. Inside, in Leah's tidy kindergarten handwriting is printed in purple crayon "Yor the besd."

"That's a keeper, despite — or is it because of — the bad spelling?"

The task turns out to be a pleasant one with Celeste along to appreciate each Halloween pumpkin, spelling test and school journal. It's noon by the time they work through it all. They carry the stuff upstairs — three plastic bins of memories and two garbage bags full of discards.

Liv gestures at a stack of boxes in the corner of the dining room.

"Ross' stuff — it's mostly paper and a ton of books. Even his master's degree thesis is in there. I don't know what he's going to do with it all. The last I heard, he's planning to work as a shepherd on Saturna Island."

"Not your problem, remember?" Celeste says breezily. "Come on. I brought us some lunch. Let's eat outside in the sun."

She unpacks sandwiches loaded with avocado, cheese, tomato and sprouts on her homemade bread, with iced tea to wash it down. They sit under the apple tree — Liv has decided to leave the Adirondack chairs here for the next owners. The tree's pink blossoms are fading — white petals flutter like confetti on their picnic.

It's a glorious day — the meadow is a brilliant green and the cottonwoods along the river are leafing out and fluorescent. She raises her face to the sun. She loves this land. It breaks her heart to see her garden plot fallow, studded with dead stalks and burgeoning weeds. Last year at this time she had already planted — the rich soil was freshly dug, with promising rows of seedlings. *Just before the unravelling.*

Liv wraps her arms around herself — she's taken to giving herself hugs recently. She feels something stuck to the back of her right arm clinging to the wool of her sweater and pulls it off. It's one of the sticky yellow husks from the cottonwoods that litter the property in the spring. She brings it to her nose, breathing in its acrid, complex aroma.

"That's a smell I will always link with this property. I'll miss it."

Celeste begins to chuckle.

"Oh, that's just perfect, Liv. That's Balm of Gilead! Remember from Moragh's story? In ancient times, it was believed to be the most powerful ointment for healing physical, emotional and spiritual pain. The irony is, nothing can heal all pain — some of it sticks to you, just like those little husks. And you just have to cope with it — exactly like you are right now. You pull them off, you're soothed and amazed by the smell, and you move on."

"Wow. That's pretty cool. And, you know, I feel like I've banished so much of the pain from my early life. I know I can do this. I don't want to leave this place — and yet I know I have to go. I have absolutely loved living here."

"I know, Liv. I wish you could stay. But you have stuff to do, a new life to live. Trust me, we are all going to be living vicariously though you, so you'll be forced to keep in touch and visit often."

"I brought you something to take along for your new home." Celeste gathers the picnic things and carries them to her car. She returns with a large, flat parcel wrapped in brown paper. It seems heavy from the way she carries it.

She places it in front of Liv, who quickly unwraps it.

"The Buddha stained glass!" Liv launches herself onto Celeste, hugging her fiercely.

"I guess I hinted often enough," she says with a laugh. "It's beautiful beyond words. Thank you."

"You are so welcome." Celeste says, and sighs. "I am going to miss you."

"Me too." Then Liv's face brightens in a smile. "I have something for you too."

Now it's Liv's turn to leap up. She emerges from the house with a large bundle wrapped in flower-print fabric in green and rose pink, tied with a large blue bow. She places it in front of Celeste.

"You've done so much for me, not only as the best friend anyone could ever hope for, but as a guide through all our sessions. I wanted to do something for you that would reflect that."

Celeste pulls the bow. The fabric falls away to reveal an intricate quilt. The design is random, a mosaic of fabulous colour and textures.

"I call it the Wyrd Quilt."

For a moment Celeste is speechless, then she spreads the quilt before her. "It's gorgeous Liv! I'll always treasure it!" One patch catches her eye and she inspects it closely.

"Hey — I remember this! Isn't this the fabric we tie dyed and made those terrible-fitting skirts from?"

"Yes! They were awful but the colours are pretty! And see here, the striped pieces are from that purple dress of Rebecca's you gave to Molly. She loved it. And these yellow ones are from the Batman shirt Micah wore every single day when he was four. I even put in one of Ross' shirts." She points to a square of green tartan flannel.

Despite the warmth of the day, Celeste spreads the quilt across her lap and inspects each section, trying to identify each of the fabrics.

She gently touches a square of thick white cotton, embroidered with a blue and yellow butterfly motif.

"Your grandmother's, right? This is fantastic — it's literally your life rendered in fabric. It's appropriate that the prevailing colour is blue, with all these denim pieces."

"Those were my old jean overalls."

"Oh my God, Liv, you didn't cut those up, did you? Your Little Mountain signature look!"

"Well, they were totally faded, ripped and worn through. I couldn't see me wearing them to college or my new job."

They sit in silence, admiring their treasures. The gifts are an acknowledgement that this will be Liv's last day on the farm, their last day as neighbours.

Celeste reaches for Liv's hand. She gently opens her fingers and places the cool soapstone in her palm.

"One more time? It occurred to me that we could go forward and get a glimpse of what's to come."

Liv feels a rush of apprehension. Nothing in her life so far has been easy and there's no indication that things will change. She considers saying no, but she trusts Celeste. This is the logical last installment of the journey they began last summer.

"Okay."

Celeste drapes the quilt over one of the chairs and bids Liv to sit.

"Once again, my friend, follow the trail to the ridge, and down to the water's edge. Count the trees you pass...Ten, nine, eight...look to your future...seven, six, five...follow your blue cord...four, three...to see what will be...two, one."

26

~ Casting Forward ~

Session No. 13 transcript, June 13, 1988
Liv, 2010

My feet are floating as I steer down the trail to the extreme right.
It's rocky and steep, and as I walk a fog envelops me. It smells of the
sea. I choose my steps carefully. At the bottom, my feet land softly on
an expanse of fine, grey sand. It's a beach in a quiet bay. The tide is
out, so the ocean glints in the distance. Down the beach beyond the
pier, I see some people, so I move toward them.

Gulls wheel overhead, making me think of Hannah. I see a
magnificent white boulder on the foreshore. I know where I am.

The sound of children's voices draws my attention. There are
several children, from toddlers to young teens, and a couple of sets of
parents.

"Grandma!" a child calls. She's clutching a kelp pod, running up
the beach to a woman who sits on a log. The woman leans forward,
laughing.

It's me. My hair is shorter, cut to shoulder length and partially white. I have wrinkles at the corners of my eyes, but it's me.

I recognize Molly beside me— gorgeous Molly, all grown up. Her hair glows like burnished copper in the afternoon sun and she's deep in conversation with a tall fellow who doesn't take his eyes off her. The angelic little girl who brought me the kelp pod, turns cartwheels in the sand yells, "Look Mom," and Molly smiles and waves at her.

Micah — a grown version of my mischievous but sweet-natured son — bounces a baby on his hip nearby, while a small-framed, raven-haired young woman reclines against a rock, smiling at them. And there's Leah, gloriously pregnant. Her porcelain skin and red lips suggest the earlier era of Grace Kelly or Audrey Hepburn. In baggy white shorts, t-shirt and a pink baseball cap, she's laughing and helping a couple of adorable little girls put the finishing touches on a sandcastle. These are my grandchildren-to-be and my heart is already exploding with love for them.

There's a man beside me on the log, but as hard as I look, I can't distinguish his features. He has a lovely, warm energy, and seems to be very much connected to me. He's chatting with yet another man and woman, both young. They have a certain familiar ease with each other and are clearly enjoying the day. Strangely, I can't make out any of their faces — they elude me.

It's enough to see this older version of myself reach out to touch him and look into his face. We lean toward each other comfortably and kiss.

I feel myself being pulled back — it's like I have no substance — I can't resist. I'm being drawn back, away from this future life by some gentle, invisible force.

Liv opens her eyes and they're shining.

"That was amazing! What a crazy feeling to see all of us in the future, the kids all grown and are seemingly strong, with their own lives. Suddenly it all seems possible."

"Wonderful, Liv. I had a feeling you would find a hopeful future. You deserve it."

They decide to walk down to the river together. The water is high, so they stay well back from the bank and watch the deep chocolate water move past swiftly, relentlessly, carrying branches and debris.

There is a sense of finality for the two friends. They will never be closer than they are at this moment.

27

~ Weaving it into the Wyrd ~

October 14, 2016

Lounging in the shade of a massive green oak tree, I look out over the valley and the small village of Mukteshwar in the Himalayan foothills. The tree's deep shelter from the burning sun is cool and so welcome. My muscles ache — for the past two weeks our non-profit crew has been stacking bricks and passing buckets of cement to build the second floor of a women's shelter — and yet, I feel absolutely and perfectly content.

The scent of wild jasmine and roses, topped with a hint of nag champa incense and wood smoke, is intoxicating. Today, I am free to indulge in being pensive. It's my birthday.

Four giggling children play nearby. They cast shy brown-eyed glances my way. Soon they begin testing their English: "Hello, lady friend." They're hoping I'll play a game with them, and normally I wouldn't be able to resist their cuteness, but today, I'm giving myself the gift of solitude for a couple of hours. My wonderful husband of twenty years, Liam, is back at the mountain lodge, arranging my birthday feast and Bollywood dance bash. I don't love parties, but I do so love the people planning this one, and there is no saying no to Indian hosts!

I'm looking back on the first thirty years of my life, pondering the second, and hoping the third thirty will play out in full. Funny how I have come to see my life in thirds. It almost feels like the first segment happened to a different person — like a past life — and, in a way, I suppose that's true.

Moving like a single, squirming entity, the village children come closer and present me with a crown they've woven out of marigolds. I place it on my head and say, "Khush raho," which translates as "Be happy." They laugh and scamper around me, but then a woman's voice calls out and they quickly run off to their family huts, probably for their midday meal.

The scent of the flowers and incense leads me into a thoughtful state and I begin to delve into my memory and consider my experiences, good and bad. Collectively, they form a huge swath of the fabric of my existence, and today I'm taking out that large, colourful tapestry, dusting it off and having a good look, to make sure the threads are properly woven into the Wyrd. Not that I plan on dying anytime soon, but one must be prepared. One never knows when Skuld will come to tie off your threads.

My grandmother Olive had a saying she loved to use: "A stitch in time saves nine." As a kid, I wondered what the heck she was talking about, unless it was actually a hole in a sock she was mending. Of course it had a much broader meaning — you shouldn't procrastinate, and you should keep your things in order and your life on the right track. How I wish she could see this shelter we're helping to build for women and children in need of protection. My grandfather died at age forty, leaving her a widow with two young daughters, my mom and my aunt. Grandma fell into a second marriage with an abusive man. She was able to extricate herself after two years and made no bones about her conviction that being on your own is way better than selling your soul. It must have driven her crazy that my mom stayed with my dad. It was obvious Grandma didn't feel much more than contempt for him.

She loved her adages, that sweet woman. One of her other favourites was: "Where there is love, there will be pain" — a sentiment I feel is so true. To experience deep love is to make yourself vulnerable to the possibility of pain. I think of the poem Ross quoted so dramatically, and interpreted so falsely, in the psych ward on the day my first marriage ended.

Look deep into your heart and you will find that which has brought you the greatest joy will also be what has caused your deepest sorrow.

Those years with Ross were some of the best of my life — they brought me three children who have grown into kind, intelligent, loving adults with children of their own. Those years led me to the realization that I needed to heal from my childhood trauma. Had I not been pushed to move forward, I may not have. Yes, there are some dark patches on this part of my tapestry — some places that look a little worse for wear, with intense and discordant colours. Still, they aren't pieces I would discard, even if I could. To be honest, I would hesitate to cut out even the worst moments of my life. I would rather mend my tapestry than have big holes in it.

Undergoing hypnotherapy while concurrently dealing with a marriage breakup would not be something I would have recommended to my counselling clients over the course of my career—yet it somehow worked in my life at that time. Celeste knew that. Thirty years later, she's still my dearest friend, and still practicing hypnotherapy.

It doesn't matter how you heal. It only matters that you do.

For me, it seems I needed to come fully undone, quickly and all at once, in order to morph into the person I was to become. Pulling off the Band-Aid, so to speak, allowed me to look at the pain I'd stuffed away since childhood. The past-life regressions helped me to look further back to my ancestral and spiritual roots and find the essential understanding my immediate family wasn't able to provide. Whether imagined, symbolic, or real, the characters in these stories gave me hope that I had the strength, resilience and deep, true, love within me to cast off the negative and choose a new path.

Bouncing around with Hannah in the North Atlantic, I learned we can recreate ourselves in the face of adversity. I learned that our distant family roots, as well as something that might be called our chosen spirit circles, can strengthen us and help us grow, or sometimes lead us awry.

Each of the past life regressions felt real to me. Just as genetic traits are passed from generation to generation, I now believe a kind of cellular memory, or consciousness, transfers from spirit to spirit.

When Ross and I went our separate ways, he took his faithful Labrador Ruby and together they made new adventures. I said some really hard goodbyes to my friends in Little Mountain and moved to the city to recreate our life as a family of four. I went from being a married farm woman to an urban, single, working parent and a full-time social work student. Moragh was with me at that time. I called upon her strength and independent spirit whenever I was struggling with self-doubt or life just got too hard.

Living in a funky two-bedroom rental suite in a rickety old heritage house, Leah, Molly, Micah and I found our way in our new life. While I grieved the serenity and constant beauty of country life, my friends, my animals and our lovely piece of land, I was stimulated, excited and busy beyond belief with college, work, getting the kids adjusted and going to group therapy at the sexual assault centre. I also had my romantic adventures — in retrospect, it probably would have been a good idea to put that part of my life on hold and just patiently wait a mere five years for Liam to arrive. But hormones.

Friends from Little Mountain would visit and maybe spend a night or two with us. We would stay up for hours after the kids were in bed, talking, sharing a bottle of wine or a pot of tea, but always laughing. They encouraged me to regale them with tales of my often embarrassing and usually hilarious romantic entanglements.

Leah, Molly and Micah struggled with our new life at first, but proved they were just as resilient as I had hoped. They didn't see their dad very often — not surprisingly, he didn't find peace working as a shepherd on a remote island. He was never the same after his hospitalization — in a short time, he lost not only his family, but his career. Teaching had become entirely impossible, and the college administration forced him into an early retirement. He bought himself a fifth-wheel trailer and moved around, eventually ending up in the Kootenays, where he had been born and raised. Even though his new gypsy lifestyle was his choice, or perhaps his illness's choice, I think losing his career and leaving his family ripped out a big piece of his heart and spirit.

Without medication, he had more lows than highs. This compelled him to seek out more drugs and alcohol, chasing down his earlier highs. Even though he still possessed enough charm to get women into his bed, he seemed to have lost the ability or the desire to keep them there for long.

When the kids did see Ross, he was unpredictable — sometimes he was high as a kite and keenly interested in their lives, really wanting to be their dad, while at other times he was wrapped up in some completely off-the-wall project and oblivious to their company. They craved his love and attention, but were less and less willing to enter the uncertainty of his world. All three suffered because of this, as did he.

Once, he sent them home by Greyhound from the Gulf Islands by themselves, rather than driving them as we'd arranged. They got on the wrong bus at the ferry and ended up lost in Vancouver and called me from a pay phone, upset and scared. After that, I didn't allow him to make the travel arrangements and I didn't encourage visits, no matter how much I needed a break. But I couldn't bring myself to deny him access altogether. Despite the pitfalls, I knew their visits gave the kids the sense that he truly loved them.

As I worked my way through my social work classes, I learned I was actually putting my children at risk by letting them be alone with a mentally unstable, addicted, alcoholic parent. Oddly, that hadn't occurred to me until then. I knew I was terrified the whole time they were with him, but it didn't occur to me that I could say no. I still had a lot of work to do in that area. They started saying no themselves once they were old enough, but they felt guilty about it, and so did I.

One of the Mukteshwar Lodge staff, Anil, has spotted me and approaches quietly, wearing a bright pink "I Love New York" t-shirt, carrying a tray. I look up and yet again I'm struck with wonder at the gorgeous backdrop of distant snow-capped mountains against the bright blue sky. My favourite Himalayan mountain, often shrouded in fog, is revealing her beauty today. She is Nanda Devi, which means "Bliss giving goddess", and the second highest peak in India. I swear the cool, delicious breeze drying my sweaty brow is coming directly from her, several hundreds of kilometers away.

"Tea, Madame?" Anil asks — interestingly, he bears the same name as the boy in Veda's story. Anil's soft voice and the aroma of the sweet chai and spicy samosas bring me back to the physical world for a few moments. I stand to stretch and thank him as I receive the colourfully painted wooden tray of goodies. He's even placed a fragrant orange rose beside the plate. He says, "Happy birthday, Madame," in perfect English, before shyly turning away to leave.

After my snack, I recline on the thick cotton blanket and let my eyes close. Looking back can be a bit tiring — plus, I'm sixty now and can have a little nap if I want to. I drift in and out. I hear the brook bubbling in the foliage nearby. Does it trickle toward the life-giving Ganges? I remember my surprise when I first saw that river and it reminded me of the silty North Fork River, which flowed past our property in Little Mountain. The colour of the water had a remarkable quality — it looked solid and impossible to gauge from a distance, transparent up close. Like human beings.

I'll never forget the feeling I had when the Honorary Chancellor of The University of Victoria, a First Nations elder, gently tapped my head with the mallet and whispered something in his language, Halkomelem, bestowing my degree. With that cherished tap, I felt I had been honoured with something far greater than a degree. It was an acknowledgement of trust in my ability to help other people with their struggles.

Looking into the audience, I beamed as I accepted my certificate, and I saw my people — Leah, Molly, Micah, Mom and Celeste. They shared my pride in that moment. This was the payback for the years when my studies made me less available as a mom, daughter and friend. I often had to take the kids to the college with me when I had evening classes, as I couldn't afford a babysitter. I'd tell them they had to quietly play in an empty classroom, do their homework or read a book. If they were able to get along and not cause an uproar, I would give them each a dollar. Most times, they were stellar. Once in a while, they weren't and I'd have to leave my class, red-faced and embarrassed.

I like to think the risks I took — writing cheques for groceries when I knew there was no money in my account, driving rattle-trap vehicles and crossing my fingers that the kids were safe with their father — helped me to empathize with the families I would be tasked with helping. Armed with equal parts of enthusiasm and idealism, I ventured forth into the world of child protection, addiction, mental health and family counselling.

Not long after we moved to the city, I was summoned to visit my father in the hospital at the coast. My brothers were much more attentive to him than I. My excuse was my busy life and living in a faraway city, but the truth was, I didn't want to be with him. On his deathbed, he cried as he said to me, "Livvy, I'm on this train and it won't stop. It's going backwards and it won't stop. It's making me see all these things I don't want to see. I'm a bad person."

He was trying, I suppose, to apologize for being such a terrible father. I don't know if he believed in God, or in heaven or hell, but I imagine he was probably fearful, envisioning the mountains of coal fueling the infernos of hell just for him.

Instead of letting him apologize, I placated him and told him he wasn't a bad father. He looked so scared and skinny and yellow and hollow. I couldn't bear to cause him more pain, so I denied us both the opportunity to speak the truth. Instead, I made the lie larger and told him he was a good father — and frantically searched for something to illustrate this fallacy.

"You were always there for... my car. You cared about my safety, so you fixed the brakes, changed the oil. Remember that time that you rescued me when I drove into that huge, water-filled ditch when I was seventeen?"

He smiled and reached for my hand, but I gently pulled it away. I was remembering the rest of the car-in-the-ditch story — I'd left out the detail that I was dead drunk at the time and so was my dad, in the throes one of his relapses. He'd been too drunk to notice I was drunk, too drunk to see that I needed some parenting. I had such a huge tolerance for insane behaviour that I didn't even feel any danger getting in a car with another drunk and enlisting yet another drunk friend of his to illegally tow my smashed-in Volvo. I left home two weeks later.

"Dad," I said to him on his deathbed that day, "You don't need to go backwards on the train, just let go and let yourself rest." I meant it — I honestly couldn't bear to see him suffer. It seemed to me he'd suffered enough. He died the next day when I was driving home. It bothered me that I couldn't cry.

What I feel now, as a mature woman sitting under an oak tree in Mukteshwar, is not as pure as forgiveness for my father. It's more like freedom from anger, bitterness and regret — a kind of detachment.

I'm so grateful to have had Celeste and then subsequent counsellors and mentors, who helped me in so many ways. I learned to not be so afraid of my own anger, or the anger of others — that these strong emotions are most often an expression of fear or unmet needs and must somehow be released. Just like my grandmother, I have my own favourite adages. One I've used a lot in my work is: "Holding onto anger is like swallowing poison and hoping the other person dies."

The foibles and fears I've retained are possibly too deep for me to completely let go of in this lifetime. I don't feel safe when I'm in my bed alone. I feel fearful and repulsed when I'm around people, even family and friends, who are drinking to the point of being drunk, especially when they get loud or speak aggressively. I just don't trust drunk people and don't want to be around them.

I also have what I have termed "casaphobia." It's a name I made up to describe the opposite of agoraphobia, where people experience anxiety being outside their own home and tend to spend a lot of time there. My anxiety pops up when I am inside my own home or indoors anywhere — I get a sudden need to go outside and walk, bike, swim or paddle my kayak, preferably in a natural area with trees or gardens or water. Then my heartbeat slows and I can breathe and think clearly again. The abuse and assaults I experienced in my younger years all happened inside four walls and it has been hard to shake the feeling that being inside walls is not safe. My past life as Veda, who was shot inside a well, probably didn't help with this particular neurosis, either.

During my years as a counsellor, I've been honoured to have had clients trust me with their stories and allow me to guide them toward healing themselves. Many of them made me think of Joey. His story gave me a visceral awareness of the reverberating, devastating effect of the residential schools. My hypno-journey with Joey helped me gain one particularly useful understanding: any notion that I know what's best for another person is fundamentally wrong, just as the policy of assimilation that produced the residential school travesty was absolutely wrong. Just like the actions of Hitler and his armies were absolutely wrong. No one can ever assume to make decisions for another person, let alone an entire culture. We must all weave the fabric of our own lives.

I realize that my life is one of white privilege. Although I came from poverty and violence and all the emotional aftermath of those things, part of the reason I was able to rise out of the ashes was that I was white and attractive according to European standards. Had I been Indigenous, black or brown-skinned, or had ancestors from a non-European culture, and had I not had the great good fortune to have Celeste in my life, chances are I wouldn't have been given the opportunity to complete my education or find the kind of support I needed to put my past behind me.

It took me a long time to really get value from my past life as Detlef. But I finally came to understand that we are all capable, under certain circumstances, of being deviant or doing harm to others. We can't be afraid of acknowledging that. In my work as a counsellor, I found this useful when I encountered people whose lifestyles and behaviour repelled me or seemed immoral. I was able to put myself in their shoes, to see their context even if I could not understand or relate to it. We all have a shadow.

The reason my tapestry includes a fair bit of social activism, I believe, is connected to Veda and her deep love of Gandhi and his teachings, as well as my experiences as a child and young woman. I'm here in these foothills today because of the threads that connect me to all those women, children and people without power or voice, who desperately need others to stand with them and speak loudly. As Gandhi said so beautifully, "Be the change you want to see in the world." To have taken the pain I experienced as a victim and transform that emotion in a controlled way to help others has been the most healing thing I have done.

One of my pet theories as a counsellor is that as long as someone has one person — maybe a parent, friend or mentor — just someone who truly cares and has unconditional regard for them — there's a far better chance they're going to be okay. Without that, sociopaths are created. I had my grandmother and I also had my mother. As hampered as our mother was by her situation and by our culture at that particular time, she loved her children and we knew it. We learned from her how to be good parents and decent human beings. Her dying wish was for her five kids to be there for each other. And through marriage collapses, health issues, holidays, happy and sad milestones, we have done that. My brothers have long since grown into good men with children and grandchildren of their own.

Rather than shutting out my childhood years, I can take them out and look at them with a smile in my heart. That doesn't mean I've forgiven everything that happened to me, but I have been able to mend the pieces of my soul that were torn by the actions of others. With help, I have woven through the tears, with sharp needles and colourful threads. My stitches bled at first, but now the images of abuse are all but invisible. They are now just a tiny piece of my story and take up no more space than any other part of the design.

The village children begin to emerge from their homes after lunch. The boys chase each other with sticks and the girls sit in a circle, singing a song. Things haven't changed that much since I was a girl. The social workers here in the Himalayas were shocked to hear that we have women's shelters in Canada, too. They were surprised that, for all our wealth and seemingly advanced society, domestic violence, sexual assault and child abuse are still huge issues in our country. This revelation seems to bring us closer together. We're not seen as people doing charity work for those less fortunate, but as like-minded people joining together for a common cause. It makes the world feel smaller and more connected.

I think back to all the young people I have counselled, many of whom had experienced sexual abuse. With some, I've shared parts of my story, hoping it will help them to see there is light at the end of the tunnel if you look for it.

I hear voices and turn my head to discover the source — a group of four women walking down a dirt path, chatting in Hindi and laughing. They carry impossibly huge bundles of sticks upon their heads. The brilliant hues of their saris and head scarves remind me of Moragh and Veda — bright and wonderful parts of my tapestry, rich in a rainbow of colour. These cheerful women find joy in each other's company despite their simple, poor existence. Like them, I have been fortunate to have female friends who have sustained me in the worst of times and nourished my happiness throughout my life.

Liam and I met under the most contrived of circumstances, the blind date. Two friends and self-appointed matchmakers chose him as my perfect match and promoted him to me tirelessly. He's a medical doctor and he wasn't an alcoholic, married or even mentally unstable. I was unsure at first, thinking that I wasn't suitable for a completely healthy partner. "A doctor? I don't think so," I reasoned with my persistent matchmakers, one a doctor and the other a nurse I was working with on a mental health outreach team. I imagined this Liam doctor guy as being brainy and conservative. Even if I gave it a chance, I expected disagreements about things like pharmaceuticals versus counselling, self-care and herbal remedies…let alone past lives! But I had to admit I wasn't doing a great job of choosing a mate for myself.

Neither Liam nor I had ever gone on a blind date before, but we self-consciously agreed and met for dinner. The waiter came by several times to take our order before we were able to focus on the menu, instead of looking into each other's eyes and thoughts. Any doubts I had dissolved before dinner arrived.

"I need to warn you that I have a fair bit of baggage," I said nervously as our orders were finally taken and the small talk made way for much larger talk. Even as I said it, I realized it sounded like a challenge — *Run, good doctor, while there's still time!* Without missing a beat and without dropping his soft green-eyed gaze, he said, "I'd be happy to help you unpack that baggage and figure out where it belongs. I've got my own and it's heavy and dusty and old and it would do me a lot of good to unpack it as well," he said and that was when I knew.

I have never known a kinder, more thoughtful, or principled man. He's utterly egalitarian — a homeless heroin addict deserves exactly the same care as a billionaire, in his opinion.

We fell deliriously in love, got married and our family grew to seven — I gained two amazing step-children and Liam embraced my three. We endeavoured to raise these five kids from the unrealistic, well-intentioned perspective of our love bubble! Yep, we made lots of mistakes and had many crazy times with five kids aged eleven through fifteen. We built a home or two and wove a vibrant life together over the past couple of decades, rich with hard lessons and wonderful moments — but that portion of my story will have to be told in its own volume.

When Micah was still in high school, Ross died of an overdose. We will never know if it was an intentional or accidental. He was sixty and alone. Not quite alone — his newest Labrador retriever, Jasper, was with him until he was discovered four days after his death. Surrounding him were syringes and vials of old medicine and an ancient leather medical bag, which was likely passed down to him from his father who was a medical doctor in Nelson. The coroner discovered traces of cold medicine, heroin, alcohol, pot and barbiturates in his system. We all agreed that it didn't seem his style to commit suicide and not leave some kind of dramatic note or message.

The shock sent us all reeling. Ross' death left a dark, empty space in his children's hearts that took many years to heal.

Before his death, Ross had recently gone into recovery and had been going to AA. He'd bought a small farm near Nelson and had begun to reconnect with the kids. He attended both Leah and Molly's high school graduations and Micah had spent two weeks with him the previous summer, fishing and fixing up an old truck. Ross had even visited Liam and I at our home and we had a few pleasant cups of coffee and talks about the kids.

"Looks like you finally have your beautiful castle on a hill and a prince to match, Queen Liv," he teased me when he entered our large new home. Even sober, he had a way of making me feel uncomfortable, but he was trying, and we knew the kids would love to see both of us getting along. I laughed and said, "Yeah. All I need now is a drawbridge to keep the riffraff out." He chuckled and so did Liam. No one had any thought that these would be our last moments with him.

Liam, the kids and I drove for nine hours to Ross' home on the Kootenay river and over the next three days, we went through his belongings, setting aside some things to store and hauling off truckloads of stuff to the dump and the Salvation Army. Friends from Little Mountain came to help and to attend the memorial service. The convoy back home through the dangerous mountain pass must have been quite a spectacle — a pick-up truck full of crazy things, including pinball and vending machines that Ross had turned into a bit of a business. Our son Micah, with his learner's driving license, rode out front on his Dad's motorbike, causing my heart to be in my mouth the entire time.

The kids were so regretful that they hadn't known their dad better and that he would never again have the chance to be a part of their lives. Molly seemed especially devastated, I believe because she had the most distant and complicated relationship with him. The loss stirred up convoluted feelings of guilt, regret — even blame — in each of us. But for them, it was the thought that he loved them and now he was gone. He would never get to follow their careers or be a grandfather to their children — a role I'm sure he would have loved. He would have been thrilled that his oldest daughter, who used to line her stuffies up on the couch and teach them how to read and how to behave, is now an elementary school teacher; his second oldest, the one who knew and understood anxiety and the need to be included and loved for who you are, now makes her living as a social worker, helping others navigate the world; and his wild little daredevil son, who now makes his living welding and pipe-fitting giant oil rigs and ships.

And so, the last vestiges of Ross took up residence in our garage. At one point, the urn containing his cremated remains fell off a shelf and spilled onto Liam's head.

"Damned Ross, I knew he'd find a way to get the last laugh," I cursed with amusement as I grabbed the Dustbuster and vacuumed up his ashes and put them back in the tin, laying Ross to rest one more time.

I like to think that, having endured my lives as an orphan, a witch, a cast-off girl, a Nazi soldier and a victim of the residential school system, and, in this current life, a sexual abuse and assault survivor, I would be in good standing for a really awesome life next time. But there is no way to know. If reincarnation exists, there are many unexplored centuries in the history of my soul, and I'd need to do much more hypnotherapy to find out the rest of the story. But the final third of my life is just beginning and I find that I want to live it as much in the present as possible, feeling grateful for every moment.

My sessions with Celeste opened my eyes to alternate ideologies. Throughout my life, I've explored a huge variety of philosophies and techniques for managing the angst of living.

In Buddhism, there's a practice called Tonglen, which seeks to transform negative emotions such as anger and fear into positive and productive energy. One starts by acknowledging you are not the only one having these feelings — you aren't alone. From there, you let them come to the surface. Breathe them in, in all their discomfort, and then breathe out compassion and love. The negative feelings dissipate and are transformed into love for yourself and for others and transmit just a little bit of healing energy to the world.

With this dreamy thought, I suddenly realize my life story is not just for me — it's asking to be told, asking for a voice. Parts of it will not be easy to share and probably not easy to hear, but maybe it could be like a Tonglen offering which, having been shared, may help others with the same pain. It could be like weaving it into the Wyrd.

I have a perfect visual memory of myself at thirty, running along that tree-lined path to Celeste's house many years ago, terrified by the present, sublimating the past and unable to look to the future. I'll tell my story, beginning with that day in 1987. This village in Northern India, dusty and poor and yet vibrant and colourful, is the perfect backdrop for such a life-rattling epiphany.

I hear Liam calling from down the hill — he wants me to come to the internet tent, where we can sometimes get a sketchy signal for a few minutes in the late afternoon. Is it my imagination or is a strand of pure blue light leading me to him and the iPad he's holding?

"It's our grandkids, Liv — they're on Facetime and they want to sing Happy Birthday to you."

I jump up and run down the path to the tent, as though I'm a much younger version of myself. I'm missing them so much and even though we'll be back home in a couple of weeks, I can't bear to miss a chance to feel their love and give them mine.

~ The End ~

*"Do not be dismayed by the brokenness
of this world.*

All things break. And all things can be mended.

Not with time, as they say, but with intention.

*So go. Love intentionally, extravagantly,
unconditionally.*

*The broken world waits in darkness
for the light that is you."*

~ L.R. Knost

Author Donna Bishop at village meeting in Almora, India.

See Shelter for Himalayan Women Project Facebook page for more
information.

Made in the USA
Lexington, KY
16 August 2019